SOME CHOOSE DARKNESS

Books by Charlie Donlea

SUMMIT LAKE

THE GIRL WHO WAS TAKEN

DON'T BELIEVE IT

SOME CHOOSE DARKNESS

Published by Kensington Publishing Corporation

SOME CHOOSE DARKNESS

CHARLIE DONLEA

KENSINGTON BOOKS
www.kensingtonbooks.com

KENSINGTON BOOKS are published by

Kensington Publishing Corp.
119 West 40th Street
New York, NY 10018

Library of Congress Control Number: 2018912563

ISBN-13: 978-1-4967-1381-0
ISBN-10: 1-4967-1381-8
First Kensington Hardcover Edition: June 2019

ISBN-13: 978-1-4967-1383-4 (ebook)
ISBN-10: 1-4967-1383-4 (ebook)

10 9 8 7 6 5 4 3 2 1

Printed in the United States of America

For Cecilia A. Donat
Great-aunt, old lady, friend

I fear I am writing a requiem for myself.
—Mozart

THE RUSH
Chicago, August 9, 1979

*T*HE NOOSE TIGHTENED AROUND HIS NECK, AND THE OXYGEN DEPRI-vation spun his head into a splendid mix of euphoria and panic. He allowed the nylon to take the full weight of his body as he eased off the stool. Those who did not understand "The Rush" would consider his pulley system barbaric, and no one but him fully knew its power. The Rush was a sensation more formidable than any narcotic. There was no other vector of life that could provide an equal experience. Quite simply, it was all he lived for.

As he lowered himself off the stool, the rope to which the nylon noose was tethered creaked with the strain of his body as it slithered through the grooved rim of the pulley while he sunk toward the floor. The rope curved over the winch, ran down to a second pulley, then back up and around the third and final crank to form an M.

Attached to the other end of the rope was another strap of soft nylon, which was wrapped around his victim's neck. Every time he lowered himself from the safety of the stool, the nylon around his neck took her weight as she levitated like magic off the ground six feet in front of him.

Her panic was finally gone. There was no more kicking or flailing. When she rose now, it was dreamlike. The Rush saturated his soul, and the image of her floating in midair enraptured his mind. He took her weight as long as he could bear, bringing himself to the brink of unconsciousness and to the edge of ecstasy. He closed his eyes briefly. So tempting was the lure to continue toward the high, but he knew the dangers of allowing himself to wander too far down that lurid path. To travel too long on its trail would prevent return. Still, he couldn't resist.

With the nylon tight against his throat, he focused his half-closed eyes on his victim hovering across from him. The noose tightened its grip, pinched his carotid, and formed spots in his vision. He let go momentarily, closing his eyes and giving in to the darkness. Just for a bit. Just for a second more.

THE AFTERMATH
Chicago, August 9, 1979

WHEN HE CAME BACK TO THE PRESENT, HE GASPED FOR AIR, BUT none would come. In a panic, he searched with his foot for the edge of the stool until his toes found the flat wooden surface. He stepped onto it and relieved the pressure from his neck, taking huge swallows of air as his victim sunk to the floor in front of him. Her legs no longer supported her when she reached the concrete. Instead, she crumpled in a heap, the weight of her body pulling his end of the rope until the thick safety knot lodged on his side of the pulley, keeping the noose slack around his neck.

He pulled the soft nylon over his head and allowed time for the redness to leave his skin. He knew he'd gone too far tonight. Despite the protective foam collar he wore, he'd have to find a way to hide the deep purple bruising on his neck. He needed to be more careful now than he'd ever been before. The public had started to catch on. Newspaper articles began to crop up. The authorities had put out warnings, and fear was rising above the warmth of summer. With the public's heightened awareness, he had begun to stalk more carefully, plan more deliberately, and cover his tracks more thoroughly. The bodies he could hide, he had found the perfect location. The Rush was more difficult to contain, and he worried that the veil covering his secret life would be pulled away by his own inability to conceal the elation he carried in the days after his sessions. He would be smart to shut things down. Lie low and wait for the panic to calm. But The Rush was too much to ignore. His existence depended on it.

Sitting on the stool, he turned his back to his victim. He took a moment to bring his emotions under control. When he was ready, he turned to the body to begin the cleanup and preparation for transport the next day. When he was finished, he locked the place up and climbed into his vehicle. The ride home did little to tame the residual effects of The Rush. When he pulled to the front curb, he saw the lights of the house extinguished. It was a good thing tonight. His body was still trembling, and he could not have managed normal conversation. Inside, he dropped his clothes in the washing machine, took a quick shower, and climbed into bed.

She stirred as he pulled the covers over himself.

"What time is it?" she asked with her eyes closed, head sunk into the pillow.

"Late." He kissed her cheek. "Go back to sleep."

She slid her leg over his body and draped her arm across his chest. He lay on his back, staring up at the ceiling. It usually took hours for him to settle down after he returned. He closed his eyes and tried to control the adrenaline that coursed through his veins. His mind replayed the past few hours. He was never able to remember it all, not clearly and not so soon after. In the weeks ahead, the details would come back to him. But tonight, behind closed lids, his eyes fluttered in wild saccades as the memory center in his mind offered brief sparks of the evening. His victim's face. The terror in her eyes. The nylon noose at a sharp angle around her neck.

The images and sounds swirled through his mind in a fast flurry, and as he further played out the fantasy, the sheets stirred next to him as she woke. She curled farther into his side. With The Rush pounding in his veins, the flushing of endorphins through the dilated blood vessels audible in his ears, he allowed her to kiss his neck, then his shoulder. He permitted her hand to sink to the waist of his boxer shorts. The Rush overtook him, and he rolled on top of her. He kept his eyes closed as she let out soft moans, which he blocked from his mind.

He thought of his workspace. Of the darkness. Of the way he could lay himself bare when he was in that place. He took on an easy rhythm and focused on the woman he had brought there earlier in the night. The woman who had levitated like a ghost in front of him.

THE SWEET SCENT OF ROSES

*T*HE WOMAN REACHED INTO THE GARDEN, PINCHED THE CLIPPERS TO THE *base of the rose, and severed its stem. She repeated the process until she had six long-stemmed red roses in her hand. She climbed the stairs to her back porch, placed the roses on the table, and sat down in the rocking chair. Staring out over the field, she watched the young girl approach, climb the stairs, and walk up to her.*

Her voice was high-pitched and innocent, the way all children's voices should be.

"Why do you always take roses from the garden?" the young girl asked.

"Because they're beautiful. And if they're left on the vine, they'll eventually wither and go to waste. If I prune them, I can put them to better use."

"Do you want me to tie them?" the girl asked.

She was ten years old and the sweetest thing to ever come into the woman's life. From her apron, the woman removed a twist tie, handed it to the girl, and watched as she carefully picked up the roses. Avoiding the thorns, the girl wrapped the tie around the stems, twisting until it bound the bouquet in a tight bundle.

"What do you do with the flowers?" the girl asked.

The woman took the perfect bundle from her. "Go inside and clean up for dinner."

"I see you pick them every day, and I tie them for you. But I never see the flowers again."

The woman smiled. "We've got work to do after dinner. I'll let you do the painting tonight, if you think your hand is steady enough."

The woman hoped the bait was enough to veer the conversation.

The girl smiled. "You'll let me paint all by myself?"

"Yes. It's time you learn."

"I'll do a good job, I promise," she said before running into the house.

The woman waited just a moment, until she heard dishes clinking inside as the girl set the dinner table. Then she stood from the rocker, carefully arranged the newly bundled roses, and walked down the porch steps and out across the field behind the house. The sun was setting and the shadows of birch trees cut across her path.

As she walked, she lifted the flowers to her nose and inhaled the sweet scent of roses.

PART I

THE THIEF

CHAPTER 1
Chicago, September 30, 2019

THE CHEST PAINS HAD STARTED THE YEAR BEFORE.

There was never a question about their source. They were stress-induced, and the doctors promised they would never kill him. Tonight's episode was particularly distressing, though, waking him from sleep with a cool chill of night sweats. He tried to suck for air, but it was like breathing through a cocktail straw. The harder he worked to inhale, the more distraught he became. He sat up in bed and fought the fear of suffocation. History told him the episode would pass. He reached for the bottle of aspirin he kept in the nightstand drawer and placed one, along with a nitroglycerine tablet, under his tongue. After ten minutes, the muscles of his chest relaxed and his lungs were able to expand.

It was no coincidence that this most recent bout of angina coincided with the arrival of the parole board letter, which sat on his nightstand. He had spent time reading the letter before he fell to sleep. Accompanying the letter was the judge's summons for a meeting. He grabbed the document now as he climbed from bed, his sweat-soaked shirt cold against his skin as he walked down the stairs and headed to his office. He twisted the combination lock on the safe under his desk and pulled open the door. Inside was a stack of old parole board letters, to which he added the latest.

The first parole hearing correspondence had arrived a decade before. Twice a year, the board met with his client, denying him his freedom and explaining their decision in a properly worded essay that would stand up against appeals and protests. But last year, a different document arrived. It was a lengthy review by the board chairperson, who described in rich detail how impressed the board was with his client's progress over the years, and how his client was the very definition of "rehabilitation." It was after reading the final sentence of that letter, which indicated the parole board's enthusiasm for their next review and the suggestion that great opportunities lay ahead for his client, when the chest pains had begun.

This latest correspondence marked the arrival of a slow-moving train that carried as its freight pain and misery, secrets and lies. That proverbial train had always been just a speck on the horizon, never making progress. But now it was a full barreling freighter growing larger by the day, impossible to stop, despite his many efforts. Sitting behind his desk, he stared at the middle shelf of the safe. A file folder was stuffed fat with pages from his investigation. An exploration that, during times of sorrow and angst like tonight, he wished he'd never embarked upon. The ramifications of his findings, however, were so profound and life-altering that he knew he would be empty had he not. And the idea that his own lies and deceptions might soon crawl from the shadows under which they had rested for years was enough to cause his heart to, literally, ache.

He wiped the layer of perspiration from his forehead and worked hard to fill his lungs with breath. His biggest fear was that his client would soon be free to continue the search. The investigation, which had been declared fruitless, would enjoy a resurgence once his client walked from prison. This, he knew, could not happen. Everything in his power must be done to prevent it.

Alone in his study, he felt a new chill come upon his body as his saturated shirt pressed to his shoulders. He closed the safe and spun the dial. The chest pains returned, his lungs tightened, and he leaned back in his chair to fight again the panic of suffocation. It would pass. It always did.

CHAPTER 2
Chicago, October 1, 2019

$\mathcal{R}$ORY MOORE INSERTED HER CONTACT LENSES, ROLLED HER EYES, and blinked to bring the world into focus. She despised the vision her Coke-bottle glasses offered—a bowed and distorted world when compared to the crispness of her contacts—but she loved the shelter her thick-rimmed frames provided. So, a compromise. After her contact lenses settled, she slipped nonprescription glasses onto her face and hid behind the plastic casings like a warrior ducking behind a shield. To Rory, each day was a battle.

They agreed to meet at the Harold Washington Library Center on State Street, and thirty minutes after Rory had dressed in her protective armor—thick-framed glasses, beanie hat pulled low, coat buttoned to her chin with the collar up—she climbed from her car and walked into the library. Initial meetings with clients always took place in public locations. Of course, most collectors had trouble with this arrangement because it meant hauling their precious trophies out into the daylight. But if they wanted Rory Moore and her restoration skills, they'd follow her rules.

Today's meeting called for more attention than normal, since it had been arranged as a favor for Detective Ron Davidson, who was not only a trusted friend but also her boss. Since this was her side job, or what others annoyingly called her "hobby," some part of her was honored that Davidson had reached out. Not everyone understood the complicated personality of Rory Moore, but over the years, Ron Davidson had broken through to win her admiration. When he asked for a favor, Rory never gave it a second thought.

As she walked through the library doors, Rory immediately recognized the Kestner doll that was housed in a long, thin box and resting in the arms of the man waiting in the lobby. The blink of an eye and a quick glance at the gentleman holding the box was all it took for Rory to run through her appraisal of him, her thoughts flashing like lightning through her mind: midfifties, wealthy, a professional of some sort—business, medicine, or law—cleanly shaven, polished shoes, sport coat, no tie. She quickly backtracked and rejected the initial thought of a doctor or lawyer. He was a small-business owner. Insurance or similar.

She took a deep breath, arranged her glasses squarely on her face, and walked up to him.

"Mr. Byrd?"

"Yes," the man said. "Rory?"

The man, a full twelve inches taller than Rory's five-two stature, looked down on her petite frame and waited for confirmation. Rory offered none.

"Let's see what you've got," she said, pointing at the porcelain doll that was carefully packaged in the box, before walking into the main section of the library.

Mr. Byrd followed her to a table in the corner. The library was only scantly populated in the middle of the afternoon. Rory patted the table and Mr. Byrd laid the box down.

"What's the issue?" Rory asked.

"This is my daughter's Kestner doll. It was a gift for her fifth birthday, and has been kept in pristine condition."

Rory leaned over the table to get a better look at the doll through the plastic window in the box. The porcelain face was badly split down the middle, the crack starting somewhere beyond the doll's hairline, running through the left eye socket and down the cheek.

"I dropped it," Mr. Byrd said. "I'm beside myself that I was so careless."

Rory nodded. "Let me have a look?"

He pushed the box toward her and Rory carefully unlocked the latch and lifted the lid. She inspected the damaged doll like a surgeon's initial assessment of an anesthetized patient lying on the operating table.

"Cracked or shattered?" she asked.

Mr. Byrd reached into his pocket and produced a ziplock bag that contained small pieces of porcelain. Rory noticed his thyroid cartilage rise and fall as he swallowed hard to control his emotions.

"These were everything I could find. I dropped it on hardwood, so I think I located all the pieces."

Rory took the bag and analyzed the shards. She went back to the doll and gently ran her fingers over the fractured porcelain. The split was well opposed and should come together nicely. The restoration of the cheek and forehead could be made to look flawless. The eye socket was another issue. It would take all her skill to restore, and she'd likely need help from the one person who was better than Rory at restoring dolls. The shattered portion, Rory was sure, would be found on the back of the head. The repair there, too, would be challenging due to the hair and the small bits of porcelain she held in the ziplock bag. She didn't want to remove the doll from the box until she was in her workshop for fear that more porcelain might fall from the shattered area.

She nodded slowly, keeping her gaze on the doll.

"I can fix this."

"Thank God," Mr. Byrd said.

"Two weeks. A month, maybe."

"As long as it takes."

"I'll let you know the pricing after I get started."

"I don't care what it costs. As long as you can fix it."

Rory nodded again. She placed the ziplock bag containing the shattered pieces into the box, closed the lid, and relatched the lock.

"I'll need a phone number where I can reach you," she said.

Mr. Byrd fished a business card from his wallet and handed it to her. Rory glanced at it before sticking it into her pocket: BYRD IN-SURANCE GROUP. WALTER BYRD, OWNER.

Rory attempted to lift the box and leave when Mr. Byrd put his hand on hers. A stranger's touch had never been well tolerated, and Rory was about to recoil when he spoke.

"The doll belonged to my daughter," he said in a soft voice.

The past tense caught Rory's attention. It was meant to. Rory looked at the man's hand on her own, and then met his eyes.

"She died last year," Mr. Byrd said.

Rory slowly sat down. A normal response might have been *I'm sorry for your loss.* Or, *I see why this doll means so much to you.* But Rory Moore was anything but normal.

"What happened to her?" Rory asked.

"She was killed," Mr. Byrd said, taking his hand off Rory's and sitting down across from her. "Strangled, they think. Her body was left in Grant Park last January, half-frozen by the time she was found."

Rory looked back at the Kestner doll resting in the box, the right eye shut peacefully, the left eye open and askew with a deep fissure running through the orbit. She understood what was happening, and knew why Detective Davidson had been so adamant that she take this meeting. It was a classic bait and switch that Davidson knew Rory would be helpless to resist.

"They never found him?" Rory asked.

Mr. Byrd shook his head, dropping his gaze to his dead daughter's doll. "Never had so much as a lead. None of the detectives return my calls anymore. It feels like they've simply moved on."

Rory's presence in the library that morning proved Mr. Byrd's statement false, since it was Ron Davidson who had convinced her to come.

Mr. Byrd brought his gaze back to her.

"Listen, this is not a setup. I reached for Camille's doll the other day because I was badly missing my daughter and needed to hold something that reminded me of her. I dropped the goddamn thing and shattered it. I couldn't bring myself to tell my wife because I feel so guilty, and I know it would send her into a fit of depression. This doll was my daughter's favorite possession through her childhood. So please believe me that I want you to restore it. But Detective Davidson told me that your work as a forensic reconstructionist is heralded in the City of Chicago, and beyond. I'm prepared to pay you anything it takes for you to reconstruct the crime and find the man who wrapped his hands around my daughter's neck and choked the life from her."

Mr. Byrd's stare became too much for Rory to handle, penetrating the protective shield of her nonprescription glasses. She finally stood, lifted the Kestner doll box off the table, and secured it under her arm.

"The doll will take a month. Your daughter, much longer. Let me make some calls and I'll be in touch."

Rory walked out of the library and into the fall morning. She felt it as soon as Camille Byrd's father had used the past tense to describe his daughter, that subtle tingling in her mind. That nearly imperceptible, but now ever-present, whisper in her ears. A murmur her boss knew goddamn well she wouldn't be able to ignore.

"You're a real son of a bitch, Ron," Rory said as she exited the library. She had been on hiatus from her job as a forensic reconstructionist, a scheduled break she forced herself to take every so often to avoid burnout and depression. This most recent pause had been longer than any of her others, and was starting to piss off her boss.

As she walked along State Street and back to her car, with Camille Byrd's shattered doll under her arm, Rory knew the vacation was over.

CHAPTER 3
Chicago, October 2, 2019

*H*ER PHONE BUZZED FOR THE FIFTH TIME THAT MORNING, WHICH she again ignored. Rory stared at her reflection in the mirror as she pulled her dark brown hair back and tied it off. She was not a morning person and on principle did not answer her phone before noon. Her boss knew this, so Rory felt no remorse for ignoring him.

"Who is incessantly calling you?" a voice asked from the bedroom.

"I'm meeting Davidson."

"I didn't know you decided to go back to work," the man said.

Rory walked from the bathroom and slipped her watch onto her wrist. "Am I going to see you tonight?" she asked.

"Okay, we won't talk about it."

Rory came over and kissed him on the mouth. Lane Phillips had been her, what? Rory wasn't traditional enough to label him a "boyfriend," and this far into her thirties, she thought the description sounded juvenile. She'd never considered marrying him, despite that they'd slept together for the better part of the last decade. But he was much more than her lover. He was the only man on this planet, aside from her father, who understood her. Lane was . . . hers, that was the best Rory could do in her own mind, and they were both okay with that.

"I'll tell you about it when I have something to tell. Right now, I don't know what I'm getting myself into."

"Fair enough," Lane said, sitting up in bed. "I've been asked to appear as an expert witness on a homicide trial. I'll be testifying in a couple of weeks, so I'm meeting with the DA today. Then I'm teaching until nine tonight."

When Rory tried to back away, he grabbed her hips.

"Are you sure you won't give me any clues about what Davidson lured you back with?"

"Stop by tonight after your class and I'll catch you up."

Rory gave him another kiss, batted away his roaming hands, and walked out of the bedroom. A minute later, the front door opened and closed.

Her phone rang two more times as she sat in morning traffic on the Kennedy Expressway. She exited on Ohio Street and snaked through the grid-pattern streets of Chicago. She pushed through the congestion until she reached Grant Park, circled the side streets for fifteen minutes until she found a parking spot too small for even her tiny Honda. Somehow she managed a brave parallel parking maneuver, unsure if she'd be able to escape the twisting and turning and bumper kissing when it was time to leave.

She walked through the tunnel that cut under Lake Shore Drive and along the picturesque path until she came to the cusp of the park. Grant Park was a magnificent piece of real estate that separated the high-rise buildings of The Loop from the lakefront. The park was always a popular destination with tourists, and this morning was no exception. Rory walked through the crowds until she spotted Ron Davidson sitting on a bench near Buckingham Fountain.

Despite that her coat was already buttoned to her neck, she pulled it tight, lifted her collar, and pushed her glasses up the bridge of her nose. It was a mild October morning and others around her wore shorts and sweatshirts, enjoying the lake breeze and bright sunshine. Rory was dressed for a brisk fall day: gray coat secured top to bottom, collar up, gray jeans, and lace-up Madden Girl Eloisee combat boots, which she wore everywhere, including during the dog days of summer. As Rory approached the detective, she pulled her slouchy fleece beanie down on her forehead. The edge of the hat touched the top of her glasses. She felt protected.

Without introduction, she sat down next to him.

"Well, Christ be the king, it's the lady in gray," Davidson said.

The two had worked enough cases together for Davidson to know all of Rory's quirks. She shook hands with no one, something Davidson had learned after a few attempts where his hand floated in the air while Rory averted her eyes. She hated meeting with department personnel other than Ron, and she had little tolerance for red tape. She had never accepted a deadline on a job, and worked strictly solo on her cases. She returned calls at her leisure, and sometimes not at all. She hated politics, and if anyone—from an alderman to the mayor—tried to pull Rory into the spotlight, she disappeared for weeks. If her skills as a forensic reconstructionist weren't so outstanding, Ron Davidson would never tolerate the headaches she caused.

"You've been off the grid, Gray."

Rory allowed the corners of her mouth to curl slightly while she stared at Buckingham Fountain. No one but Davidson called her "Gray," and over the years Rory had warmed to the nickname—a combination of her attire and her detached outward persona.

"Busy with life."

"How's Lane?"

"Fine."

"Is he a better boss than me?"

"He's not my boss."

"Yet you spend all your time working for him."

"Working *with* him."

Ron Davidson paused for a moment. "You haven't returned a call for six months."

"I told you I was on hiatus."

"There were a few cases I could have used your help on."

"I was getting burned out. I needed a break. Why do you think most of the detectives who work for you aren't worth a shit?"

"Ah, I missed your candor, Gray."

They sat in peaceful silence for a few minutes people-watching the tourists who passed through the park.

"Will you help me?" Davidson finally asked.

"You're a real bastard for doing it that way," Rory said.

"You hadn't returned a call for half a year. You've been too preoccupied with Lane Phillips and his Murder Accountability Project. So, I got creative. I thought you'd appreciate it."

More silence.

"Well?" Davidson asked again when enough time had passed.

"I'm here, aren't I?" Rory kept her focus on the fountain. "Tell me about her."

"Camille Byrd. Twenty-two-year-old gal who was strangled. Body was dumped in the park here."

"When?"

"Last year, January. Twenty-one months," Davidson said.

"And you guys have nothing?"

"I made some threats and banged some pots, but my guys are stumped on this one, Rory."

"I'll need the files on the case," Rory said, still looking at the fountain, but noticing the bend in Davidson's neck as the head of Chicago Homicide looked up subtly and exhaled in relief.

"Thank you," he said.

"Who is Walter Byrd?"

"Wealthy businessman and a personal friend of the mayor's, so there's been some urgency on the squad to put this one to rest."

"Because he's rich and connected?" Rory asked. "There should be urgency for any parent whose child is killed. Where was her body found?"

Davidson pointed. "East side of the park. I'll show you."

Rory stood and allowed Davidson to take the lead as they walked. They made it through the park until they came to a grassy knoll off the walking path. A row of birch trees flanked each side of the area, and Rory's mind calculated the ways someone could transport a body to this location.

Davidson walked onto the grass. "Her body was found here."

"Strangled?"

Davidson nodded.

"Rape?"

"No."

Rory walked to the location where Camille Byrd's body had been found, and turned in a slow circle, taking in the lakefront and the boats resting on the water. She continued to turn and saw the Chicago skyline. Fat white clouds hovered like overinflated balloons in the otherwise-blue sky. She imagined the girl's body found in the dead of winter, bloated and lifeless and frozen through. She imagined the bare trees of January, the foliage stripped by cold.

"Dump her here. Why?" she said. "It's such a risk with no protection from the trees. Whoever did this wanted her to be found."

"Unless he killed her here. Something got out of control. A heated argument. He kills her and runs."

"That's a lovers' quarrel," Rory said. "And I'm assuming your guys exhausted that angle. Talked to all her boyfriends, current and past? Workmates, old flames."

Davidson nodded. "Covered and cleared, all of them."

"Then it wasn't someone she knew. She was killed elsewhere and brought here. Why?"

"My guys don't know."

"I need everything, Ron. Files, autopsy, interviews. Everything."

"I can get you all of it, but I've got to put you back on the payroll to do it. Make it official that you're working again. Then I can get you anything you need."

Rory went silent again as her eyes took in the scene. So many things were firing in her brain. She knew herself well enough not to attempt to tame the influx of information. She wasn't aware of everything she was learning. She knew only to take it all in, and then, in the days and weeks ahead, her brain would sort out the things it was calculating and inventory the images it was capturing. Slowly Rory would organize it all. She'd study the case file. She'd get to know Camille Byrd. She'd put a name and narrative to this poor girl who had been strangled to death. She'd see things the detectives had missed. Rory's uncanny mind would piece together bits of a puzzle everyone else had deemed unsolvable until she had reconstructed the crime in its entirety.

Her phone rang, pulling Rory back from the inner workings of her mind. It was her father calling. She thought about letting it go to voice mail, but decided to answer it.

"Dad, I'm in the middle of something. Can I call you back?"

"Rory?"

She didn't recognize the voice on the other end of the call, only that it was female and panicked.

"Yes?" She took a few steps away from Davidson.

"Rory, it's Celia Banner. Your father's assistant."

"What's wrong? My dad's number came up on my phone."

"I'm calling from his house. Something's wrong, Rory. He had a heart attack."

"What?"

"We were supposed to meet for breakfast, he never showed. It's bad, Rory."

"How bad?"

The silence was like a vacuum that sucked the words from Rory's mouth. "Celia! How bad?"

"He's gone, Rory."

CHAPTER 4
Chicago, October 14, 2019

*I*T TOOK A FULL WEEK AFTER THE FUNERAL BEFORE RORY FOUND THE time, and the gumption, to enter her father's office. Technically, it was her office as well, but since she hadn't handled a formal case in more than a decade, Rory's involvement in the Moore Law Group was not immediately evident. Her name was on the letterhead, and she drew a 1099 every year for the limited work she did for her father—mostly research and trial prep—but as her role at the Chicago Police Department and Lane's Murder Accountability Project demanded more of her attention over the years, the work she did for the firm became less obvious.

Besides Rory's occasional employment, the Moore Law Group was a one-man firm with two employees—a paralegal and an office administrator. With an anorexic staff and a manageable roster of clients, Rory assumed the dissolution of her father's law practice would require a bit of time and expertise, but would, ultimately, be conquerable in a couple of weeks of concentrated work. Rory's law degree, something she earned more than a decade ago, but had never truly put to use, made her the perfect and only candidate to take care of her father's business affairs. Her mother had passed years before and Rory had no siblings.

Rory entered the building on North Clark Street and rode the elevator to the third floor. She keyed the door and pushed it open. The reception area consisted of a desk in front of tan metal file cabinets straight out of the seventies, and was flanked by two offices. The one on the left was her father's; the other belonged to the paralegal.

She dropped a week's worth of mail onto the front desk and headed into her father's office. Her first order of business would be to shuffle the active cases to other law firms. Once the firm's docket was cleared, there would be the matter of paying bills and settling payroll for the staff with whatever funds were stashed away. Then Rory could close the lease on the building and shut the place down.

Celia, the office administrator and the one who had discovered her father dead in his home, had agreed to meet at noon to go through the files and help with reassignment. Rory settled her purse on the ground, popped open a Diet Coke, and got started. By noon, a mountain of paperwork surrounded her as she sat at her father's desk. She had emptied the file cabinets from the reception area, and the contents were now organized into three stacks—pending, active, and retired.

She heard the front door open. Celia, a woman she'd met a handful of times over the years, appeared in the doorway to her father's office. Rory stood.

"Oh, Rory," Celia said, rushing past the stacks of files to embrace her in a tight hug.

Rory kept her arms straight at her sides and blinked several times behind her thick-rimmed glasses while the strange woman invaded her personal space in ways most of Rory's acquaintances knew not to.

"I'm so sorry about your father," Celia said into her ear.

Celia had, of course, uttered the same sentence at the funeral a few days before. Rory had been just as stoic in the dimly lit funeral hall, standing next to the coffin that held the wax sculpture of her father. When she felt the warmth of Celia's breath in her ear now, and sensed what she guessed were the woman's tears spilling onto her neck, Rory finally put her hands on Celia's shoulders and broke free from her grip. She took a gathering breath and exhaled away the anxiety that was rising from her sternum.

"I've been through the file cabinets," Rory finally said.

A confused look came over Celia's face as she looked around the office and recognized the amount of work Rory had done. Celia patted the front of her jacket to collect herself, wiped her tears. "I thought . . . Have you been working on this all week?"

"No, just this morning. I got here a couple of hours ago."

Rory had long ago stopped attempting to explain her ability to conquer tasks like this one in a fraction of the time it took others. One reason she never practiced law was because it bored her to death. She remembered classmates spending hours studying textbooks that she memorized in a single skimming. And others taking months-long review courses to prepare for the bar exam, which Rory passed on her first attempt without opening a book to prepare. Another reason she avoided lawyering was because she had a strong aversion to people. The idea of haggling with another attorney over the jail sentence of some two-bit criminal made her skin crawl, and the thought of standing before a judge to plead her case caused her to wheeze with angst. She was better suited working solo to reconstruct crime scenes, her final opinions coming in the form of a written report that ended up on a detective's desk.

Rory Moore's world was a walled-off sanctuary she allowed few to enter, and even fewer to understand. Which was why this morning's discoveries were particularly disturbing. She learned that her father had several active cases heading to trial in the coming months that would need immediate assistance. Rory had already considered the likelihood that she'd be forced to dust off her diploma, swallow down the bile, and actually make her first appearance in court to explain to a judge that the lead counsel had died and the case would need an extension at best, a mistrial at worst, and that she'd require some guidance from Your Honor to figure out what the hell to do from there.

"A couple of hours?" Celia asked, tugging Rory back from the recesses of her mind. "How is that possible? This looks like every case we've ever taken on."

"It is. Everything I could find in the file cabinets. I wasn't able to check the computers."

This was a lie. Rory had no trouble logging on to her father's database. It was password protected, but barely, and Rory had quickly hurdled the minor security precautions to cross-reference the cases in the file cabinets with those on the hard drive. Despite that she had every right to access the computer files, being so far removed from the daily workings of the firm made it feel like trespassing.

"If it's in the cabinet, it's in the computer," Celia said.

"Good, then this is everything." Rory pointed to the desk and the first stack of folders. "These are pending cases. Should be simple enough to call these clients and explain the situation. The firm won't be taking them on and they'll have to look elsewhere for representation. I think it would be professional to make a list of other firms that handle these types of cases, so our clients have somewhere to start."

"Of course," Celia said. "Your father would want that."

"The second stack is the retired files. A simple form letter explaining that Frank Moore has died should suffice. I'll leave those two piles for you to handle?"

"Not a problem," Celia said. "I'll take care of it. What about those?"

Rory looked at the final hoard of records she had set on her father's desk. The sight started her hyperventilating. She felt the walls of her carefully constructed and meticulously cinder-blocked existence vibrating with unwanted trespassers from beyond.

"These are all my dad's open cases. I teased them out into three categories." Rory placed her hand on the first pile. "Currently negotiating plea deals—twelve." With her spoken words, she felt her underarms warm with perspiration as she touched the second group of files. "Awaiting court appearances—sixteen." A bead of sweat rolled down her spine to dampen the small of her back. "And finally"—she moved her hand to the last pile—"preparing for trial—three." Her throat caught when she said "three" and she coughed to hide her fear. The three cases going to trial would need immediate assistance.

A fearful look came over Celia when she saw the blood drain from Rory's face, as if the heart disease that claimed her father surely ran in the family and might strike twice in the same month. "Are you okay?"

Rory coughed again and regained her composure.

"I'm fine. I'll find a way to deal with the active cases if you could handle the rest."

Celia nodded as she picked up the mound of pending cases. "I'll start contacting these clients right away." She carried the stack to her desk in the reception area and went to work.

With her father's office door closed, Rory fell into his chair and stared at the files and the four empty Diet Cokes that had fueled her morning work. She clicked the computer to life and searched for criminal defense attorneys in Chicago who would be willing to take the cases.

CHAPTER 5
Stateville Correctional Center, October 15, 2019

*F*ORSICKS WAS HIS ALTER EGO. HE HAD ANSWERED TO THE MONIKER FOR so long now that he wasn't sure he would respond any longer to his real name. The nickname originated from the number that had been assigned to him the first night he arrived, stamped onto the back of his jumpsuit in large block font: **12276594-6.**

Before prison guards knew an inmate's name or the crime for which he had been convicted, they knew his number. His had been shortened to the final two digits in the series—"four-six"—which had morphed over the years into what most inmates and some uninformed guards believed to be his last name—"Forsicks."

He walked into the prison library and clicked on the lights. It was his home within the walls of the penitentiary. He had run the place for decades. Lifting weights and ballooning his body had never interested him, and joining the animals in the prison yard to colonize into sects of gangs was equally unappealing. Instead, he found the library, befriended the elderly lifer who ran the place, and bided his time. The lifer started wheezing during the winter of 1989 and never saw the last decade of the twentieth century. A guard rapped on the bars of Forsicks's cell the next morning to tell him the old man was gone, paroled to the heavens. The library was Forsicks's to run. *Don't screw it up.* He wouldn't.

For thirty years, the library had been under his control. In total, he had logged four decades on the inside without a single incident. The stellar track record had turned him nearly invisible, like the superheroes he read about in comic books he managed to score every month. He despised comics and graphic novels, but made sure to read them just the same. They gave him a softer persona and helped hide the longings that still loomed in his soul.

Prior to jail, he had set his life around The Rush—the feeling that washed over him after he spent time with his victims. The Rush had controlled his mind and shaped his existence. It was something from which he could never escape. After he was caught, though, he had no choice but to conform to life in prison. Withdrawal had been agonizing. He longed so badly for the feeling of power and dominance The Rush had once provided, for the incongruous sense of righteousness he enjoyed when he slipped the nylon noose around his neck and offered himself up to the lure of euphoria that only his victims could provide.

But after the dizzying withdrawal had subsided and he settled into the years in front of him, he looked to something else to fill the void. It quickly became obvious what it would be. The secret that had destroyed his life lay buried somewhere outside the walls of this prison, and he decided to spend the final chapter of his life unearthing it.

He sat at his desk in the front of the library. Only in America could a man who murdered so many be given such freedom—a desk and an entire prison library over which to rule. But after so many decades in this place, only a scant few on the inside knew his story. Even fewer cared. His anonymity was another reason he never corrected anyone who called him Forsicks. It added to his cover. The world had turned the lights out on him years ago. Only recently had the halogen of the past started to flicker back to life. Alone in his library, he unfolded the *Chicago Tribune* and found the headline on page two: 40 YEARS AFTER THE SUMMER OF 1979, THE THIEF SET TO WALK FREE.

His gaze passed over his old nickname, "The Thief." He couldn't ignore what the title did to him, the subtle stream of adrenaline it provided. But he was also aware of the downside to such a perfect signature—it was sure to draw attention and stir up memories. As headlines started popping up and talking heads began discussing the summer of '79, he would need to find a way to avoid the protestors and escape those who planned to haunt and torture him. He needed just a small window of anonymity after his release to complete his final journey, the planning of which he had dedicated his life in prison. It was a voyage he'd waited decades to embark upon, and had foolishly believed others could accomplish for him. But The Thief was the only one who could unearth the thing that haunted him, the secret that had ruined him.

This many years after his reign of terror, his victims were faceless and anonymous. Even when he visited the darkest parts of his mind and tried to conjure some of The Rush that used to fuel him, he could only scantly remember any of the women. They were all dead and gone, erased from his memory by time and indifference.

Only one remained vibrant in his memory, clear and present as if forty years were merely a blink of the eye, a single beat of his heart. She was the lone standout he could never forget. She ran through his thoughts during the quiet days in the library, and haunted his dreams when he slept. She was the only one he remembered, and his looming freedom presented a long-overdue opportunity to sew up loose ends with her.

CHICAGO
August 1979

*A*NGELA MITCHELL STARED AT THE TELEVISION. SHE STOOD WITH HER friend Catherine Blackwell and watched the news report. On the screen, a reporter stood in front of a darkened alley as the sun set on the summer night. Trashcans rested against chain-link fences, and weeds pushed through the cracks of the uneven pavement.

"Another woman," the reporter said, "has been confirmed missing. Samantha Rodgers, a twenty-two-year-old from Lincoln Park, was reported missing on Tuesday after she failed to show up for work. Authorities believe she is the fifth victim in a string of unexplained disappearances that started in the first week of May."

The reporter walked along the boulevard. A few pedestrians passed behind her and stared into the camera with stupid grins, unaware of the tragedy being reported.

"The disappearances started May second with the abduction of Clarissa Manning. Since then, three other women have gone missing from the streets of Chicago. None have been found, and it is suspected that their disappearances are all related. Now, Samantha Rodgers is feared to be the latest victim of a predator the authorities are calling The Thief. The Chicago Police Department continues to warn young women not to walk the streets alone. The authorities are asking for any leads in the whereabouts of the missing women, and have set up a tip line."

"Five women in three months," Catherine said. "How have the police not been able to find this guy?"

"They have to know something," Angela said in a quiet and reserved voice. "They're probably keeping the details away from the public so as not to tip this guy off to what they know."

Angela's husband walked into the room and clicked off the television. He kissed her lightly on the forehead. "Come on. Dinner's ready."

"It's just terrible," Angela said.

Angela's husband ran his hand over her shoulder and pulled her close for a quick hug. He cocked his head toward the kitchen, making eye contact with Catherine as he left the room.

Angela continued to stare at the blank television screen. The reporter's profile was burned into her mind, an afterimage that allowed Angela to recall every detail of the woman's face, the alley, the green street signs in the background, and even the dumb looks on the faces of the passersby who had walked through the frame. It was a gift and a curse to remember everything she saw. She finally blinked the reporter's image away, allowing it to fade from her visual cortex just as Catherine tugged lightly at Angela's elbow, pulling her toward the dinner table.

CHICAGO
August 1979

*F*OUR OF THEM—ANGELA AND CATHERINE, ALONG WITH THEIR HUS-bands—sat around the dinner table. Thomas, Angela's husband, had finished grilling chicken and vegetables, and they settled for the air-conditioned safety of their dining room rather than the original plan of eating on the back patio. The summer heat was sti-fling, the humidity thick, and the mosquitoes unrelenting.

"Sorry to spend another summer night inside," Thomas said. "We wait all year for winter to leave, and still find ourselves stuck in-side."

"I've been spending all my days outside lately," Bill Blackwell, Catherine's husband, said. "One of our foremen quit a couple of weeks ago. I've been running his crews, so a break from the heat is fine with me."

"We haven't hired anyone to replace him yet?" Thomas asked.

Thomas and Bill were partners in their concrete business, pour-ing foundations for new homes, paving industrial parking lots and indoor garages. Their business, started when they were both twenty years old, had grown to a midsized company with a unionized labor force.

"I've got a request in to Local 255. They're working on it, but until we hire someone I'm running the crews, which means I'm outside all day. And with temperatures in the midnineties, I'm very happy to be sitting inside tonight."

"If it helps," Thomas said, "I had to work the Bobcat when one of our guys was sick this week."

"That doesn't help," Bill said. "Driving a Cat is not the same as running the crews. If I get any more mosquito bites, I'll contract malaria."

"Should we be more sympathetic toward our hardworking men, Angela?" Catherine asked.

Angela stared at her plate, a detached look on her face.

"Angela," Thomas said.

When she didn't respond, he reached out and touched her shoulder, startling her. Angela looked up suddenly. The expression on her face made it seem like she was surprised to see others in the room.

"Bill was just saying how bad the mosquitoes are," Thomas said in an encouraging voice. "And that he's working harder than I am down at the shop. I need my wife to defend me here."

Angela tried to smile, but ended up simply nodding at Thomas.

"Anyway," Catherine said, pointing at her husband's neck, "if you get any more bug bites, you'll not have to worry about malaria as much as needing a blood transfusion. It looks like Dracula got to you."

Bill put his hand to his neck. "I had an allergic reaction to the bug spray," he said.

Thomas kept his hand on Angela's shoulder, an attempt to coax her into the conversation. She put her hand on top of his, and offered another false smile.

"I'm not sure insect repellent works on vampires," Angela said.

This brought chuckles from the group. Angela tried to engage in the dinner conversation, but all she could see was the afterimage of the television reporter still burned in her mind, and all she could concentrate on were the women who had gone missing this summer.

CHICAGO
August 1979

W HEN THEIR GUESTS WERE GONE, ANGELA CINCHED THE TOP OF THE garbage bag and tied it off. Her husband wiped his brow with his forearm as he stood in front of the sink and cleaned dishes. Entertaining was a new experience for her, and something to which Angela was still adapting. Before meeting Thomas, she had never enjoyed the experience of close friends, or any friends at all, for that matter. She had spent her life on the outskirts of societal norms. Vivid memories from Angela's youth reminded her why traditional friendships were impossible.

When Angela was age five, a girl had approached her in the kindergarten classroom to offer a Betsy McCall doll and the invitation to play together. To this day, Angela could feel the overwhelming sense of discomfort from someone standing so close to her, and the revulsion that came at the thought of touching a doll so many other children had handled. Even before kindergarten, Angela had taken to carrying her possessions in plastic sandwich bags to keep them safe from germs and filth. Her parents had learned that Angela's tantrums—complete sensory detachments—were quelled only when her belongings were safe inside the plastic bags. The habit continued through grade school, and kept her sealed off from friendships as tightly as her possessions were protected from the world.

So, hosting Catherine and Bill Blackwell for dinner had taken Angela as far out of her comfort zone as she'd been in months. But it was a good thing. It was making her life more normal. She had Thomas to thank for her transformation. Angela would forever be aware of the sideways glances she encountered from most of the world, but she took solace in the fact that Thomas accepted her, despite her many idiosyncrasies. Through her marriage, a new world had opened up. Catherine was the first person she called a friend. Around others Angela managed to control many of the unique habits that plagued the rest of her time. Catherine had seen some of these idiosyncrasies, and had accepted them. Like Angela's aversion of physical contact by anyone other than Thomas, and her affliction to loud noises, and the way she could become transfixed by something her mind wouldn't stop working on—as had occurred tonight when she watched the reporter explaining that another woman had gone missing. She had been unable to concentrate on anything else for the rest of the evening.

Despite her friendship with Catherine, Angela had never warmed to Catherine's husband, who was one of Thomas's closest friends. But this, too, seemed to be a nonissue for Catherine. They met frequently for lunch while their husbands worked.

"That was fun," Thomas said.

"Yeah."

"You and Catherine are becoming good friends?"

"We are. And her husband is nice, too."

Thomas came over to her. "Catherine's husband has a name, you know."

Angela averted her eyes, staring at her feet.

"I know tonight was hard for you. But you did great. I also know Catherine provides a level of comfort for you, but you can't only talk to her and me. You have to talk to everyone who's in the house. It's just polite."

She nodded.

"And you have to call people by their names. Bill, right? Catherine's husband's name is Bill."

"I know," Angela said. "He just . . . I'm not used to him, that's all."

"He's my business partner, and he's a good friend, so we're going to see him a lot."

"I'll work on it."

He kissed her forehead again, like he had when she watched the reporter covering the latest disappearance, and went back to the dishes.

"I'm dropping this outside," Angela said, lifting the tied-off garbage bag.

She headed out the kitchen door, which led to the backyard. She walked across the small plot of grass, and noticed the utility door to the garage was open. It was dark now and light spilled from the garage and through the door frame to form a trapezoid on the grass outside the door. When Thomas was grilling the chicken, Angela remembered Catherine's husband—*Bill*, as Thomas had just reminded her—walking freely in and out of the garage. It was another part of the night that made her uneasy, knowing the garage was a mess of clutter and junk. Angela had a hard time with things that were not strictly organized, and she was so embarrassed by the appearance of the garage that she had considered closing the door at one point during the evening as a nonverbal way of asking Catherine's husband to stay on the patio.

Angela shut the utility door now and pushed past the chain-link fence to enter the darkened alley. Lifting the top of the trashcan, she placed the garbage bag into the empty bin. A cat hissed and darted from behind the cans. Startled, she dropped the trashcan top, causing a loud metallic ruckus to echo through the alley while she let out a scream. Dogs barked from adjacent lots.

Angela took a deep breath and looked down the alley. A streetlight glowed at the far end of the block, casting swaying shadows of tree limbs onto the ground. In her mind Angela pictured a satellite image of the city limits, and referenced her location now as she stood in the shadowed alley on the far fringes of the city. Angela's thoughts turned to the diagram she had meticulously created, in which she placed red dots to mark the suspected location of each abducted woman. She had highlighted in bright yellow the area that joined them all. Her neighborhood was far outside the colored pentagon.

With a rumble in her chest and a tremor in her hands, Angela retrieved the top of the trashcan and haphazardly threw it back in place before running through the yard and into her kitchen. Thomas had finished the dishes and she heard the Cubs game playing in the living room. When she peeked in on him, Thomas was in a deep recline in the La-Z-Boy, which meant he'd soon be snoring. With her fingertips alive with adrenaline, she snuck into her bedroom and knelt at the foot of the bed. Opening the trunk, she found the stack of newspaper clippings and her map of the city.

She'd spent the entire evening suppressing her obsessive-compulsive needs. Angela's freshly learned self-restraint had done her well. It opened up a new world with Thomas, and had allowed her to forge a friendship with Catherine. But Angela knew she could not completely ignore the needs of her mind and the demands of her central nervous system, which screamed for her to organize and list and break down the things that made no sense. She saw things as either straight and ordered with sharp, ninety-degree angles, or in complete disarray. The calls of her mind to piece together in rigid order anything that did not line up smoothly had always been loud and impossible to ignore. But lately, those screams had been deafening. The idea that there was a man who had eluded the police, and who had thrown the city into a state of paralysis, was the very definition of chaos. And ever since Angela had allowed her fierce and unrelenting psyche to consider this man, whom authorities called The Thief, she had been able to think of nothing else.

She brought her stack of newspaper articles to the small desk in her bedroom, clicked on the light, and spread them out in front of her. Angela read them all for the hundredth time, determined to find what everyone else had missed.

CHICAGO
August 1979

ANGELA SPENT THE FOLLOWING MORNING AT HER KITCHEN TABLE surrounded by the previous week's newspaper clippings about The Thief. She had read them late into the night as Thomas slept on the La-Z-Boy. Now he had left for work and Angela was back at it. Both the *Tribune* and the *Sun-Times* lay before her as she meticulously worked the scissors around the corners of each article. She'd even managed to score a *New York Times* that had a brief write-up about the events in Chicago, the article drawing parallels to the "Son of Sam" killings from three years earlier. Angela read and reread the news pieces, concentrating on the five women who had gone missing, and cataloguing everything that had been reported about each victim. She collected photos and created her own biographies. She knew so much about each woman that she felt connected to them.

Angela worked hard to hide from Thomas the full scale of her affliction. There had been stretches in the past when her obsessive-compulsive disorder had consumed her, overwhelming her mind in ways that prevented routine rituals of daily life. During the darkest times, the illness tethered Angela to the completion of redundant tasks her brain insisted were necessary. And the more she tried to break free from those tumultuous duties, the more paranoid she became that something terrible would happen if she interrupted the cycle of meaningless assignments. The loop of paranoia fed itself until Angela was lost to its power.

She felt that pull happening again now, and knew she needed to tame this current bout of obsession if she hoped to avoid a relapse. But she felt helpless when her mind focused on the missing women and the anonymous man who was taking them. Angela believed she could find a link between the victims. What she would do with her discovery, Angela hadn't decided. Perhaps she would share her findings with the authorities. But Angela was careful not to get too far ahead of herself. Thinking too far into the future opened her mind to wild speculation that caused angst and fear. If Thomas noticed her missing lashes and thinning eyebrows again, he'd worry about a relapse. This would send her back to her therapist's office, which would spell the end to her research. She couldn't let that happen. The women who stared back from the newspaper clippings deserved her attention, and Angela was powerless to ignore them.

After the press clippings were catalogued and ordered, she packed up her files and placed them back in the chest at the foot of her bed. It was 10:00 A.M. when she brought her coffee out to the garage. She carried with her two homemade breakfast sandwiches wrapped in foil. The garage was a detached two-car unit behind their bungalow-style home. A cement walkway led from the patio off the kitchen and ran to the utility door at the back of the garage, the front of which opened into the alley. The previous night, Angela had allowed her imagination to create irrational nightmares of what waited in the dark shadows after the cat ran from behind the trashcans. This morning, the sun was bright and her fear was gone.

She walked through the utility door and hit the opener on the wall, causing the large garage door to rattle upward, and allowing the morning's sun to brighten the area. Because she rarely ventured into the garage, it was incongruent to the home she kept. If the space were hers and not Thomas's, Angela would have it ordered and meticulous the way everything else in her life needed to be. Instead, it was a mess of cluttered shelving filled with tattered books and dusty storage containers; there were paint cans coated with the drippings of a home project from when she and Thomas had painted the bedroom; there was car repair equipment, which

Thomas had stacked in the corner, and an old couch they had meant to sell, but had never gotten around to. The couch was now filthy from dust and dirt, and covered by old magazines and newspapers. It was her morning project.

Wednesday was garbage day, and Angela's task was to drag the old couch into the alley for the garbagemen to haul away. The breakfast sandwiches were her bribe to the guys for hauling away such a large piece of trash. Before she could get to the couch, though, Angela started with the magazines and newspapers that covered it, dumping them in the trash. After ten minutes, the couch was empty of the clutter that had covered it. Positioning herself near the entrance of the garage, she grasped the arm of the couch and pulled. It was weighty and her progress was slow, but after ten minutes, Angela managed to drag the couch into the alley. She needed to move it another twenty feet to the garbage area, but she had spent her strength hauling the heavy piece of furniture this far. She walked into the garage to catch her breath and regain her energy.

As she took deep, recovering breaths, she looked anxiously at the cluttered shelves, knowing that Thomas would be upset if she took her obsessiveness for order to the rest of the garage when she had told him she planned only to move the couch out to the garbage. But her fingers tingled as she looked at the chaotic shelving. Inspecting the items, she found things she had forgotten existed—old glassware from before she had married, and holiday decorations she and Thomas had never used.

On another set of shelves, Angela stumbled over old wedding gifts that were both impractical and unwanted. She found a picnic basket flanked on each side with compartments for wine bottles. Never in her life had she been on a picnic, and the idea of sipping wine while sitting among insect-infested grass caused her skin to crawl. She lifted the top of the basket. Something inside caught her eye. A closer inspection revealed a thin jewelry box.

She looked around the garage, and then out into the alley, as if she had just discovered a hidden treasure and worried about another learning her secret. She pulled the box from the depths of the basket and opened it. A sliver of morning sunlight slanted through the side window of the garage and struck the diamonds of the necklace, brilliantly highlighting the green peridot they encircled. It wasn't unusual for Thomas to make extravagant purchases. He'd done so in the past and Angela's birthday was just a week away. She immediately felt guilty for having spoiled his surprise.

"Can I offer you a hand?"

The deep, unfamiliar voice caused Angela to jump. She dropped the necklace back into the basket and spun around, finding herself face-to-face with a man she did not know. Her lungs expanded in an unintentional gasp, and a whine escaped into the air. The man stood in the alley by the couch, but his presence felt much closer. He had deep-set eyes darkened by the morning light, which shined down from behind him and silhouetted his form. The black presence of his shadow crept across the garage floor, coming so close to Angela that her skin tingled with goose bumps.

"Looks like you're stalled."

"No, no," Angela said without thought. She was backing away toward the utility door behind her, her feet staggering. As a general rule, Angela Mitchell avoided eye contact whenever possible. But the charcoal holes in the man's face were too cryptic to ignore.

"I'll just give it a push with you," the man said. "Help you get it over to the trashcans. You're throwing it away, yes?"

Angela shook her head. Her mind flashed to the biographies she had amassed on the missing women. The newspaper articles she had scanned and studied. The map of the city she had marked with the locations of the disappearances, and the bright yellow pentagon she had highlighted to demark the area of the city to avoid. She was filled now with the same sense of dread as when the stray cat had hissed from behind the trashcans. Last night, she had sensed another's presence, and she had run back into the house before her mind could dwell too heavily on the feeling. And since then, Angela had worked hard to compartmentalize the thought, to suppress the idea that someone had been present with her in the alley, watching from the shadows. To allow her mind to concentrate on that fear, to permit her psyche to continuously strike the flint that might throw sparks onto the tinder of her anxiety, had the power to drive her mad. Once that thought was ignited, she would be unable to stifle the flames.

Years before, a vagrant thought like that could send her into a weeks-long state of paranoia and obsessiveness where she'd lock herself in her home, checking and double checking the door locks, climbing from bed in the dark of night to make sure every window was secure, lifting the phone one hundred times in a row to make sure a dial tone was present to prove it was functional. Angela had worked too hard over the last few years to allow her new life to be ruined by the inner workings of her convoluted mind. But now, as she stared at the man in the alley, she wished she'd paid closer attention to the warnings her brain had sent last night.

"My husband will be right out," she managed to say. "He'll help me the rest of the way."

The man looked beyond Angela, through the frame of the open utility door behind her, and to the back of the bungalow. He pointed at the house. "Your husband is home?"

"Yes," Angela said too quickly.

The man took a step forward to the precipice of the garage, bringing his murky shadow closer until it bent off the floor and climbed up her legs. Angela could almost feel it.

"You sure I can't help?"

Angela backed farther away; she turned and hurried through the utility door and into the backyard. She ran to the kitchen door and fumbled with the handle until she pulled the door open and stepped into the safety of her home, immediately locking the door behind her. She peeled the curtains to the side to peek outside. The man stood next to the abandoned couch, staring through the open garage door at the back of Angela's house. Over the pounding in her ears, the squeaking brakes of the garbage truck broke through as it turned into the alley. The stranger looked behind him and hurried away as the truck approached.

Angela's hands were shaking. She couldn't bring herself to go back outside to talk with the garbagemen, to deliver the sandwiches in exchange for them taking the couch. Instead, she ran to the bathroom, lifted the lid to the toilet, and vomited until her eyes teared and her sternum ached.

CHAPTER 6
Chicago, October 16, 2019

*R*ORY MOORE PULLED NEXT TO THE UNMARKED SQUAD CAR, DRIVER'S side to driver's side. She rolled down her window and pushed her nonprescription glasses up the bridge of her nose. It was dark and shadowed inside her car. She was sure Detective Davidson couldn't see her eyes, always a plus.

The detective handed her a manila envelope through the window.

"Autopsy and tox results," he said. "Plus all the notes and interviews taken on the case."

Rory took the package, saw Camille Byrd's name printed on the bottom of the folder, and thought of the girl's shattered Kestner doll and her father's pleas for help. Rory dropped the file on the passenger seat.

"You're officially on the case," Ron said. "I filled out the paperwork this morning."

"When was the last time any of your guys looked at any of this?" Rory asked.

Davidson ballooned his cheeks as his exhaled a defeated breath. Rory knew he was embarrassed by the answer he was about to offer.

"It's over a year old, with nothing new in months and over five hundred new homicides so far this year. It's cold."

Rory's mind flashed back to the morning in Grant Park when Ron had shown her where Camille's frozen body had been found. Rory's heart ached, the way it did for the victim of every case she took on. It was why she was so selective. Within the tiny world of forensic reconstruction, no one could do what Rory Moore routinely accomplished. She had breathed fresh life into cases that were colder than a Chicago winter. It was simply in her genes. Her DNA was programmed to see things others missed, to connect dots that looked scattered and incongruent to everyone else. She left the straightforward reconstructions—the car wrecks and suicides—to others in her profession who were better suited to handle such trivial cases, the ones detectives could figure out on their own with a little effort and a lucky break. Those clinical cases never challenged Rory. She reconstructed cold case homicides, cases others had abandoned and given up on. But she accomplished this by developing a deep and personal connection with the victim. She accomplished this by learning their story, discovering first who they were. Why they were killed always followed. It was a taxing technique that drained her emotionally and often brought her closer to the victim for whom she was seeking justice than she was to anyone else in her life. But it was the only way Rory knew how to do her job.

Rory knew that Ron Davidson, who ran the Homicide Division inside the Chicago Police Department, was under pressure from every direction, political and social, to pull Chicago's unsolved murder rate out of the toilet. The city had one of the nation's lowest homicide solve rates; so when Rory agreed to take on Camille Byrd's icy cold, unsolved homicide, it represented an opportunity for Ron to knock a case off his docket without expending many resources. Rory reconstructed crimes on her own, rebuffing assistance from any of the Homicide detectives. For years, the force had kept Rory on retainer, and if she weren't so selective about the cases she took on, she'd have a new one every week.

"I'll take a look and let you know what I find," Rory finally said.

"Keep me posted."

Rory's window began its ascent.

"Hey, Gray," Davidson said.

Rory stopped the window halfway up, looked through the glass at him.

"Sorry about your dad."

Rory nodded and started the window back up before the two cars drove off in opposite directions.

CHAPTER 7
Chicago, October 16, 2019

*R*ORY WALKED INTO THE NURSING HOME AND ENTERED ROOM 121. The lights were dim, and the television cast the room in a blue glow. A woman lay still in the bed, her eyes open but not acknowledging Rory's presence. Rory approached the hospital bed, which sported tall guardrails on either side to protect its occupant. She sat in the adjacent chair and looked at the woman, who continued to stare at the television as if Rory were invisible.

She reached out and took the woman's hand.

"Aunt Greta. It's me, Rory."

Her great-aunt inverted her lips, sucking them into her mouth the way she did after the nurses had removed her dentures.

"Greta," Rory said in a whispered voice. "Can you hear me?"

"I tried to save you," the old woman said. "I tried, but there was too much blood."

"Okay," Rory said. "It's okay."

"You were bleeding." Her great-aunt looked at Rory. "There was too much blood."

A nurse walked into the room. "Sorry, I tried to catch you before you came in. She's having a bad day."

The nurse adjusted the pillows behind Greta's head, placed a white Styrofoam cup with a straw extending out of it on the over-bed table.

"Here's your water, hon. And there's no blood around here. I hate blood, that's why I work in this place."

"How long has she been like this?"

The nurse looked at Rory. "Most of the day. She was fine yesterday. But, as you know, dementia takes them back to another part of their life. Sometimes just briefly, other times for much longer. It'll pass."

Rory nodded, pointed at the Styrofoam. "I'll get her to drink."

The nurse smiled. "Call me if you need anything."

As soon as the nurse was gone, Rory's great-aunt looked at her again.

"I tried to save you. There was too much blood."

Greta had been a nurse, and though it had been many years since she practiced, the dementia, which was ravaging her mind, pulled her back to the darkest moments of her profession.

Greta went silent and looked back at the television. Rory knew it would be one of those visits. Her great-aunt was ninety-two years old, and her mental capacity varied widely. Sometimes she was as sharp as ever. Other times, like tonight and over the past two weeks since Greta had learned about the passing of Rory's father, she was lost in the past. In a world that Rory could not penetrate. The best chance over the last several years to catch her in a coherent state came at night. Sometimes Rory came and went in a matter of minutes. Other times, when Aunt Greta was alert and talkative, Rory stayed into the early hours of morning, talking and laughing like she remembered doing as a child. Few people fully understood Rory Moore. Her great-aunt Greta was one of them.

"Greta, do you remember what I told you about Dad? About Frank, your nephew?"

Greta chewed some more on her capsized lips.

"The funeral was last week. I tried to bring you, but you weren't feeling well."

Rory saw her great-aunt's chewing grow faster.

"You didn't miss anything. Except me squirming in the corner trying to avoid everyone. I could have used you for cover, old lady."

This brought a quick glance from Greta and the subtle twitch of a smile. Rory knew she had broken through on a night that had offered little opportunity.

"What better way to deflect attention from myself than to wheel in a little old lady everyone loves?"

Rory felt her great-aunt squeeze her hand. A tear formed on Greta's eyelid and then rolled down her cheek. Rory stood and quickly pulled a tissue from the box to wipe Greta's face.

"Hey," she said, trying for the eye contact she normally worked to avoid. "I've got a tough one I need your help with. It's a Kestner doll with a bad fracture through the left eye socket. I can fix the break, but I might need some help with the coloring. The porcelain is faded and I'll need to color over the epoxy. You want to lend a hand?"

Greta looked at Rory. She stopped chewing her lips. Then she nodded with a subtle bob of her head.

"Good," Rory said. "You're the best. And you taught me everything I know. I'll bring your colors and brushes next time I visit and you can take a look."

Rory sat back down in the bedside chair, reached for Greta's hand again, and spent an hour watching the muted television screen until she was sure her great-aunt had drifted off to sleep.

CHAPTER 8
Chicago, October 16, 2019

S HE PULLED TO THE FRONT OF HER BUNGALOW AND PARKED ON THE street, which was lined with her neighbors' cars. It was just past eleven o'clock, and Rory felt good about her visit with Greta. She didn't always feel that way when she left her great-aunt's side. Alzheimer's and dementia had stolen most of her personality, turning her at times into a nasty old woman who could spit insults like a drunken sailor one moment, and babble incoherently the next. Despite the ferocity of the abuse, the vile version of Aunt Greta was preferred to the vacant-eyed, hollow soul Rory often found when she visited. Each of Greta's personalities was tolerated because occasionally, like tonight, there was a glimpse of the woman Rory had loved her whole life. It had been a good night.

The dog across the street barked as Rory walked up her steps and keyed the front door, grabbing the mail on her way in. She dumped the stack of envelopes, along with Camille Byrd's autopsy report, onto her kitchen table and pulled a glass from the cabinet. The middle shelf of her refrigerator held six bottles of Three Floyds Dark Lord, an impossible-to-find imperial stout that Rory managed to keep well stocked through an Indiana connection. Each twenty-two ounce bottle was positioned label out and in flaw-less rows—the only way Dark Lord should be shelved. She plucked one from the front, popped the cap, poured it into the tall glass, and topped it off with blackcurrant cordial. With an alcohol con-tent of fifteen percent, the beer was stronger than most wines and it took only a couple of glasses to obtain the desired effect. At the kitchen table, she pushed the stack of mail to the side and pulled the manila envelope she had received from Detective Davidson in front of her. Two full swallows of stout and a deep breath, then she dove in, opening the file to the first page of the autopsy report.

At the time of her death, Camille Byrd was a twenty-two-year-old recent University of Illinois graduate. She'd finished college in May and was still hunting for a place to put her communications major to use. She lived in Wicker Park with two roommates. The medical examiner determined the cause of death to be throttling, or manual strangulation. Manner of death, homicide. No evidence of sexual assault.

Two more swallows of stout and Rory turned the page. She read through the ME's findings. Classic signs of asphyxiation were noted—bloodstained fluid in the airway, swelling of the lungs, petechiae on the face, and subconjunctival hemorrhage in the eyes. Severe bruising was noted to Camille's neck, along with fractures to the hyoid bone and larynx, confirming the conclusion of strangulation. The presence of "fingerprint" markings left no doubt. Rory pulled an autopsy photo in front of her. She re-read the findings. Camille Byrd had gone missing one night, and her body was discovered the next. Rigor mortis and lividity allowed the time of death to be gauged at twenty-four hours prior to her body being discovered. Whoever killed Camille Byrd had done it quickly. Leukotriene B4 was detected in skin samples, Rory read, indicating that the bruising on the neck took place antemortem—before the girl had died, and now present forever more as the healing power of her body faded with her last breath.

She spent an hour in her quiet house, flipping through the rest of the medical examiner's report before she switched to the detective's notes. The autopsy report had been computer generated; the Homicide Division of the Chicago PD still worked with paper charts. Opening the file brought an assault of ugly, curt penmanship that was difficult to decipher. Rory was certain of some Freudian link between male detectives' atrocious penmanship and their mothers, as if their childish writing was evidence of a man's constant need for pampering.

For an hour, and over another Dark Lord spiked with blackcurrant cordial, Rory read about the life of Camille Byrd. From her childhood, to the day she went missing, to the morning her frozen body was found in Grant Park. She took notes, single-spaced, one sentence after the other, until she filled an entire page. Unlike the detective's writing, Rory's was perfect cursive. However, with no spaces between sentences and few punctuation marks, she was sure her notes looked nearly as indecipherable as the detective's piggish scribble.

When she closed the file, Rory knew she was a long way from knowing Camille Byrd as well as would be necessary to find the answers she was looking for. But tonight was a start. Stacking the reports to the side, Rory finally closed her eyes. She settled her mind and allowed the facts to take hold. That night, she would dream of Camille Byrd the way she always dreamt of the victims she studied. This was how every reconstruction began. She chose each case carefully, and devoted her full attention to it until she reached her conclusion and turned everything over to the detectives to finish the job.

After twenty minutes of meditation, she opened her eyes and took a deep breath. She carried the files into her office and placed them neatly on her desk, removed the 8-by-10 photograph of Camille Byrd and pinned it to the large corkboard on the wall. Pocked with holes from previous reconstructions, the board had told many disturbing stories over the years. Tonight the echoes from previous cases went unheard as Rory stared at the photo of Camille Byrd, who stared back from some unearthly place, waiting for Rory's help.

She hit the lights on the way out of the office. With the rest of the house dark, she grabbed another beer from the fridge and headed to the den. The room contained only indirect lighting, no overhead bulbs or lamps, just carefully positioned spotlights. The first switch Rory tripped brought to life the built-in shelves and silhouetted two dozen antique China dolls that stood on the ledges. Positioned three per shelf and in seamless columns, the recessed lighting cast each doll in a perfect combination of luminance and shadow. Every doll's porcelain face shined under the spell of the lighting, both the coloring and polish flawless.

Exactly twenty-four dolls stood on the shelves. Any less left a vacancy that gnawed at Rory until the empty slot was filled. She'd tried it before—removing one doll without replacing it with another. The unfilled space created an imbalance in her mind that prevented sleep and work and rational thought. The nagging annoyance dissipated, Rory had discovered, only after she filled the vacancy with another doll to make the shelving complete. She'd come to terms with this affliction years ago, and had finally stopped battling it. It had been embedded in her since she was a young child standing in Aunt Greta's house staring at doll-lined shelves. Rory's love of restoration originated during her formative years when she spent her summers with Greta bringing broken dolls back to perfection. Now Rory's den had looked the same for more than a decade and was a replica of Aunt Greta's house from years ago, the built-ins lined with some of her most triumphant restorations. Never a vacancy present.

A thin drawer was positioned under each shelf, in which rested "before" pictures of each doll featured on the ledge above. The 8-by-10 glossy photos depicted cracked faces, missing eyes, jagged tears that spilled white stuffing, stained garments, missing limbs, and faded porcelain that had shed its glaze over years of life. The images in the drawers stood in stark contrast to the immaculate dolls standing on the shelves above, which Rory had meticulously brought back to life.

Sitting at her workbench, she turned on her gooseneck lamp and directed its beam to the ruined Kestner doll Camille Byrd's father had used to lure Rory into reconstructing his daughter's death. She took another sip of Dark Lord and began her cursory examination, photographing the damaged doll from every angle until finally laying it flat and taking a conclusive picture that would become the "before" image against which her restoration would be gauged. The beer buzz, coupled with the preoccupation of a new project—both Camille Byrd's childhood doll, and the woman herself—was enough to penetrate the deep folds of Rory's brain and distract her from the gnawing image of the files waiting for resolution in her father's law office. The distraction of a new project was just sufficient to push into the shadows of her mind the thought of her father dying alone in his home.

CHAPTER 9

Stateville Correctional Center,
October 17, 2019

*H*IS KILLING SPREE DECADES AGO HAD, FOR A SHORT TIME, MADE him a celebrity. But soon after his conviction, the world moved on and had mostly forgotten about The Thief. Only in recent months had his star begun to rise again as journalists relived the summer of 1979 by recounting the women who had been informally counted as his victims. Family members were tracked down. Friends, now gray and wrinkled by age, spoke of long-forgotten kinships with those they lost. Ambitious newscasters replayed old footage in an attempt to recapture the panic of the city during that sweltering summer when The Thief ran loose through the shadowed streets of Chicago, stealing young women never to be seen again.

And now, as his celebrity began its slow ascent, he would need to rely on the one man who had helped him most over the years. He had access to the prison e-mail system, but it was a tedious process to receive and deliver messages, and prison rules placed strict word counts on his e-mails. It was faster and easier to write his letters by hand and send them through the post office, which he had done several times in the last three weeks without a response. The United States Postal Service—jail mail—had always been his swiftest form of communication. Faster even than a phone call, which required him to make a formal request, wait for approval, and then schedule a date and time to use the prison pay phone. It had always been his preference when he needed to get ahold of his attorney to simply pen a letter, stuff it in an envelope, and drop it in the mail. But after two weeks without a reply, he decided to petition for a phone call. With his final parole board hearing fast approaching, his attorney had been in constant contact with him regarding the details of his impending release. But for the last two weeks, his attorney had been silent and unreachable.

The Thief lay on his bunk now and folded his hands across his chest as he waited. There was an imbalance in the universe. He could feel it in his gut. Passing time had never been a challenge. At least, not for many years. But of late, since the parole board had stamped him *approved,* time became something more difficult to manage. His sentence was coming to an end, and he allowed himself to taste what waited on the outside. It was a dangerous practice to entertain thoughts about the freedoms that might soon come to him. It was especially dangerous to imagine the satisfaction of finding her. Still, despite the hazards, he closed his eyes as he lay on his bunk and imagined finally coming face-to-face with her. What a joyous moment it would be. The woman who had put him here would finally receive retribution.

"Forsicks," the guard said, interrupting his thoughts. "You got phone privileges today?"

He sat up quickly and stood from his bed.

"Yes, sir."

The guard turned his head and in a booming voice yelled down the length of the cell block. "One-two-two-seven-six-five-nine-four-six." His voice echoed off the walls and conjured prisoners to the front of their cells, where they stuck their arms through the bars and rested their elbows on the metal as they watched what was transpiring.

Forsicks's cell door rattled open and the guard motioned for him to take the lead as they walked down the long galley. Seeing nothing exciting, the other prisoners melted back into their cells. A door buzzed as they approached the end of the gangplank and Forsicks pushed through it. Another guard was waiting for him on the other side. He did a quick pat down, and then motioned him toward an isolated pay phone on the wall.

Forsicks went through the practiced routine of navigating the automated prison phone system that allowed outgoing collect calls, dialed the number from memory, and listened to the staticky ring through the receiver. After the eighth loop of buzzing, the call went to voice mail, where he learned that his attorney's mailbox was full.

The universe was off. Something was wrong. All of his fantasies about finding her began to fade.

CHICAGO
AUGUST 1979

*T*HE VOMITING CONTINUED FOR THE ENTIRE WEEK AFTER HER EN-counter with the stranger in the alley. Her head swam with vertigo and her stomach roiled with nausea every time Angela thought of that morning. The dirty couch had sat abandoned for the entire day. The garbage men hadn't touched it. The couch sat at an odd angle at the precipice of the open garage door, and Angela imagined they assumed it was there temporarily while the garage was being cleaned. She had watched through the slit in the curtain that covered the kitchen window as the garbage truck stopped in the alley and the guys emptied her overflowing trashcans into the back of the truck before hopping back onto the fender as the driver continued down the alley. Angela couldn't bring herself to open the kitchen door and run to the alley to ask them to haul the couch away.

It was early afternoon when Angela had heard the honking that day. Her neighbor was attempting to pull his car into the garage directly across from Angela's, but couldn't make it past the couch to cut the tight angle. As was typical in Chicago, the constant honking of one's horn was the chosen solution to nearly every problem a driver faced, from slow-moving traffic, to kids playing ball in the street, to a deserted couch in an alley. When the honking reached five nerve-racking minutes, Angela had finally gotten up the nerve to leave the house. She pulled the couch back into the garage, shut the door, and hurried back inside to bolt the door behind her. *Once. Twice. Three times, to be sure.*

She told Thomas about the day's adventure as soon as he'd gotten home. He suggested they call the police, but when they discussed it further, Angela was at a loss for exactly what she would be reporting. That a stranger, and likely a neighbor, had been kind enough to offer his assistance? That a cat had frightened her the night before and filled her with the sense that she was being watched? Angela knew how that conversation would go. She could already see the sideways glances the officers would give each other while Angela stuttered through her explanation, all the time doing her best to avoid eye contact. The nervous plucking of her eyebrows would be looked upon like a contagious disease until the officers excused themselves to speak with Thomas in private about his paranoid wife, who was clearly making more out of things than was there. The further she discussed the incident with Thomas, the more absurd it sounded to call the police.

More pressing now, a week later, was Angela's fear that she was on the verge of an obsessive-compulsive breakdown. That she even recognized its imminent approach, like thunderclouds on the horizon, could be considered progress. Years before, the affliction would descend upon her without warning to steal a week or a month as the demands of her mind sent her on meaningless tasks of redundancy. But in the new paradigm of her life, Angela not only sensed the collapse approaching, she fought like hell to prevent it. While she battled her condition, she also worked hard to hide the worst of her symptoms from Thomas. The lack of eyelashes was camouflaged by a thick application of mascara to the few follicles that remained, and a shadowing pencil bolstered her thinning eyebrows. Despite the sweltering heat, Angela had taken to wearing jeans and long shirts in lieu of shorts and tank tops in order to hide the bloody scabs that marked her shoulders and thighs from her nervous scratching.

The masking of her symptoms, however, was a venomous crutch that made things worse. The better Angela was able to conceal her habits of self-mutilation, the more dramatic her dependency on them became. She tried to stop herself with subtle tricks that had worked in the past. She kept the tips of her fingers slick with Vaseline to make more difficult the grasping of her eyebrow follicles.

And she clipped her nails down to the soft pads of her fingers to make them benign tools as she dug into her skin. She was managing thus far to keep the worst of her breakdown hidden.

The vomiting, however, was becoming a problem. Thomas noticed it the other morning. When he checked on her, Angela had told him it was the result of bad Chinese food. In reality, the nausea came every time she worked herself into a frenzy with thoughts of the stranger from the alley. Each morning after Thomas left for work, Angela spent hours pulling the curtains of the kitchen door to the side so she could stare out into the alley. A routine developed: pull curtain, check alley, secure lock, lift phone, listen for dial tone, repeat. The only thing that broke the cycle was the need to vomit. Her stomach turned whenever the image popped into her mind of the man standing in the alley and peering through the open garage door and into her kitchen, which sent her to the bathroom in violent flurries of retching.

It was during a rare moment of lucidity a week after her encounter in the alley, when Angela had discovered an expired bottle of Valium from her previous doctor. Swallowing a tablet every six hours, Angela found, took the edge off, allowed her to sleep at night, and brought her mind back from the encounter in the garage. It was a temporary fix until she could reason with herself and calm her mind. She had beaten the obsessiveness before. She could do it again.

Under the calming effects of the Valium, Angela convinced herself that it was possible, and even likely, that her encounter in the alley was nothing more than a Good Samaritan offering his help. And it was very *un*likely that the horror of the missing women could stretch this far out to the fringe of the city limits, where she lived a quiet life. She took a deep breath and tried to steady her shaking fingers as she poured her morning coffee. She stopped her gaze before she could look for the hundredth time out the back window and into the alley. Instead, she forced her thoughts to focus on the missing women and the profiles she had created. It had been days since she thought of them.

She retrieved the press clippings from the chest in her bedroom and spread them across the kitchen table. For two hours, Angela studied the missing women and the notes she had made about each of them. Perhaps it was the clean slate of her mind coming off a lost week of paranoia, or the Valium freeing her thoughts to flow in ways they hadn't in the weeks before, but as she read through the profiles, she saw something she had missed previously. Her mind ran through the catalogued information, like scrolling through microfilm at the library. Articles she had read over the past years suddenly came together in her mind and she saw a pattern that had always been there, waiting to be discovered, but to this point had gone unnoticed. Her mind raced and she jotted notes, but the bleached-out exertion from fighting her OCD for the last week had frayed her neurons and brought self-doubt. Surely, she was wrong.

Pushing her insecurities aside, Angela scribbled notes frantically as thoughts spilled from her mind, fearful that if she didn't capture them on the page they'd be lost forever. She recalled with great clarity the newspaper articles she had read years earlier and scribbled names and dates from the images that sped through her mind. When she finished, she looked at the clock. It was approaching the noon hour. She had sat down at the kitchen table three hours ago, but it felt like only minutes.

Quickly dressing in jeans and a long-sleeved shirt, Angela stuffed her notes into her purse. A wave of nausea came over her as she imagined leaving the house, but she had no choice. She had to get to the library to confirm her suspicions. She knew, too, she would have to take another precaution. She needed confirmation that her thoughts were lucid and coherent, and not the result of her paranoia. And that confirmation could come from only one person.

Angela picked up the phone and dialed her friend Catherine's number.

"Hello?"

"Catherine," Angela said in a soft voice.

"Angela?"

"Yes, it's me."

"Are you feeling better? Thomas told Bill that you've been ill since the night we had dinner together."

Perhaps, Angela considered, she hadn't been hiding her symptoms as well as she imagined.

"I'm fine, but I need to talk with you. Can we meet?"

"Sure. Is something wrong?"

"No. I just need some help. Can I stop by in a while?"

"Of course," Catherine said.

Angela hung up without saying good-bye, ran to the bathroom, and then vomited.

CHICAGO
August 1979

*A*NGELA MITCHELL SPENT TWO HOURS AMONG THE LIBRARY SHELVES, pulling books and skimming pages. She sat at the microfilm station and spun old rolls of newspaper articles that dated back to the summer of 1970, nearly a decade earlier. She scribbled notes until her uncanny mind saw clearly the pattern she suspected existed. She spent thirty minutes plotting her findings onto graph paper and creating a line chart that translated her findings to paper form so others might understand her discovery.

She organized her notes, returned the microfilm to the shelf, and hurried from the library. Catherine's house was just two blocks from her own, and at 3:00 P.M., Angela pushed through the wrought iron gate that led to the front stoop. Even before Angela could knock, Catherine opened the door.

"Woman, it's ninety degrees outside," Catherine said as Angela walked up the front steps. "Why are you covered in denim?"

Angela looked at her jeans and button-down shirt. She was less concerned with how her fashion choices would react to the sweltering heat as she was with hiding the scabbed-over claw marks that covered her arms and legs.

"I'm behind on laundry," she finally said.

"Come into the air conditioning." Catherine pushed open the screen door and waved Angela inside.

They sat at the kitchen table. "So what got you so sick? Stomach bug?"

"Yes," Angela said, glancing quickly into Catherine's eyes, her first bit of eye contact, then back down to the table. "But I've been over it for the last few days. You know how Thomas worries."

Thomas had pushed hard during the first year or two of marriage for Angela to mix with his friends' wives. But Angela had always felt judged by them. They whispered about her when they thought she wasn't listening, and treated her like a child when she didn't respond to their boisterous ways. Catherine Blackwell was different. Angela felt accepted when she was with Catherine, who never asked foolish questions or gave confused looks when Angela grew quiet with anxiety. Catherine had always made her feel comfortable, and stood by her whenever anyone treated Angela badly. The first time the two ventured to lunch together, a condescending waitress had scolded Angela for not speaking loudly enough.

Speak up, honey.

Her name is Angela, not Honey, Catherine had said. *And she's almost thirty years old, not twelve.*

From that moment, Catherine Blackwell was not only her protector, she was Angela Mitchell's closest friend.

"Can I get you something to drink?"

"No, no," Angela said. "Thanks, though."

"So what's so urgent?"

"I know this is going to sound crazy," Angela said, pulling a folder from her purse. It held newspaper clippings and her biographies of the missing women, in addition to the reams of paper from her latest research trip to the library. "But I've been looking into the women who have gone missing."

This caught Catherine's attention. "Looking into them how?"

"I've been collecting bits of information about them from the papers and from newscasts."

Catherine pulled one of the pages across the table. It was a *Chicago Tribune* article about Samantha Rodgers, the latest girl who had disappeared from the streets of Chicago. Catherine had watched one of the news reports about the missing girl with Angela when they all had dinner together the week before. The girl's picture was at the top of the article, a crease bent through her photo, where the clipping had been folded and stashed in Angela's binder.

"Why are you collecting all this?" Catherine asked.

Angela looked up.

"I'm obsess—" Angela caught herself. Speaking the word "obsessed" out loud would be confessing to her friend the dark affliction that had plagued her life. It was unlikely, Angela understood, that Catherine hadn't already recognized the signs of her condition, but Angela stopped herself, nonetheless.

"I can't stop thinking about them," she finally said.

"Why?"

"It's hard to explain. When my mind gets focused on something, it's hard for me to . . . let it go. So I started collecting information about the girls, and I think I've found something."

Angela spread the information across the table. She had printed articles from newspapers and microfilm at the library, as well as pages from the books she had referenced, and her own notes that filled the first third of her spiral notebook.

"Five girls have gone missing since spring. Here are the dates each disappeared." Angela pointed to a different page. "Here is a list describing each victim—age, race, ethnicity, occupation, and physical characteristics, like hair color, skin tone, eye color. You get the idea."

Angela pushed the handwritten list to Catherine.

"The police say each disappearance is random. They believe the same man has taken all of these women, but they believe there is no connection between each woman. From what I can tell, they're right about that. The women, in relation to one another, have no association. But the police say The Thief strikes unsystematically. That's not true."

Catherine looked at Angela. "How long have you been working on this?"

"All summer. Since the women started to go missing. It's all I do, really. All I've been able to think about. But in reality, I realized this morning that I've been working on it much longer than just this summer. I just wasn't aware of it until now. Until I put it together."

"What did you put together?"

Angela lifted a random sheet of paper from within the scattered Xeroxed pages. "Look at this. I categorized all the characteristics of each missing girl—age, race, occupation, physical qualities—all the things on that list you're looking at—and then I went back to look not just at missing persons cases, but also homicides in and around Chicago that involved women who match those characteristics."

Angela produced the handmade chart she had created at the library.

"Look here." She pointed at the graph paper. "On the bottom of my graph are years starting in 1960 and going all the way through to today, the summer of 1979." Angela ran her finger from left to right across the bottom of the page. "On the vertical axis is the number of homicides of women who fall into the category of these missing women. Again, age, sex, race, physical characteristics. Now look, from 1960 to 1970, the number of homicides that involved women who match these descriptions was flat."

On the graph, a horizontal line ran from 1960 to 1970 without any substantial spikes or dips.

"But in 1970," Angela said, "there was a sudden uptick in homicides involving these types of women."

On the chart, Angela's handwritten line spiked upward dramatically in 1970.

"These are *all* the homicides in Chicago?" Catherine asked.

"No. In 1970, there were more than eight hundred homicides in and around Chicago. This graph only represents homicides involving women who match the characteristics of the five women who have gone missing this summer." Angela tapped the page again, tracing her finger over her graph. "The increase in homicides begins in 1970 and continues until 1972, then tapers out but stays high relative to the entire decade of the 1960s. Then, this year, 1979, there is a sudden drop again back to levels equal to the sixties."

Catherine was nodding her head as she listened. "I see the increase and the decrease. But what does it mean?"

"Here's my theory," Angela said. "The same person who is taking women this summer has been killing these types of women since around 1970. Between 1970 and 1978, he was careless and brazen. But since the beginning of this year, he's been more diligent. Instead of the police finding a body some weeks after a girl goes missing, now the women just disappear with no bodies being discovered."

Catherine squinted her eyes as she began to see Angela's theory come together. "You're saying this person's reign of terror spans, not just to this summer, but for the entire decade."

Angela made eye contact again. Her second time. "Yes."

Catherine sat back in her chair. "This is some crazy stuff you're telling me."

"But you see how it's possible, right?" Angela asked.

"When you present it to me this way, yes. That's assuming all your facts are correct."

"They are."

"And you got all this information from the library?"

"It's all there for anyone to find. You just have to look in the right places and with the right ideas in mind. This guy, The Thief, he has a *type*. And he's been preying on a specific type of woman for ten years."

"So why has this guy suddenly become so careful this year? Why is he hiding the bodies so much better?"

"Good question," Angela said. "What happened last year? What was the big story around here?"

Catherine shook her head. "I don't know."

Angela pulled more pages from her folder and passed them to Catherine. "Out in Des Plaines?"

Catherine's eyes widened slightly when it came to her as she read the headline: KILLER CLOWN CLAIMS 33 AS MORE BODIES DISCOVERED.

"John Wayne Gacy," she said.

"Correct. The police discovered a serial killer named John Wayne Gacy, who killed more than thirty young men and buried them in the crawl space of his home."

"And what? The Thief got spooked by Gacy's arrest?"

"Correct. Police activity picked up. The public was more diligent. And if the authorities had any ability to see patterns, they would have picked up on this one." Angela tapped her homemade chart again. "So he changed from a killer to a thief. He still kills these women, I'm certain of it. He just hides their bodies better."

"Angela, sweetheart," Catherine said. "I don't really know what to say. If this is correct, even if it's only partially accurate, you need to take this to the police."

Angela looked at Catherine again. "That's why I need your help."

"Anything."

"I can't go to the police. They'll look at me . . ." Angela made brief eye contact again. "You know what they'll think."

"Bring Thomas with you."

Angela was already shaking her head. "I can't tell Thomas about this. He's already worried about how I spend my days. If he knows I've been obsessing—"

The sound of her own voice uttering *that word* again caused Angela to scratch her shoulder through the fabric of her shirt. Frustration flared when her benign fingernails, clipped to the nubs, were unable to produce the searing pain she hoped for.

"Thomas would think this is an unhealthy way for me to spend my time."

"But if it's true, Angela. If what you've discovered is true, this transcends what Thomas thinks about how you spend your time." Catherine tapped the graph. "If this is true, then telling the police could save lives."

The front door opened and Catherine's husband yelled into the house.

"Catherine, you home?"

"In here, hon."

In a panic, Angela began gathering her research and stuffing pages back into the file folder as Bill Blackwell walked into the kitchen. He wore dirty jeans and a shirt covered in bits of concrete. Angela immediately recognized the appearance, since it was how Thomas often came home after work. Catherine's husband wore a bandana, which hung loose around his neck. Angela remembered the red marks on his skin and his remarks from the other night about mosquitoes and an allergic reaction and his foreman quitting, which forced Bill to run the crews. Angela hadn't even been aware that night, preoccupied as she was with her thoughts of the missing women, that she had comprehended Bill Blackwell's words. Angela's mind worked that way, absorbing everything around her and storing it all in the deep recesses of her brain. The catalogued information randomly floated from her subconscious until she was aware of its presence. It happened to her often. Her mind would whisper to her that she was aware of something, even if she didn't quite grasp precisely what it was she understood. Then, later, the stored image or nugget of knowledge would break loose from the anchor in her mind and rise to the surface. But there was something else that caught her attention now. Angela tried not to look, tunneling her vision to the task of organizing her papers so she could leave as quickly as possible.

"Angela," Bill said. "How are you? I didn't know you guys were getting together today."

Angela smiled and offered a quick glance at Bill Blackwell. Then the other image that had caught her attention came into focus. She saw another man in the background.

"This is Leonard Williams," Bill said as the man walked into the kitchen. "He's been working up at the Kenosha shop for me. I stopped home for a quick bite to eat before heading out to a job on the west side."

When Leonard Williams appeared from the hallway and entered the kitchen, Angela immediately recognized him as the man from the alley who had tried to help with the couch. His dark eyes were less shadowed now than they had been when the morning sun had backlit his frame that day, but the dark charcoal of his orbits was unmistakable. Angela's throat closed in a momentary spasm of panic, and for an instant, she was unable to breathe, causing her eyes to widen and bulge as she stared at the stranger from the alley. The man who had pushed her into a week of hysterics that had ignited her obsessive-compulsive habits.

She finally pushed air into her lungs and returned to shuffling papers into her purse, some of which scattered to the floor. She hurriedly tried to retrieve them and stop others from falling, but succeeded only in scattering more pages from the table.

"Wow, wow, wow," Bill said. "Take it easy."

He glanced wide-eyed at Catherine before picking up a few loose papers from the kitchen floor and handing them to Angela, who took them quickly without looking at him. Angela didn't need to look into Bill Blackwell's eyes to see the disgusted look on his face. She sensed it. It was an expression that sent Angela back to her childhood. Most people had looked at her this way throughout her adolescence, and today Angela felt much of the confidence she had earned in the last few years slipping away. She muttered a nearly silent thank-you while stuffing the pages into her bag.

"Let me help you," Catherine said, taking control of the situation and organizing the pages into a neat stack for Angela to place back into her purse.

"Angela stopped by for coffee," Catherine said. "Just a quick visit."

Bill looked at the dry coffeepot, empty since this morning.

"Got it," he said. "You feeling better? Thomas said you were under the weather."

Angela nodded quickly. "Yes. Thank you." She looked at Catherine. "Call me later so we can talk."

"Will do."

Angela walked past Catherine's husband and the man from the alley, hurried to the front foyer, pushed through the screen door, and raced down the steps, quickly walking along the sidewalk with her purse clutched under her arm.

Inside the house, Bill Blackwell stood next to Catherine and watched Angela rush down the block. He kept his voice quiet so Leonard Williams, whom Thomas had just hired as a foreman, wouldn't hear. He didn't want his words getting back to his partner.

"I'd never say anything to Thomas, but what the hell is wrong with her? Is she a little . . . dense? Like retarded?"

Catherine turned her head and stared into her husband's eyes. "She's anything but stupid, you idiot."

"Then why does she act like that?"

"Because she's a goddamn genius, Bill. And people treat her like a leper."

CHAPTER 10
Chicago, October 21, 2019

*R*ORY ENTERED THE SMALL LAW FIRM AND CLICKED ON THE LIGHTS. She walked past Celia's desk and into her father's office, where the stacks of files had shrunk since her initial visit. She still remembered the day Celia had dribbled tears onto her neck. A week later, the thought continued to bubble her skin with goose bumps and call for extra scrubbing each morning in the shower.

Despite her hysterics, Celia was quite efficient. She and the paralegal had notified all of the firm's current clients about the death of Frank Moore, and the need for them to find new counsel. From Celia's diligent work and research, nearly every client was either represented by a new firm or had strong leads on where to take their cases. A letter had gone out to all former clients explaining the news. In just one week, Celia's work was completed, her desk emptied, and the rest of the dissolution of Frank Moore's firm rested on Rory's shoulders.

Rory, too, had been busy. She'd placed calls to all clients whose cases were approaching trial and explained the situation—extensions were being filed until new counsel could be assigned. Nearly every case had been shuffled, and when she walked into her father's office this morning, there was only a single, lone folder waiting on his desk. It was as enigmatic as it was troubling, and so far, Rory had not been able to reassign it. Mostly because the judge she had spoken to about the case had requested a meeting before Rory did anything else, but also because the closer Rory looked into the details of the file, the more curious she became about how this case had fallen into her father's hands.

She spent an hour at her father's desk, searching the Internet for any information she could find about the client. Rory had never known of the case during her time at the firm. But given her limited role within the Moore Law Group, this was not startling news. She had never heard of most of her father's clients, but this one carried such magnitude that she was interested to know how he had kept such tight wraps on it. Her father's history with this client was extensive, and untangling the firm from the situation would not be as simple as a few phone calls looking for reassignment.

At 10:00 A.M., Rory shut down the computer, grabbed the lone file that remained on her father's desk, and locked the empty law office on the way out. She climbed into her car and drove downtown to the Daley Center. Inside, she made it through security, and, a few minutes later, rode the elevator with the security guard to the twenty-sixth floor, where the Circuit Court of Cook County was located. The guard led her down a hallway to the judge's chambers and knocked on a closed door. A moment later, the door opened and a distinguished-looking older man appeared, white hair and wire-rimmed glasses. He was dressed in a suit and tie.

"Rory Moore?" the judge asked.

"Yes, Your Honor," Rory said as the guard tipped his hat and was gone.

"Russell Boyle. Come on in."

Rory walked into the judge's chambers and took a seat in front of his desk. The judge sat in his deep-set leather throne and swiveled to face Rory.

"I've been trying to get ahold of your father for a couple of weeks. Sorry to hear about his passing. I was just made aware of the circumstances."

"Thank you."

"Thank *you* for coming down here on such short notice. I don't mean this to sound harsh, but for many reasons other than the obvious, your father's death comes at a terrible time. Frank and I

were working on a delicate case, and the situation needs attention."
Judge Boyle lifted a file from his desk.

"Yes, sir," Rory said. "It's the last bit of my father's business that
I'm trying to take care of."

"Are you familiar with this case?"

"No, sir. I wasn't familiar with any of my father's cases."

"Weren't you a partner in the firm?"

"A partner? No, sir. My father's law firm was a one-man shop. He
had no partners. Certainly not me. I did some side work for him
when he needed help, but I wasn't active in the firm."

"What was your role at the firm, Ms. Moore?"

Rory tried to find the correct words to describe what, exactly, she
did for her father. Her lightning-fast mind and borderline photo-
graphic memory allowed her to read briefs and comprehend the
law and its loopholes better than her father had ever understood it.
When Frank Moore got stuck on a case, he asked his daughter for
help. Despite that she had never stepped foot in a courtroom, Rory
had always been able to put together a winning strategy for just
about every case for which her father had sought her counsel.

"Mostly research," Rory finally said.

"But you *are* an attorney, Ms. Moore. Is that correct?"

The technical answer was *yes*, but all she wanted to do was lie.

"I'm not practicing any longer."

"Are you licensed in Illinois?"

"Yes, sir, but only as a supplement to my employment with the
Chicago Police Depart—"

Judge Boyle handed Rory a file in midsentence. "Good. Then
you're more than qualified to handle this situation."

Rory took the file.

"Let me get you up to speed. Your father's client is preparing for
parole, and it's a touchy situation."

Rory opened the file and began reading.

"He's due in front of the parole board one final time to review
my recommendations for the conditions of his release, which is
scheduled for November third. The hearing will be the day before.
Your father and I were hashing out the details, and I'm afraid
you're going to have to put on your lawyer shoes for the hearing.
It's mostly a formality, as the board will go along with all of my rec-

ommendations, and I've already approved all of theirs. But, nonetheless, we all need to cross our *t*'s and dot our *i*'s on this one. You'll have to appear with him."

"Sir, I'm not sure that's a good idea."

"I've dragged my feet on this for as long as possible, but the parole board has made their decision and I've spoken to the governor about it. There's no way to stop this from happening, so I'm going to make sure it goes as smoothly as possible now. There was a shitload, excuse my French, of details I worked out with your father. Many terms of the release were negotiated. We had everything just about settled."

Judge Boyle pointed at the file in Rory's hands.

"Make yourself familiar with the details so we can discuss the final terms next time you and I meet."

"Your Honor, I'm working to reassign all my father's cases. I'm not taking them on myself."

"I'm afraid that's not an option in this case. Unless you think you can find someone to handle it for you by next week."

"Can I request an extension?"

"Your father has already requested several. I can't kick this down the road any longer. There's too much attention on the case. Your client has been in the news lately, and he's due in front of the board in two weeks. Before then, and when you're familiar with the case, you and I will talk about the specifics of his parole. Let's get this man's affairs in order, and get his file the hell off my docket."

"Sir, I'm not suited for a courtroom. Or parole boards. Or for lawyering, in general."

Judge Boyle was already out of his majestic leather chair and on his way to the door of his chambers.

"I suggest you find a way to remedy that situation before you come out of retirement next week."

He opened the door and stood next to it. Rory took her cue to leave, her knees buckling slightly when she stood. After she gained her bearings, Rory cleared her throat.

"What did this guy do that makes a simple parole so complicated?"

"He killed a whole slew of people back in 1979. And now a few idiots on a parole board think it's a good idea to let him out of jail."

CHICAGO
August 1979

ANGELA JOGGED THE TWO BLOCKS HOME FROM CATHERINE'S HOUSE, raced up her steps, and pushed through her front door. She rattled the frame closed and twisted the dead bolt with trembling fingers. Her breathing was labored from her frantic march home, during which she constantly looked over her shoulder to make sure no one was following her. With the door securely latched, she leaned her forehead against the frame, her breaths shallow from having come face-to-face with the stranger from the alley. She tried for the last week to stop the image of his deep-set eyes from trickling into her mind. She'd done a good job today of replacing that image of the stranger's face with those of the missing women as she worked out her theory that The Thief had been lurking for much longer than this summer. But now, since seeing the man at Catherine's and knowing Thomas and Bill had hired him, Angela's tightly tethered paranoia had broken loose.

She spent an hour checking the locks and windows, picking up the phone a hundred times in a row. She called Thomas's office, but there was no answer. Her index finger became raw from punching the numbers on the phone. She settled into a mindless loop of dialing Thomas's office number into the phone, pacing to the back door, peeling the curtains to the side, and staring out into the alley. Back and forth for hours until she finally heard the deep rumble of Thomas's Ford truck turn down the alley, and saw the garage door begin to open. The growl of her husband's truck, a noise that usually irked her the way all loud noises did, today brought comfort.

Angela's skin was burning as she waited for Thomas in the kitchen. When the door opened, Angela immediately recognized the concern on her husband's face.

"What's the matter?" he asked, rushing to her.

"I saw him again," Angela said, but Thomas was paying no attention to her words.

He grasped her wrists gently and examined her hands, lifting them to his face to get a better look. For the first time, Angela noticed her bloody fingertips. Thomas moved his hands to her upper arms, pulling her sleeves away. Angela had unknowingly removed the long-sleeved, button-down shirt she had worn to the library, which Catherine had questioned. She stood now in a white T-shirt, the sleeves of which were soaked with bloodstains from where she had dug at her shoulders and opened the scabs that were hidden there.

"What's going on?" Thomas said. "You're covered in blood, Angela."

She felt him wipe her forehead and eyebrows, where her bloody fingertips had left crimson streaks from pulling at her lashes.

"He was at Catherine's. Bill hired him."

"Slow down," Thomas said, looking into her eyes. "Slow down and breathe."

Angela swallowed hard and tried to control her frantic respiration. She was like a child who had cried ferociously and was now trying to speak. She exhaled a few times and allowed Thomas's grip on her shoulders to right her mind.

"I was at Catherine's house today."

"Okay?"

"And Bill came home."

"Okay?"

"And he was with the man from the alley. From when I tried to get rid of the couch."

"Who was it?"

"Bill said he works for you. He runs the warehouse up north."

Thomas furrowed his brow, and then cocked his head. "The Kenosha warehouse? That's Leonard."

"He was in Catherine's house. He looked right at me."

"Leonard Williams? Are you talking about Leonard?"

"Yes!" Angela screamed. "He was the man from the alley."

"Angela, it's okay."

Thomas tried to pull her into his chest, but she resisted like a child working to prevent a parent from lifting them.

"But . . . I saw him in the alley."

"Leonard lives in the area. He was probably out walking that morning. This is good news, Angela. You see? Leonard is harmless. He runs one of our warehouses. That's all."

Angela felt Thomas pull her close again, this time allowing it. She rested her head on his shoulder, her chest still heaving, but no comfort came from her husband's embrace. Worry was all she could do and all she could feel. It was all her mind would allow. It filled her chest, her head, her soul.

Thomas whispered into her ear. "I think it's time you start seeing your doctor again."

CHAPTER 11
Chicago, October 22, 2019

*I*T WAS MIDMORNING ON THE DAY AFTER HER MEETING WITH JUDGE Boyle, court was in session, and the hallways were vacant when Rory walked through the Dirksen Federal Courthouse in The Loop. Her combat boots rattled with her gait and echoed off the walls. Rory found the courtroom, pulled her gray coat tight to her neck, opened the heavy door, and slid silently into the back row. The pews were mostly empty, but for the first three, which were lined with young men and women Rory guessed were students of the distinguished Lane Phillips. Groupies, she thought, who followed the good doctor everywhere he went. Lane's court appearances brought high fervor for the young lads who hoped to see their mentor in rare form on the stand. Rory admitted that a Dr. Lane Phillips court appearance could rival any other type of entertainment.

Lane was testifying as an expert witness for the prosecution in the case of a double murder that took place the year before—a man was accused of killing his wife and mother in a fit of rage. Rory hadn't seen much of him in the last week because he had been preparing for his time on the stand.

"Dr. Phillips," the attorney asked from behind the podium. "You mentioned earlier that your specialty is in forensic psychology. Is that correct?"

"Correct," Dr. Phillips said from the witness chair.

Lane Phillips was approaching fifty, but looked like he was in his thirties, with mismanaged hair and the remnants of a once-prominent dimple on his right cheek, which flashed when he smiled. His casual attitude toward anything that came his way made him popular with the students, who looked up to him like a deity. His laissez-faire style—messy hair, black jeans, worn sport coat, and no tie—surely spoke to the young audience that filled the front pews. Whenever Lane spent the night at Rory's place, he never took more than ten minutes to shower and dress in the morning. His efficiency made Rory Moore, who was far from girlish, look like a beauty queen.

Lane's appearance stiffly contrasted with the sharp-suited attorney cross-examining him, whose hair was perfect and whose cuff links shined brightly as they peeked from under the sleeves of his tailored suit. Even before Rory took into consideration the discussion between the two men, it was obvious they were rivals.

"Is it also true, Doctor, that you serve often as an expert witness in high-profile cases?"

"The profile of a case is not a variable in my decision to serve as a witness."

"Very well," the attorney said, walking from behind the podium. "But it is true that you often testify as an expert witness in cases of homicide, is it not?"

"Yes, that's true."

"Usually, your expertise is sought to help the jury understand the mind-set of the one who stands accused of murder. Is that correct?"

"Oftentimes, yes," Dr. Phillips said. Lane sat upright with his hands folded in his lap, oozing a calm confidence against the attorney's aggression.

"In this case today, you've offered the jury quite a detailed *look*, so to say, into the mind of my client. Is that fair to say?"

"I offered my opinion on your client's mind-set when he killed his wife and mother, yes."

The attorney let out a subtle laugh. "Objection, Your Honor."

"Dr. Phillips," the judge said. "Please limit your comments to the questions being asked and offer no more conjecture on guilt or innocence."

"Excuse me, Your Honor," Dr. Phillips said, looking back to the attorney. "I offered my opinion on what someone might be think-ing *if* they had shot and killed their wife and mother."

This got a subtle reaction from the students.

The attorney nodded his head and offered a small smile as he ran his tongue against the inside of his cheek.

"So, as in today's earlier testimony, and in the many other cases in which you've served as an expert into the criminal mind, one might guess that you are employed by a government agency. Say, the FBI?"

He shook his head. "No."

"No? Wouldn't a distinguished mind such as yours be put to good use in the Criminal Investigative Division or the Behavioral Science Unit within the Federal Bureau of Investigation?"

Dr. Phillips opened his palms. "Perhaps."

The attorney took a few steps forward. "You must, instead, be in private practice, then? Counseling such individuals on a regular basis. Surely, *that* is how you came to be such an expert on the crim-inal mind."

"No," Lane said calmly. "I'm not in private practice."

"No?" The attorney shook his head. "Then please tell us, Dr. Phillips, with all of your advanced degrees and your many publica-tions in forensic psychology, where exactly do you work?"

"The Murder Accountability Project."

"Yes," the attorney said, gathering papers and reading from them. "The Murder Accountability Project. That's your pet project that has supposedly developed an algorithm to detect serial killers. Do I have that right?"

"Not really, no," Lane said.

"Please enlighten us, then."

"First, it's not a pet project. It's a legitimate LLC corporation that pays my employees and me a salary. And I didn't *supposedly* de-velop anything. I *actually* developed an algorithm that tracks simi-larities between homicides across the country to look for trends. These trends can then lead to patterns, which can help law en-forcement solve homicides."

"And all these homicides you help to solve, how many of the ac-cused perpetrators do you deal with personally as a psychologist?"

"My program identifies trends to help law enforcement track potential killers. Once we see a pattern, the authorities take over the case."

"So the answer to how many of these alleged murderers you end up counseling as a psychologist would be *zero*. Is that correct?"

"I'm not directly involved with any of the accused that my program has helped identify."

"So calling yourself an expert in psychology when you no longer practice the profession is a bit misleading, is it not?"

"No, sir. Misleading is dressing in a shiny suit and calling yourself an attorney, when really you're just a hack throwing insults to distract the jury."

Lane's students tried unsuccessfully to mute their laughter.

"Dr. Phillips," the judge said.

Lane nodded. "Excuse me, Your Honor."

The attorney, unfazed, went back at his papers. "You are also a professor at the University of Chicago. Is that correct?"

Lane looked back at his rival. "Yes."

"A professor of what, exactly?"

"Criminal and forensic psychology."

"I see," the attorney said again, walking back to the podium with a trying-too-hard confused look on his face and scratching his sideburn. "So you run a business that claims to identify killers, but you don't work in any capacity of psychology with those killers. And you *teach* the psychology of the criminal mind to young college students. I'm struggling to understand where your *practical* experience comes from, Dr. Phillips? I mean, you've offered so much information about my client's mind-set, and what he must have been thinking in the days leading up to the night his wife and mother were killed. Insights such as the ones you offered have to come from *practical, clinical* experience working with men and women convicted of violent crimes. But it looks to me like the prosecution has put on the stand a so-called expert witness who runs a business that sells algorithms and data to the police, and who teaches psychology to college kids. Doctor, have you heard of the axiom 'those who cannot *do*, teach'?"

"Objection!" the prosecutor said as she stood from behind the table.

"Withdrawn, Your Honor. I have no more questions for Dr. Phillips."

The DA was heading to the witness-box. "Dr. Phillips, prior to taking a university faculty position and starting the Murder Accountability Project, where were you employed?"

"At the Federal Bureau of Investigation."

"For how long?"

"Ten years."

"And what was your role within the Bureau?"

"I was hired as a forensic psychologist."

"And your job was to analyze crimes to determine the type of person who may have committed them. Is that accurate?"

"Yes, I was a profiler."

"During your tenure at the Bureau, you worked on over one hundred fifty cases. What was your clearance rate in those cases, where your expertise in profiling the perpetrator led to an arrest?"

"I had a close rate of ninety-two percent."

"The national average for clearance rate of homicides is sixty-four percent. Your success rate was thirty points higher than that. Before your tenure with the Bureau, Dr. Phillips, you wrote a thesis on the criminal mind titled *Some Choose Darkness*. That thesis is still widely heralded as a comprehensive look into the minds of killers and why they kill. Please tell us, Dr. Phillips, how you gained such insight."

"I spent two years during my PhD studies on sabbatical, during which I traveled the world interviewing convicted killers, understanding motive, mind-set, empathy, and patterns of how a human being decides to take another's life. The dissertation is a well-received and peer-reviewed document."

"In fact," the DA said, "more than ten years after your thesis was published, it is still popular in the forensic community. Am I correct?"

"That's correct."

"In fact, your thesis is used as the main training tool around which the FBI teaches new hires who join the Bureau as profilers. Is that correct?"

"Yes."

"In addition to your dissertation, you also compiled your findings on serial killers of the last one hundred years into a true-crime book. Is that correct?"

"Yes."

"As of the latest printing, how many copies of that book are in print?"

"About six million."

"No more questions, Your Honor."

CHAPTER 12
Chicago, October 22, 2019

*R*ORY ENTERED THE TAVERN ON THE AFTERNOON AFTER LANE'S courtroom appearance. She and Lane sat at the corner of the bar and ordered drinks. Rory took off her beanie hat and removed her glasses. There were few people in this world Rory Moore felt comfortable around, Lane Phillips was one of them. The bartender placed a Surly Darkness stout in front of her, and a light beer in front of Lane. Rory made an ugly face when she looked at Lane's beer.

"What?" he asked.

"Your beer is the same color as urine."

"That dark stuff hurts my stomach."

"*You* hurt my stomach," Rory said. "Why do you put yourself through that crap?"

"On the stand? Every expert witness has his credentials questioned. It's part of the gig. Gotta have thick skin to deal with it, and you have to see it for what it is. The defense is attacking me to distract the jury from the fact that his client killed his wife. If my credentials need to get shredded in order for my opinions to be heard, that's okay with me, as long as the son of a bitch is found guilty."

"I hate bullies."

"He's just doing his job."

"Lawyers are the scum of the earth," Rory said, taking a sip of stout.

"Says the lawyer next to me. And he's right, by the way. I haven't practiced psychology for years. And I haven't dealt directly with the criminally insane for more than a decade."

"That might be about to change. I need a little help."

"With the Camille Byrd reconstruction?"

Rory thought briefly of Camille Byrd, whose photo she had pinned to her corkboard days before. Her father had died of a heart attack just after she agreed to take the case, and tying up his affairs had been an all-encompassing task. A pang of heartache struck as Camille's face popped into her thoughts. Rory had all but abandoned the case, and the guilt of leaving a cold case unattended suddenly felt heavy on her shoulders. She made a mental note to put in some hours on the reconstruction, once she had this last file of her father's settled.

"No, something else," she finally said.

Rory reached into her purse and pulled out the file Judge Boyle had given her.

"I've got my father's firm pretty well settled, besides this one case."

She pushed the folder across the bar, and saw Lane's posture straighten. Paging through a criminal's file gave him a thrill. And despite any stiff-suited attorney trying to convince people otherwise, Lane Phillips was one of the best at dissecting the mind of a killer. He'd resigned from the FBI not because his profiling skills were suspect, but because he was too proficient at it. Diving into criminal minds left him shaky and tormented by what he found there. He understood their minds so well that it left a haunting impression he had difficulty shaking off. So when his true-crime book, which chronicled the minds of the most notorious serial killers of the last one hundred years, including personal interviews with many of them, sold more than two million copies during its first year in print, he quit the Bureau and started the Murder Accountability Project with Rory. The MAP was an effort to track unsolved homicides and identify patterns that might highlight similarities between crimes, often pointing to serial killings. Rory and Lane's skills complemented each other. She was able to reconstruct homicides better than anyone in the country, and Lane

Phillips was one of the world's foremost authorities on serial killings.

"Ever hear of this guy?" Rory asked as Lane paged through the file.

"Yeah. They called him The Thief. But, Christ, that was forty years ago. Your father represented this guy?"

"Apparently. I'm still sorting the details. Garrison Ford, the big criminal defense firm, originally handled the case. My father worked at Garrison Ford after leaving the public defender's office, but his tenure was short. Just a couple of years. When my father left to start his own firm, he took this case with him."

Lane turned a few pages in the file. "When was the last time your father worked at Garrison Ford?"

"Nineteen eighty-two," Rory said. "And he's had this guy as a client ever since."

"Doing what?" Lane asked.

"That's what I'm trying to figure out. After Garrison Ford mounted an unsuccessful defense at trial, my father worked on appeals and represented him at parole hearings. The guy also has a small fortune from before he was put away, and it looks like my dad oversaw the money. Set up a trust and protected it for three decades. Settled some debts, looked after some property, and paid himself out of the trust for legal services rendered."

Lane turned the page. "And visited this guy a lot. Look at all these visitor log entries."

"Yes, my father had quite a relationship with this man."

"So what's the issue? Pawn this case off like you've done with all the others."

"I can't. This guy's been granted parole. My father was working with the judge on the details when he died, and His Honor is under some pressure to get it off his docket, so he's not letting me delay it."

Lane took a sip of beer as he continued to page through the file.

Rory picked up her stout. "Tell me about this guy. I looked him up. He was convicted on a single count of Murder Two. Doesn't seem like it would be so spectacular that he made parole after forty years. But when I talked with the judge, he said the guy killed a whole bunch of people."

"Oh, boy," Lane said, looking up from the file and staring at Rory. "What?" Rory asked.

"Something's piqued your interest about this case, hasn't it?"

"Stop it, Lane."

"I know how you operate, Rory. Something about your father's involvement in this case has planted itself in that brain of yours and now you can't let it go."

With her father gone, Lane Phillips was the only other person who fully understood Rory's obsession with things unknown. His history as a psychologist stopped Rory from pretending he was incorrect. Dr. Phillips knew the workings of the human brain well, and Rory's, in particular, better than most. This quirk in her personality was what made her such a sought-after forensic reconstructionist. Until she had all the answers about a case, she was helpless to stop her mind from working to find them. Especially if an initial glance at a case held something that made no sense, and her father's involvement with the man the papers called The Thief made no sense at all.

"Tell me about this guy," she said again.

Lane wrapped his hand around the bottom of his beer mug, spun it in place as he collected his thoughts on the long-ago case. "The prosecution pushed for Murder One, the jury came back with second-degree for the lone victim. But this guy was suspected in many other cases of missing women," Lane said. "Five or six . . . I'd have to look it up."

"Five or six homicides? Nothing in his file mentions other victims. And it would be impossible to make parole if he killed so many."

"He was *suspected* of more killings, never charged. And you won't find anything formally linking him to the other killings. Just rumor and conjecture."

"Why did they go after him for only one homicide if they thought there were more?"

Lane closed the file. "A few reasons. The city was in a panic in the late seventies. You had the Son of Sam still lingering on people's minds—he was the nut who killed a bunch of people in New York in 1976. Then, here in Chicago, we had the horror of John Wayne Gacy having killed and buried thirty-some boys in his crawl space. Then, during the summer of 1979, women started disappearing and the city bubbled with fear. The whole summer was filled with heat and anxiety. Eventually, toward the end of summer, the police found their man. But the way they discovered him was very unorthodox, and it was entirely thanks to an autistic woman who pieced it all together."

Rory leaned forward across the bar to listen more intently. She was more interested now than she had been.

"The method in which this woman gathered and delivered the evidence was very strange, and the DA knew none of the evidence would stand up in court. Most was flat-out inadmissible. Neither side wanted a trial. If the prosecution failed to convince the jury of his guilt, this guy would walk. If they succeeded, he'd be eligible for the death penalty, which was still around in 1979. So a trial was risky for both sides. In the end, the DA made the choice to go after him on the single homicide. They had shaky evidence, a lot of circumstance, and no body."

"No body?"

"No. That's why it was such a risk to go to trial, and why they went after him for only the single victim. No bodies were ever found, besides one that they could never tie to him in any meaningful way. And with no body, the jury came back with a guilty verdict for Murder Two. The conviction sent him away for sixty years, but allowed for parole after thirty. The sentence put the city's fears to rest."

"And now, after ten years of parole hearings and forty years in jail, he's about to be granted his freedom."

Lane shook his head. "I studied this case for my book, but the details never made it past the final edits. That woman who figured it all out. Goddamn, I still remember the headlines. 'Schizophrenic Woman Brings Down The Thief.'"

"Schizophrenic?"

"No one knew anything about autism back then. Plus, 'Schizophrenic' sold more papers."

Rory looked into the black abyss of her Surly Darkness stout, lifted the mug, and swallowed the rest of the beer. She wanted to order another. She longed for a touch of dizziness to soften her thoughts about this autistic woman she knew nothing about. She knew those curiosities were taking root in her mind and that they would be impossible to ignore. She stared up at Lane.

"What ever happened to her? The autistic woman?"

Lane tapped the file with his finger. "Her name was Angela Mitchell. He killed her before she had a chance to testify."

CHICAGO
August 1979

*T*WO DAYS AFTER HER BREAKDOWN, ANGELA WAS AT THE DOCTOR'S office, sitting on the table in a thin gown and pulling at her eyelashes.

"Relax, darling," the nurse said as she prepped the syringe. "I just need two vials. You won't feel a thing."

Angela looked the other way when the nurse pressed the needle to the inside of her elbow, but it wasn't the threat of a needle that had her on edge. Her panic attack had set Thomas's radar on high alert, and he'd forced her to see the doctor before things got out of control. Little did he know that things were far beyond that. Baring her paranoia to Thomas had set loose even more angst now that she was at the clinic. She'd been through this routine before. Most of her adolescence had been spent in doctors' offices and on psychiatrists' couches. Back when she was under the rule of her parents, doctors and shrinks were her way of life. Her parents believed that if Angela saw enough of them, and the right ones, they could psychoanalyze her back to health. When none of the therapists could do for their daughter what Angela's parents demanded, they admitted her to a juvenile psychiatric facility.

Angela was seventeen when her parents forced her into that place, and she spent seven months there until she discharged herself on her eighteenth birthday. It was only with the help of a dear friend that Angela had escaped that life. She had been on a (mostly) smooth trajectory for the last several years. Since meeting Thomas, she'd tightly managed her anxiety and had even felt like she was starting to fit into society. Her autism was something no one understood, including the many doctors who pretended otherwise, and Angela had long ago stopped trying to explain to others how her mind operated. She had learned over many years of criticism and failure that no one could fully comprehend the way her thoughts were organized. Yet, here she was again, waiting for a doctor to explain what was wrong with her.

She knew, though, that Thomas meant well. His eagerness for her to seek psychiatric help was simply his way of trying to protect her. He didn't know her full history. Angela had tried her best to keep hidden the dark days of her teenage years. And until just recently, the ruse had worked. Thomas had opened her life to new opportunities. He made her feel safe. But despite the progress, the events of the summer had made her realize how frail a hold she had on it all. The missing women who had run through the folds of her mind, and the idea that they were part of a longer string of violence, had started Angela down a road with no turnoffs. Despite Angela recognizing that her obsession with these women was unhealthy, she felt a connection to them that she couldn't ignore.

The stranger from the alley, who had reappeared in Catherine's kitchen, had set loose her anxiety in ways that transported her through the years and back to her adolescence. The obsessive-compulsive disorder she thought she had tethered and stowed in a locked-off compartment of her psyche had been reawakened to wreak havoc, like when she was younger. On top of it all, she feared that her affliction would push Thomas away. She feared now that Thomas had gotten a clear look at her paranoia; the anchor that had steadied her for the last couple of years was breaking free from its mooring to leave Angela adrift and alone. So many worries ran through her mind, she had trouble keeping track of them all.

"All done, darling," the nurse said, bringing Angela's thoughts back to the present. The nurse held two vials of deep red blood in her gloved hand.

"The doctor will be right in."

A few minutes later, the doctor entered the room and performed a cursory exam.

"Have you had panic attacks in the past?" the doctor asked while he scribbled in the chart.

"No," she said. "I mean . . . when I was younger, but they didn't call them that."

The doctor took a minute to finish writing, and then looked at Angela. "You used to take lithium as a teenager. Was it effective?"

Angela, who normally would shy away from a man staring at her, peered back with an intensity that surprised even herself. The horrors of her teenage years fueled her rage.

"No! He forced me to take it, and my parents went along with him."

"Who?"

"The psychiatrist my parents sent me to. The one who kept me locked away in the psychiatric hospital. He believed I had a behavioral disorder, and that I was a manic-depressive. They used lithium to sedate me. Besides putting me to sleep, it gave me wild hallucinations."

The doctor paused before nodding. "Yes, not everyone responds to it." He pulled a prescription pad from the breast pocket of his jacket and jotted on it. He tore the page free and handed her the slip. "This is for Valium, it will take the edge off with none of the side effects of lithium."

He jotted again onto the pad and tore a second slip free.

"And here is the name of a psychiatrist. I think you should talk with someone. I've been referring many of my female patients to him lately. The missing women from the city have gotten a lot of people spooked. Talking with someone will help. In the meantime, push fluids until the vomiting passes. The Valium should help, and, Mrs. Mitchell," the doctor said as he stood, "the police are good at what they do. They'll catch this guy. That will be the best cure for everything you've got going on."

On the way out of the clinic, Angela crumpled the paper that held the shrink's name, dropped it in the trash bin, and climbed into her car. She walked into the pharmacy ten minutes later to fill her Valium prescription.

CHAPTER 13
Chicago, October 23, 2019

*R*ORY PUT A CALL IN TO DETECTIVE DAVIDSON. HE OWED HER AFTER the setup with Camille Byrd's father; now she was calling in the favor. She needed everything he could find on the old case from 1979. Having scoured the dark corners of Cook County federal buildings in search of what Rory needed, Ron came through, delivering three boxes of information to her door earlier in the afternoon. Now the boxes were stacked next to her desk while Rory pored over the details.

She had emptied the first box and spread the contents onto her desk. The facts about the 1979 case fascinated her. More than anything, the enigmatic woman named Angela Mitchell, who had managed to identify a serial killer, drew all of Rory's attention. Rory felt a strange connection to the woman from four decades ago. Angela Mitchell had done, essentially, what Rory did now—she put names and narratives to victims in order to reconstruct crimes.

The defense team who represented The Thief, of which her father was a member, had created a biography of Angela Mitchell. It described her as a "socially awkward twenty-nine year-old woman who suffered from autism and a limited ability to understand her surroundings." An obsessive-compulsive personality disorder, the report continued, limited her abilities to handle the activities of daily living; and at the time during which she collected the "evidence" the prosecution had been allowed to present at trial, she was on heavy doses of Valium. The report went on in length about Angela's troubled adolescence, her time spent in a juvenile psychiatric hospital, and her estrangement from her parents. Taken on its surface, the account painted an unflattering image of Angela Mitchell.

The more Rory read, though, the more connected she felt to the woman from years ago. Their stories were similar in many ways. Although Rory was never estranged from her parents, quite the opposite, and she had never been forced into a psych ward, Rory's childhood had been plagued by many of the same ailments as Angela's. Instead of shipping Rory off to doctors and hospitals, her parents had sent her to Aunt Greta's house during the summers and on most weekends. Although no medication was forced on Rory, Aunt Greta offered different remedies for Rory's social anxiety. Without her great-aunt, Rory's childhood might have been written about using the identical language as Angela Mitchell's.

She pushed the thought of Angela Mitchell's supposed Valium addiction from her mind, working hard to prevent the comparison to the glass of Three Floyds Dark Lord stout that rested in front of her. It was three o'clock in the afternoon and Rory was on her second glass, her head vertiginous with the early effects of the alcohol. In a show of rebellion to her own thoughts, she lifted the glass, took a long swallow, and then spent two hours on the 1979 file, lost in the details of Angela Mitchell and what she had managed to do. Rory made it through two full boxes, but left the third untouched for now. She turned to her desktop and typed the name *Angela Mitchell* into the search engine. After scrolling through pages of links that had nothing to do with The Thief from 1979, Rory finally came across a few general articles that rehashed some details about the case. None of the online hits held revelations that were not already in the boxes next to her.

She was ready to shut down her computer when she came to a link for a Facebook page titled *Justice for Angela*. The page had twelve hundred followers and the last post had been made two years prior, a short paragraph dated August 31, 2017:

> Today marks the 38th anniversary of my dear friend
> Angela Mitchell's disappearance. So many decades later,
> and there are still no leads on the case. Few members of the
> Chicago Police Department even remember Angela, and

those that do are long retired and gave up hope long ago of
discovering what really happened to her during the summer
of 1979. Those of us who are part of this online community
looking for answers know that no resolutions were provided
during the farce of a trial that took place in 1980. With each
passing year, it seems more and more likely that the only
one who could shed light on the truth is sitting in jail. He, of
course, refuses to utter a word about Angela.

As always, anyone with tips or information about Angela
Mitchell can comment on this thread and I'll follow up with
you personally. The smallest detail, even this many years
later, could be helpful.

The Facebook post included a grainy image of Angela Mitchell.
It was actually a photo of a photo. The person who posted it had
used a cell phone to capture the old Polaroid picture, which was
yellowed and faded by age, the camera's flash reflecting off the
upper corner of the plastic photograph. Rory looked at Angela
Mitchell. She was a petite woman, who, in the photo, stood next to
a taller woman, who Rory assumed was the author of the Facebook
post. In the snapshot, Angela smiled shyly at the camera, her gaze
slightly down and to the left, unable, Rory understood, to stare directly into the camera's lens. Rory had the same affliction.

Lane had been correct with his assumption earlier at the bar.
The seed of curiosity had been planted in Rory's mind, and stopping it from growing was as impossible as stopping the sun from rising. She was initially curious about the case because of her father's
involvement. But now, since learning more about the mysterious
woman at the center of it, Rory felt the familiar pull of interest she
knew she couldn't ignore. It was the same feeling she encountered
at the start of a reconstruction. Some part of her mind would be
unable to rest until she knew everything there was to know about
Angela Mitchell.

She finally looked away from the gritty Facebook image and did
something she would never normally consider. She clicked the
mouse over the comment section and typed quickly: My name is Rory
Moore. I need some details about Angela Mitchell. Please contact me.

Rory hit the return key before she could reconsider, scrolled to the top of the Facebook page, clicked the *About* icon, and pulled up information on the person who created the page. The woman claimed to be Angela Mitchell's closest friend from the summer of 1979. Her name was Catherine Blackwell.

CHICAGO
August 1979

*T*HE VALIUM WAS HELPING. SHE HADN'T VOMITED IN THREE DAYS, AND the headaches came less often. The medication was dulling the urge to dig at her scabbed shoulders, and the drug's overall effect was blunting her paranoia and keeping Thomas's concerns at bay. Angela was taking twice the suggested dosage, though, and she worried not only about overmedicating herself, but also about what would happen when the pills ran out. Thomas had been watching her closely since the breakdown, and Angela worked hard to keep things together and convince him that since her visit with the doctor she was feeling well. That she had her short relapse under control. That the identity of the stranger from the alley, while at first disconcerting, had now led to relief. And, most important, that she didn't need to see a psychiatrist.

The acting and camouflaging of her symptoms was exhausting, and Angela wasn't sure how much longer she could keep up the ruse. But a reprieve was coming. Thomas was scheduled to inspect a work site in Indianapolis over the weekend and meet with the builder, who was planning a 150-home subdivision. Thomas and Bill were bidding on the job and he would be gone all of Saturday and most of Sunday. Talk of canceling the trip had started after Thomas came home a few days before to find Angela covered in blood and melting down in ways she had never before displayed to her husband. But desperately needing both time away from Thomas's suffocating concern, and the opportunity to explore her suspicions about Leonard Williams, Angela had used all her willpower and double the usual dosage of Valium to put up a façade of normalness and well-being. Now, Saturday morning, Angela gave one more push while she and Thomas sat at the kitchen table and drank their morning coffee.

"Just go," Angela said. "I'm feeling much better."

Thomas looked at her. "You're taking the medication, right?"

"I am. It's helping."

"I'm worried about being gone overnight. Bill should be able to handle this without me."

"I'll be fine," Angela said, trying to hide the urgency in her voice. "And we need this contract. It would make our year."

"We're doing fine," Thomas said. "It would be nice, but we don't *need* it."

"Go," she said, looking him in the eye the way she seldom did anyone else. "I'm okay."

An hour after she watched Thomas back his truck out of the garage and drive down the alley on his way to Indiana, Angela pulled away from the curb and headed for the highway. Thomas and Bill had four warehouses spread between Kenosha, Wisconsin, the north and west sides of the city, and Hammond, Indiana. Leonard Williams ran the warehouse in Kenosha, so with Thomas gone, Angela was on her way to the Wisconsin location.

Kenosha was about an hour and a half from the city, and Angela consulted her map after she turned off the highway. Eventually she turned down the long road that led to her husband's Wisconsin office and construction warehouse. A trail of dust floated behind her vehicle as she drove. Situated at the end of a long industrial park, the office was one of many single-story buildings that lined the gravel road. When Angela pulled up to the office on Saturday morning, hers was the only vehicle present. She put the car into park, but left the engine running and the air-conditioning raging as she listened to the radio. There had been a development overnight in the case of the summer's missing women and WGN offered the latest details.

"We can confirm," the reporter said through the radio, "that the body found early this morning is suspected to be that of Samantha Rodgers, who had gone missing three weeks ago and was considered to be The Thief's fifth, and most recent, victim."

Sitting in her car, Angela's mind flashed to the night she and Catherine had watched the news report in her living room about the missing woman named Samantha Rodgers. She had since created a biography on the woman and Angela knew all the details about her disappearance: the date she went missing, the last place she was seen, the last time her parents and friends had spoken with her, and the exact location where the cab had dropped her the night she disappeared—Western and Kedzie, a mere block from her apartment. Angela knew the details about Samantha Rodgers before the reporter spoke. In fact, she knew much more than the news story offered. Angela knew the girl so well that her heart ached at the idea that there was no hope she would be found alive.

"We are still waiting for the Chicago Police Department to confirm the victim's identity, but it is widely believed that the body of Samantha Rodgers has been found in a wooded area in Forest Glen, miles away from the victim's apartment in Wicker Park. We will stay on top of any new developments and interrupt regularly scheduled programming with any breaking news."

As Angela shut off the car's engine, she realized her heart was drumming. When she pulled the keys from the ignition, they jingled with the tremor in her hand. She steadied herself as she climbed from the car and looked around. She knew the warehouse would be quiet at this time on a Saturday morning, the work crews were already out to job sites.

She walked across the gravel lot. The office door was locked when she tried the handle. Before she left her house, Angela had retrieved a set of keys attached to a Chicago Bears keychain, which rested in the back of the kitchen drawer. Pulling the ring from her purse, she went one-by-one until she inserted the correct key into the door handle and twisted it open. She slipped into the office and closed the door behind her, looking back through the window and out into the parking lot. Her car sat all alone, the dust storm she had caused by driving down the industrial road had dissipated to a white cloud that hazed the area. Angela took a moment to look toward the far end of the road, which was empty and quiet. She locked the door and turned away from the window.

She went past the desk in the front office and pulled open the drawers to the file cabinets that lined the back wall. It took ten minutes of fingering through the files for Angela to find the employment records. Mitchell-Blackwell Construction had seventy-seven employees. It took only a minute to locate the file that held the name *Leonard Williams;* she pulled the file and sat on the floor to read it.

The first page held a Xeroxed photo of Leonard Williams's driver's license. A feverous chill claimed Angela's shoulders as she stared at the dark-set eyes and expressionless face of the man who had approached her weeks ago in the alley behind her home. Angela learned that he was fifty-two years old, previously employed by another construction outfit in the western suburb of Wood Dale, and had come to Mitchell-Blackwell with glowing letters of recommendation from his previous employer. He was married, with two children. As she paged through the thin file, something pulled at her mind. It was the way her brain operated. There was something she had seen, but not recognized. Some bit of relevance that had buried itself in her subconscious, but which hadn't yet floated to the surface of her awareness. Angela had always been able to sense this acute mindfulness of something critical, even if she wasn't able to immediately identify it.

She blinked away the glitch in her thoughts, ignored the soft whisper that echoed in the far-off parts of her mind, and continued to flip through the file—1099 forms, employment contracts, workmen's compensation paperwork, and union credentials—until it finally dawned on her. Until the whisper turned into a scream. She turned back to the opening page of the file and looked at Leonard Williams's driver's license again. Her vision narrowed to focus on his address. He lived in Forest Glen, the same neighborhood where Samantha Rodgers's body had just been discovered.

CHICAGO
August 1979

ANGELA JOTTED LEONARD WILLIAMS'S ADDRESS ONTO A PIECE OF scratch paper, replaced the file, and closed the cabinet. She walked around the secretary's desk and to the side door that led to the warehouse, pushed it open and entered the cavernous space. The rafter ceilings were three stories high and light penetrated the grimy windows in a cloudy gray film that left Angela squinting in the murkiness. She found the light switch and clicked the warehouse to life with fluorescent bulbs that blinked and warmed.

Giant trucks occupied the space, and pallets of dry concrete lined the walls, packaged in green bags and stacked high. Other equipment she didn't recognize or understand hung from the walls and stood in tall piles in the middle of the warehouse. Angela walked around the equipment. This was the place Leonard Williams operated and supervised.

In the back she came to a filmy window that looked out onto the parking lot. She saw her car isolated in the gravel lot, and again looked to the end of the long road that led from the main thoroughfare to the warehouse. It was desolate, and the emptiness of the place suddenly brought Angela aching lungs and shallow breaths. She felt the twinge of an impending attack, and fought against the pull of her mind to go to that dark place and entertain disturbing thoughts of Leonard Williams from the morning in the alley, his shadow climbing over her legs as he came closer to her, his black eyes, and his body silhouetted by the steep angle of the sun. But she felt something else, too—something that made it easier than normal to get past the roadblocks in her mind. The same stutter in her thoughts from a few moments earlier—while she looked through Leonard Williams's file, and unknowingly saw his address—was happening again now as she stared out the window. Something screamed for her attention.

She was in the corner of the warehouse, with the back wall immediately to her left and the sidewall with the grimy window in front of her. Something was off. As Angela looked again out at the parking lot, she remembered the image from when she had climbed from her car. She had parked at the edge of the warehouse, yet her car was many feet to the left of the window she was staring through. Angela looked at the back wall and realized the warehouse did not end where she stood, but continued beyond this point.

Moving away from the window, she walked along the back wall. It was covered in wooden shelving that rose up a full story. Heavy equipment and pallets of material filled the shelves. A forklift was parked nearby to claim the items from the higher shelves. As Angela walked along the back wall, she noticed a break in the shelving, in front of which sat a pallet of concrete. Behind the pallet a tarp hung like a curtain and partially covered a door. An eerie feeling came over her as she looked back through the warehouse toward the office. The rafters creaked with the wind. The roll of her stomach returned. She had swallowed two Valium on the way over, and resisted the urge to fish another from the bottle. She turned back to the partially hidden door, squeezed her small frame past the stacked bags of concrete, and tried the handle. Locked. She opened her purse and pulled out the keys attached to the Chicago Bears ring. She stuck one after the other into the doorknob until, on her fifth try, the lock twisted open.

Angela pushed the door, allowing it to swing on the hinges and glide into the darkened room until it struck the wall after a full 180-degree turn. She reached her arm in and felt for a light switch. The overhead lights brought the space to life, and she slowly walked into the large storage area. Rows of shelving lined the walls. Another wall was lined with barrel-sized oilcans. The floor was caked with mud, unlike the dusty concrete slab of the warehouse.

On the floor next to the large oilcans was a dirty tarp, a shovel, rope, and a stack of cinder blocks. She lifted the top from one of the cans and peered inside. It was dark and empty. As Angela slowly turned in the storage room, her skin was itchy and flushed. She took deep breaths to settle her stomach, but still bile rose in her throat. In the darkened corner, she saw a strange contraption hanging from the tall ceiling. She walked closer to get a better look. Bolted to the ceiling was an M-shaped wooden beam. Five pulleys were fastened at each point of the M, through which thick rope was strung. The rope hung down from each end of the beam like the loose limbs of a willow tree. Six feet separated the two ends of the rope. Angela walked even closer. Attached to each end of the rope was a strap of red nylon tied in a noose. It reminded her of some contraption from medieval times.

Angela held the nylon noose in her hand, pinching the soft, red material between her thumb and forefinger, when she heard a thud outside. She released the noose, ran to the door of the storage room, and peeked out into the warehouse. It was still dingy and gray, and the large overhead doors were closed. She heard the pounding once again. Squeezing between the shelving and pallet of concrete that hid the storage room door, Angela ran back to the window and looked out at the parking lot. One of the concrete trucks had returned and was dumping waste into a reservoir across the parking lot. The truck was backed up against a retaining wall, with its tank at a ninety-degree angle as workers barked orders to the driver.

Angela ran the length of the warehouse and into the office. She locked the door on the way out and hurried to her car as the workers continued their dumping fifty yards away. She steadied herself by leaning on the hood and breathing in the humid summer air. When the nausea passed, Angela climbed into the driver's seat and reached for her purse. She pulled out her bottle of Valium, swallowed another pill, and tore out of the parking lot, accelerating down the industrial road and kicking up a cloud of dust in the process. The M-shaped contraption and dual nooses burned in her vision like the afterimage of a flashbulb, just like the reporter's image from the night she watched the news report about Samantha Rodgers. And then something else . . . another whisper, far in the recesses of her mind, just a slight murmur, asking to be heard. She knew she should stop and listen to it, attempt to decipher what it was trying to tell her, but she was hardly aware of it as she sped along the gravel road, fighting to breathe and control her shaking hands, let alone able to comprehend its muddled message.

CHAPTER 14
Chicago, October 24, 2019

*R*ORY HAD NEVER APPRECIATED POSTCOITAL AFFECTION AND, IN FACT, needed her space after intimacy. Having slept together for ten years, Lane no longer questioned Rory's stealthy escape from the bedroom after sex. During the early phase of their relationship, she used to wait until Lane was asleep before attempting her getaway, but now it was just expected. She was slow and quiet as she slipped from beneath the covers, pulling a tank top over her head and tiptoeing downstairs.

In the kitchen, she opened the refrigerator, spilling soft light across the floor as she grabbed a Dark Lord. In her office, Rory sat at her desk and opened the file that waited there. With the rest of the house dark, her workspace was lit only by the soft auburn glow of the desk lamp. She took a sip of stout and began reading.

The Thief had hired the law firm of Garrison Ford immediately after his arrest. The 1979 retainer had been $25,000, which was paid with a cashier's check. The total fee for representation, which included the failed defense and the contentious trial, was close to $120,000—also paid via cashier's check in four lumps between the summer of 1979 and the winter of 1981. All of this information was contained in the third and final box Ron Davidson had delivered, along with the file from her father's office and the information Judge Boyle had provided.

Rory took a sip of beer and turned the page. The best she could piece together, her father had become involved with The

Thief during the appeals process, after the sixty-year sentence had been handed down. Garrison Ford continued to bill for services into 1982, when her father left the firm to start his own practice. Cross-referencing documents she unearthed from her father's file cabinets at his law office, Rory found a transition of invoicing that started in the later half of 1982. The first check was written to the Moore Law Group on October 5, 1982, to finance the second round of appeals.

Rory found that all reimbursements—old Xerox copies of hand-written checks—were full lump-sum payments. Over another beer, she learned that in addition to being a cold-blooded killer, her father's client was also a millionaire. At the time of his arrest, he had a net worth of $1.2 million. The man's financials were intimately detailed in his file because, in addition to handling appeals and representation at parole hearings, the man had also hired her father to look after his fortune during his incarceration, a task that included resolving debts, bringing his estate into order, and liquidating assets. Dipping into the dark side of criminal defense, Rory saw how her father had structured this man's fortune in an oasis of LLC corporations and trusts to hide assets and protect against the threat of civil lawsuits. Sheltered as it was, had the families of his other alleged victims gone after him, a large portion of his money would be off-limits.

But no civil suits were ever filed. Without bodies, Rory knew, a civil suit would be deemed frivolous. The remains of only one woman were found during the summer of 1979. Her name was Samantha Rodgers, and although there had been an attempt, Rory read, to tie The Thief to this woman, the attorneys at Garrison Ford had managed to convince the judge that any evidence linking their client to Samantha Rodgers was purely circumstantial. The judge agreed and the prosecution dropped their pursuit, instead focusing on Angela Mitchell.

Her father's client's money stayed protected, and, all told, when the killer settled into his cell in the early 1980s, he did so with more than $900,000 resting in a bank account. Through the 1980s, Rory's father had drawn from those funds to pay his legal fees during the lengthy appeals process, which dragged on for a decade.

In addition to checks rendered for legal services, Rory also came across additional payments categorized as "retainer fees." Over the course of the 1980s, the Moore Law Group had been paid more than $200,000. It was a steep sum to simply file appeals. The roots of her curiosity stretched deeper into her mind as she recognized that her father's connection to this man went beyond the typical attorney-client relationship.

What were you doing for this guy, Dad?

Rory read the details of the appeals her father had crafted, which highlighted the prosecution's weaknesses. They included, conveniently, that the district attorney could produce no physical evidence against his client, including the body of his alleged victim. Adding to the absence of Angela Mitchell's remains, Rory's father had argued that the woman was mentally retarded, as was stated in the 1979 brief. The term "cognitively challenged" was still decades away, and labeling her as "autistic" was less dramatic, too medical, and didn't fit the narrative. A mentally retarded schizophrenic was much more powerful. But no matter which adjectives had been used to describe Angela Mitchell, none were quite right. As Rory learned more about what the woman had done, and the lives she had surely saved, nowhere in the documents was Angela Mitchell described as "hero."

According to the statement by the prosecutor, Angela had spent the last days of her life compiling evidence that pointed a strong finger at the 1979 killer. She was killed during the process.

CHICAGO
AUGUST 1979

*I*T WAS SUNDAY MORNING, LESS THAN TWENTY-FOUR HOURS SINCE HER bizarre discovery in the warehouse, and Angela had not slept a minute. She was up all night updating the biographies of the missing women, and adding everything to her notes that she had found in the last three days about Leonard Williams. After leaving the warehouse yesterday, she had spent hours at the library, spinning microfilm and researching hanging and strangulation deaths associated with women in and around Chicago. Below the graph diagram Angela had put together depicting the trend of killings over the last decade, she now added relevant information from her library research. She was trying to make sense of the contraption she had found in the hidden storage room, and believed she was onto something. Of the women on her graph who fit the description, who fell into the profile, and who had been killed in and around Chicago, most had been strangled. On the last page of her file, Angela had drawn the odd, M-shaped wooden beam with the dual hanging nooses.

Ever since rushing from the warehouse to pore through microfilm at the library, the entire time she was creating her documents and graphs and working out her theory about Leonard Williams, all through the night and up until this morning when she arrived at Catherine's house, that soft whisper in her mind nagged and annoyed. Angela never stopped her work to listen, and feared the voice that was calling her was a side effect of the Valium, which she was swallowing at an alarming rate. Or it was the logical and reasonable part of her mind working to be heard, trying to tell her that she was overmedicating herself and that her ideas about the missing women were ridiculous.

She sat at Catherine's kitchen table now, pushed the whisper of that voice away, and showed her work to her friend. Catherine sat patiently and listened to Angela tell the story of her trip to the warehouse, her discovery that Leonard Williams lived so close to where Samantha Rodgers's body had been found, that of the women who had been killed and who matched the description of the missing women from this summer—all had been strangled. And finally she showed Catherine the bizarre image she had drawn of the dual noose contraption.

Catherine took a sip of coffee when Angela finally looked at her. "You know I always support you," Catherine said. "But . . ."

"But what?" Angela asked.

"I think everything that's going on this summer has set you off."

"What do you mean?"

"I think you're very nervous about what's going on. So am I. But I think you feel like it's your responsibility to figure this out, and, Angela, some of what you're showing me is . . ."

"Is what?"

"It's hard to digest. All the research you've done on the missing women, and how they might be connected to a decadelong string of murder."

"I think they are."

"But now you're telling me you think you know who did this, and that it's a man who works for Bill and Thomas."

Angela looked away from Catherine and back to her notes, her cheeks suddenly red and searing. She gathered the papers and stuffed them into the file folder. Her research and her theories, all contained in the file folder, sat on the kitchen table like some foreign and unwanted artifact found in the wild. Neither knew quite what to do with it or how to handle it—if it were worth anything at all, or just a useless bit of something unearthed and dragged inside.

"I think Leonard Williams scared you in the alley," Catherine finally said, placing her hand on Angela's. "And I think that's made you look at him in a way that most wouldn't see him. From what I know, he's a family man. He's got a wife and kids, Angela. He's not some deranged serial killer. I don't think you've done anything foolish, let me be clear. But reasonably looking at all of this, I don't know that I totally agree with everything you're suggesting. Angela, I'm not sure . . . I'm not sure I totally believe all of this."

Angela swallowed hard at the rejection. Her surroundings faded as memories of her childhood flooded her mind. Her teachers' disparaging comments anytime Angela made a remark in school, her parents' constant refusal to listen to Angela's reasoning on any subject, her psychiatrist's outright dismissal of her pleas for help when the lithium drew wild hallucinations in her vision. All the images from her childhood carried her away, and only when she heard talking did she come back to the present. When she did, she found Bill Blackwell standing next to Catherine.

There was a far-off echo. Angela tried to hear it, but it was hollow and muted. She saw Bill's lips moving and realized the man was speaking to her. She blinked her eyes.

"The second time in a week that I come home to a surprise," she heard Bill say. "Is Thomas back from Indiana yet?"

Angela focused her eyes on the bandana around Catherine's husband's neck. She realized the soft echoing voice she had heard a moment before was not that of Bill Blackwell, but instead the whispered voice she had been hearing since her visit to the Kenosha warehouse. It was finally loud enough to decipher. It was screaming, in fact, as she stared at the man in front of her. Angela's mind flashed to the night they all ate dinner in her home. She remembered Bill's red neck, explained then as an allergic reaction to insect repellent and the remnants of mosquito bites. She remembered his bandana from the last time she sat in this kitchen with Catherine. And now today, she looked at his bandana-covered neck to see deep red marks on his skin. Marks that could come from a noose.

Angela stood quickly. The kitchen chair toppled backward and ricocheted off the kitchen floor. She backed away and, without saying a word, turned and hurried out the front door. Her thick file folder remained on the table.

CHAPTER 15
Chicago, October 25, 2019

*R*ORY MADE IT THROUGH THE SCREENING PROCESS AGAIN AND ENtered the judge's chambers after the security guard had escorted her through the hallways. Now she sat, just like she had at their original meeting, in front of the desk while the judge took to his throne behind it, the high-back leather chair rising well above his head as he sat.

"Lots to cover," Judge Boyle said. "Have you made yourself familiar with your client?"

"Your client." The sound of it bothered Rory in many ways. She didn't have "clients." Her life revolved around "cases." Her life revolved around helping *victims,* not the men accused of killing them. An acidic burn rose up her esophagus and settled in the back of her throat. But Rory swallowed it down. Her interest in Angela Mitchell was stronger than her GERD, and her father's mysterious role in The Thief's life had won a spot in her psyche. She knew she couldn't dump this case until she learned what, exactly, her father had been doing with this man for all these years.

"Yes, sir," Rory finally said.

"Excellent. Your father and I had worked out many of the stipulations relating to this man's release. Here are a few of them."

Judge Boyle handed a single piece of paper across his desk. On it was a long list of bullet points. He read from his own copy.

"There was a request to forgo a halfway house as a living requirement. Considering your client's notoriety, his age, and his financial means, I've agreed to this request. He is required to stay in Illinois for twenty-four months, however. Your client owns a home in the state, out near Starved Rock State Park. It's about an hour outside of the city. Frank had requested that your client be allowed to keep this as his residence, and I've agreed. However, there is a list of stipulations that will need to be met. You and the social worker, as well as your client's assigned parole officer, will need to visit the property ahead of time and make certain it meets the requirements."

"What requirements, sir?"

Judge Boyle pushed another sheet of paper across his desk.

"It needs to have a landline for phone, as your client will be required to check in daily with his parole officer for the first three months. Internet access is not mandatory, but suggested. The property needs to have a USPS mailing address. POB addresses are not allowed. Photos of the home will also need to be taken and placed in the formal file. Your trip to the home should be scheduled this week. You'll coordinate it with Naomi Brown, the social worker?"

The judge posed the statement as a question, but Rory understood his tone to be less of a request than an order. She nodded.

"There is a substantial sum of money that your client will have access to upon his release. Your father had financial power of attorney for the last four decades. Now that Frank is gone, the money will be handled exclusively by your client. That's over eight hundred thousand dollars, counselor. He's never been in this new world of digital banking. He'll need some help getting settled. So, of course, release the funds to him, but I'll expect you to be his steward. For the first eighteen months after his release, you'll be required to provide me with financial updates to prove that he will not squander his fortune or become"—the judge paused—"a victim . . . of financial predators looking to take advantage of him. The State of Illinois has spent enough money on this man. I'd like to make sure we spend no more after he is released."

Rory made notes.

"Finally," the judge said, "he is sixty-eight years old. He obviously has the means not to work, and his notoriety prevents him from meaningful employment. It's best for now that your client disappear for a while. Maybe forever. The property near Starved Rock has been held in a trust, so his name is not attached to it. He will be difficult to track down after release. Of course, everyone in authority who needs to find him will have easy access. But the trolls will be looking for him, and it's up to you to help him stay anonymous. Your father had done a lot of work, to this end."

The judge closed the file and stood, as if he had even more pressing issues to attend to. "Is there anything else?"

"Yes," Rory said. She swallowed down the acid again. "I'll have to see him before the formal parole hearing to go over a few other things. To my knowledge, he doesn't even know his attorney has died."

The circumstance of seeing a stranger in the close quarters of a visitation room, of having to look him in the eye and explain that she was his new attorney, was something Rory would have normally run from. Typically, she'd have done anything to avoid such a thing, arms up and slithering from its hold like a child escaping her mother's grip. But Rory was after something. She didn't give a shit about the man they called The Thief. She wanted to know what her father was doing for him, because she knew damn well it wasn't simply tending to his legal needs.

"That can be arranged," Judge Boyle said. "I'll put in the request so that it's expedited."

CHICAGO
August 1979

*A*NGELA'S BIRTHDAY FELL ON TUESDAY, TWO DAYS AFTER CATHERINE had rejected her, the way everyone from Angela's adolescence had done. Two days after she saw Bill Blackwell's neck, and the ugly red gouges he hid with a bandana. Two days since Angela had put all the haunting pieces to this summer together. Two full days, and she had done nothing. It had been two days of very little sleep, her mind allowing only thoughts about the missing women, and questioning her belief that Bill Blackwell was part of it all. That the peculiar practice of dual hanging was the method he had used to kill the women. Two days of questioning her theory that the disappearances were part of a much broader string of homicides, which dated back an entire decade. Two days of panic and doubt. And if Angela doubted herself, she couldn't blame Catherine for rebuking her.

"Is the wine okay?" Thomas asked, bringing Angela back from her thoughts.

Knowing she didn't like crowds, Thomas made early dinner reservations. Now, on her birthday, they sat at a candlelit table, sipping red wine, while the restaurant was only sparsely occupied. Angela did her best with the acidic cabernet that was upsetting her frail stomach.

She smiled. "It's good."

She had been close to confessing everything to Thomas when he arrived home on Sunday night. But instead, she kept things bottled up, allowing her mind to run wild. She had, Angela knew, lost all control of her thoughts. Not even the Valium was able to corral her psyche. The lack of sleep had her ragged and on edge.

She wrestled with her uneasy stomach through dinner, and then declined dessert.

"You don't want dessert on your birthday?" Thomas asked.

"I'm not in the mood for sweets. But you go ahead."

"No, we'll skip it tonight. I have something for you," Thomas said, producing a small wrapped present from the breast pocket of his jacket.

Everything that had transpired since that day in the garage when Angela had attempted to move the old couch out to the alley for trash pickup—her encounter with Leonard Williams, her overwhelming bout of obsessive compulsion that had stolen an entire week, the forming of her theory about the missing women dating back for a decade, the report of Samantha Rodgers's body being found, and, most recently, her bizarre discovery in the warehouse, her research about the disturbing practice of dual asphyxiation and thoughts of Bill Blackwell being involved in all of it—had caused Angela to forget about the necklace she found in the old picnic basket.

The events of the past week had nearly caused her to forget her birthday altogether. Now, as she sat with the gift in front of her, she was grateful for having forgotten about the necklace. Had it been present in her mind, she wouldn't have been able to play off being surprised.

"Can I open it?" she asked.

"Of course," Thomas said.

Angela pulled the wrapped box in front of her. She carefully tore away the paper and opened the top of the small box. She squinted her eyes at the diamond earrings that rested on the felt interior, with no attempt to hide her confusion.

"You don't like them?" Thomas asked.

She looked up at her husband, who was staring with a confused look on his face that matched Angela's.

"No, no," she quickly said. "I love them. I just . . ." She shook her head. "They're beautiful."

"We can exchange them if they're not what you like. You pointed them out a few months ago when we were shopping. I thought they'd make the perfect surprise."

Angela nodded. "They do. They're perfect."

As she slipped the diamonds through the piercings in her earlobes, her mind could think of nothing but the necklace she had found hidden at the bottom of the picnic basket in her garage.

Angela lay in bed pretending to enjoy her husband's attention. Although their sex life had never been passionate, she and Thomas shared chemistry in the bedroom and their lovemaking had always been enjoyable. But tonight, her mind was elsewhere. When he rolled off her, she lay with her head on his shoulder until she was certain he was sleeping. Then, to the sounds of his rhythmic breathing, Angela slipped out of bed. She pulled on her robe and sunk her feet into stockings. It was just past eleven, a time of night she would never typically consider venturing outside. The thought of making the journey to the garage in the dead of night had her fingertips tingling and the scabs on her shoulders begging to be ruptured. But another urge overshadowed her fear and trumped even the strongest pull from the self-destructive parts of her mind—curiosity.

She knew sleep would never come, even with the liberal use of Valium, until she understood the mystery of the necklace. Angela avoided the light switches until she made it to the kitchen, where she turned on the dim light over the stove. She felt the flush in her cheeks and the familiar queasiness in her stomach as she looked through the kitchen window to the garage. Her pounding pulse and the audible rush of blood through the vessels of her head were her body's way of begging Angela to wait until morning, but she could not.

Unlatching the back door, she stepped out into the night. The sweltering summer heat relinquished none of its power even this late, and Angela felt the humid air dampen her face. The neighborhood was quiet. She kept the patio light extinguished and carried a small flashlight with her. An impending panic attack made her breathing shallow. She hurried to the utility door at the back of the garage and ducked inside, bringing the interior to life with her flashlight.

The dirty couch was still against the wall. She turned her attention to the cluttered shelves and found the picnic basket. Pulling it from its spot, she opened the top and shined her light inside. The thin necklace box remained just where she had left it. Angela reached into the basket and pulled it out. Opening the box, she found the necklace as it reflected the flashlight's brightness.

In the darkened garage, she reached up to pinch the dangling earrings that hung from her lobes. She swallowed a sudden bolus of saliva that had formed in the back of her throat as she contemplated what it could mean. Thomas had been working late this summer, at least two or three nights a week. She remembered a string of phone calls last month when no one spoke after Angela had answered. A few times the caller had hung up just after Angela had uttered the word "hello." She knew he'd hired a new secretary that summer. Now, as Angela stood in the darkened garage, she fought against the screams of her mind that told her Thomas was having an affair. The nausea returned and her stomach rolled. She retched once, then quickly dropped the necklace back into the basket and replaced it on the shelf. She raced through the utility door and vomited onto a small patch of grass in the backyard.

Breathing heavily, she gulped the sticky summer air until a second wave of nausea passed. Then she hustled back into the house. She closed and locked the kitchen door just as the lights flashed on. When Angela turned around, Thomas stood in the kitchen, wearing only his boxer shorts.

"What's going on?" he asked.

Angela patted her nightgown, a nervous reaction to hide her confusion. It did just the opposite. "I thought I heard the trashcans rattling again. The top had fallen off," she said, immediately judging her lie to be somewhere between awful and completely unbelievable.

"Why didn't you wake me?" he asked.

"I just . . . didn't want the neighbors to hear it. Mr. Peterson has been edgy since I blocked the driveway with the couch."

Thomas walked to the back door and pulled the curtains to the side.

"The utility door to the garage is open," he said, looking at her.

"Is it? I hadn't noticed." Angela felt her stomach roiling again.

Thomas unlocked the kitchen door and walked out to the garage. The sticky night air drifted into the house as Angela watched him enter the garage and turn on the lights. He disappeared out of sight for a full minute, during which the knot in her stomach tightened and pulled her to the washroom. She vomited again before steadying herself against the wall and resting her forehead on the back of her hand. She heard the floorboards squeak and, through watery eyes, saw Thomas standing in the bathroom doorway.

"Are you all right?" he asked.

"Not feeling well again."

"This is why you should have woken me," he said, taking her under the arm and leading her back upstairs. She allowed him to guide her into bed.

"I saw that you vomited outside," he said as he pulled the covers over her. "I'm calling the doctor in the morning. I know you've been resisting, Angela. But it's time to see the psychiatrist. Someone has to help you through this, and I don't know what else to do for you."

Angela had nearly run through her Valium. She'd need more, so she didn't protest. As Thomas climbed into bed next to her, Angela closed her eyes, but never slept.

CHAPTER 16
Chicago, October 25, 2019

*T*HE FRACTURE HAD COME TOGETHER NICELY, BUT IT HAD TAKEN A larger amount of epoxy than she preferred using. The additional adhesive was needed to ensure the eye socket of Camille Byrd's childhood doll remained intact. Rory was unable to get herself into the correct mind-set to reconstruct the woman's murder, so she concentrated on Camille Byrd's doll instead. Once Rory immersed herself in the restoration, she found the doll's eye was the most challenging to repair. She had rebuilt the eye socket with a papier-mâché-and-plaster combination, a technique Sabine Esche had written about. Now that the epoxy and plaster had set, and the eye was seated in the orbit, Rory was pleased with the result. When the doll was laid down, there was just a slight delay in the closure of the eyelid, which only the most astute observer would notice.

She sanded the adhesive so that the seam of the original fracture was smooth. When Rory closed her eyes and ran her fingers over the doll's cheek, the fracture was undetectable. The *feel* of the doll's face had been perfectly restored. The *appearance* of Camille Byrd's childhood doll, however, still left much to be desired. The additional epoxy and heavy polishing had left a badly discolored patch that ran, like a stream on a map, from the hairline down to the edge of the jaw. The curved ribbon of tarnished porcelain looked like a poorly healed scar. Rory knew the skills she had utilized to repair the fracture and reconstruct the eye socket were unmatched. She also knew where her weakness lay, and that was in bringing porcelain back to its original state. For this task, she would go to a master. To the one person who was better than she was.

It was approaching midnight when Rory walked into the nursing home. She had gained permission from the staff, and had been granted the access code to the front entrance, to visit so late at night. The nurses knew Greta rarely slept at night, and that Rory's best chance for a coherent conversation usually came after midnight. Her last two visits with Aunt Greta had been failures. Since the passing of her father, Rory had trouble connecting with her great-aunt. With no children of her own, Aunt Greta's family consisted of her nephew—Frank Moore—and his daughter. Rory's father had been more like a grandson to Greta, and Rory like a great-grandchild. Over the course of her life, Rory had learned many things from Greta, including her love for restoring china dolls. It had once been their most cherished activity, restoring old dolls that had lined the walls of Greta's house. Their mutual love of antique-doll restoration was the foundation of their relationship, and was how the two had become so close through Rory's childhood. Now, since dementia had stolen Greta's mind, the old dolls Rory brought to her bedside provided a different conduit to the past. They provided access to a part of Greta's history that was filled with joy, rather than the agonizing moments of Greta's life that the dementia usually dredged up.

Tonight's visit also carried selfish undertones. Since she had requested a meeting with The Thief, a tremor had taken hold of Rory's hands, the way they used to tremble as a child. Anxiety had plagued her since a young age, and the only way Rory managed her childhood was through the calming nature of Aunt Greta and the dolls they restored together. Rory's parents had known the effect Greta had on their child, and had shuttled Rory away when signs of her disorder became apparent. After a long weekend, or sometimes an extended stay that lasted a week or more, Rory would return to her parents' house restored and renewed, much like the dolls she and Greta worked on. Tonight Rory needed the same healing powers Greta had delivered to her when she was a lost child.

Rory carried Camille Byrd's Kestner doll into the darkened room. Aunt Greta sat upright in bed with her eyes open, staring at nothing. Rory visited during the night not only because it was the most likely time to catch Greta in a coherent state, but also because Rory knew that sleep rarely came to her great-aunt during the small hours of night. The thought of Aunt Greta lying awake, staring into space, was never a comforting one. The woman had given Rory so much in life that Rory refused to allow her to spend the last stretch of her life alone.

"Hey, old lady," Rory said when she approached the bedside.

Greta's eyes flicked to the side, catching a glimpse of Rory for just an instant.

"I tried to save you. There was too much blood."

"I know," Rory said. "You did the best you could. And you helped many, many patients during your career."

"There's too much blood. We have to go to the hospital."

"Aunt Greta, everything is okay now. Everyone is safe."

"We have to go. I need help. There's too much blood."

Rory paused a moment as she stared at her. Finally she took her hand and squeezed gently. "You promised you'd help me with a restoration. Do you remember?"

Rory placed the box containing the Kestner doll on the bed. She immediately saw her aunt's demeanor change. Greta looked down at the doll, whose damaged face was visible through the window in the lid.

"I had to use a lot of epoxy to fix the fracture, which required a great deal of sanding to smooth. I have it repaired perfectly, but need some help getting the porcelain back to its original color."

Greta sat more upright in bed as Rory opened the box, removed the doll, and placed it on her aunt's lap. Rory found the controls and lifted the back of the bed upward so that Greta was fully erect.

"I brought your pastels," Rory said, removing from her backpack a large assortment of fingernail polish–sized glass bottles filled with different colors. She wheeled the bedside table over and set the paints on the surface.

"I need better light," Greta said. Her voice was scratchy and hoarse, different now than the high-pitched ramblings when she was trapped in the throes of dementia.

Rory pulled over the lamp, clicked on the overhead lights, and watched her go to work. She was immediately transported to her childhood, to Greta's home, to the room lined with dolls, and the workstation where she and Greta had spent hours and hours.

"Hey," Rory said while Greta painted a foundation coating over the repaired fracture. She kept her eyes on the Kestner doll as she spoke. "I've got to do something that's got me . . . scared."

Rory never used the words "nervous" or "anxious." To do so would be to admit too much. Greta kept working, not even a glance in Rory's direction. She was lost in the restoration.

"I've got to meet with someone Dad used to work with. A client."

Rory waited a moment for any indication that Greta had heard her.

"He's a bad man. An evil man, from what I know. But I have no choice but to meet with him."

Greta finally stopped stroking her brush over the doll's face to look at Rory. "You always have a choice."

Rory paused a moment. "I guess that's true."

Greta went back to the doll, all her concentration channeled on coloring the repaired fracture streaming down from the eye socket.

Of course, Greta's words were accurate. Rory could have simply told the judge that she would not take the case. Was she legally obligated to do so? It was a gray area. Being a partner in her father's law firm put Rory next in line to take his cases, but had she simply refused to do so, there was little Judge Boyle could have done. The truth was that Rory had already made the choice. She was meeting with this man for a reason. She had chosen to visit him face-to-face because there was something her father had been hiding. Rory wanted to know what it was, and the only person who could tell her was the man sitting in jail, waiting on his parole.

Greta spoke again as she attended to the doll, her brushstrokes even and purposeful as the fissure began to disappear. "Nothing can scare you unless you allow it to scare you."

Rory smiled and sat back in her chair. She loved the rare moments when she was able to connect with Greta, whose mind lately had seemingly been ravaged and stolen.

Two hours later, the first coat was finished and drying. To a casual observer, Camille Byrd's doll looked perfect. But Rory knew it would take two more coats of paint and polish before it was truly flawless. For this, she was grateful. It meant she would soon have an opportunity to reconnect with her great-aunt again.

CHICAGO
August 1979

*T*HE DAY AFTER HER BIRTHDAY WAS SPENT UNDER THOMAS'S WATCHFUL eye. Angela did her best to keep things together as she acclimated herself to the idea of seeing a psychiatrist. There was no way to avoid it, and she knew Thomas would press the issue. Wild bouts of memories came back to her as she remembered her teen years spent under the authoritarian rule of her doctor, in whom her parents had placed their trust that he would control her wild outbursts, her self-inflicted wounds, and morph their introverted child into a "normal" outgoing teenager.

Angela had swallowed the last of her Valium after her venture to the garage the night before, and when the sun brightened the frames of the bedroom windows this morning, she was eager for the world to pull her from another night of torment. Alone in bed now, once the nine o'clock hour came, she heard Thomas making phone calls. One of his calls was to Dr. Solomon, Angela knew, asking for a referral to a shrink. Angela had never mentioned to Thomas that Dr. Solomon's original recommendation had found its way into the trash, or that the doctor's last few phone calls had gone unreturned.

Angela finally climbed from bed as Thomas continued to talk on the phone, his deep voice rumbling from the kitchen. She showered and dressed. When she walked downstairs, Thomas was drinking coffee at the kitchen table and analyzing a spreadsheet for work.

"I made coffee," he said. "Are you feeling better?"

"A little, yes," Angela lied as she poured a cup and sat across from him.

"I called the doctor," Thomas said. "He's out of the office until tomorrow. I left a message. I think I should go with you when you see the psychiatrist."

Angela didn't protest, just nodded.

"And I've got a problem with the job in Indiana. They need me to come down and have a look. At this time of morning, I'll miss rush hour, will get down there by early afternoon. Then I'll get back by tonight. Shouldn't be later than eight."

Angela felt for the first time that she might have overdone it with the Valium. A wave of indifference had come over her since she swallowed the last of the pills after her trip to the garage the previous night. The necklace hidden in the picnic basket, and thoughts of Thomas's infidelity, ricocheted through her mind. She thought of his late nights at the office, and his spree of out-of-town jobs that had him frequently spending nights away from home. Add that to Catherine's dismissal of her findings, and Angela felt alone and isolated with no one to turn to. That wasn't true, she reminded herself. Through the fog of hazy thoughts, she knew she'd always have one person in her life she could trust. And the offer to help Angela *at any time, for any reason,* had been unconditional. Angela had never thought she would need that help. Not since she had been saved, when she was eighteen, had she needed help. Since then, she had been on her own, free from the confines of her parents and the shrinks and the psychiatric facility where they held her prisoner. But this morning, for the first time in years, Angela needed help. After all these years, she wondered if the offer still stood.

"Will you be okay by yourself?" Thomas asked. "I can call Catherine to see if she could stay with you today."

"No," Angela said.

Her mind wandered back to her childhood when her parents watched her like hawks, always fearing the worst if they left Angela alone. And Catherine was no longer someone she could confide in.

"I'll be fine."

Thomas nodded, taking a long look at his wife. "The girl at Dr. Solomon's office said he sometimes returns calls from home, so if the phone rings, make sure to answer it. She said he's been trying to reach you, that he's called a couple of times."

Angela stared at her coffee. She felt the walls of her world constricting on her. She had erased Dr. Solomon's messages from the answering machine with the illogical thinking that if she erased the messages she'd never have to talk with him. With the nonsensical reasoning that deleting Dr. Solomon's voice and his request for a return call would prevent her from having to return to the world of psychiatrists. Finally Angela looked up at her husband and shrugged. "He hasn't called, that I know of. But I'll make sure to answer if the phone rings."

Thirty minutes later, she watched as Thomas backed out of the garage and into the alley. He pulled slowly away, headed back to Indiana for the day. The rumble of the truck's engine was barely out of earshot by the time Angela was on the move. She had been unable to follow the news for the past couple of days, knowing that Thomas would not like the idea of stirring her paranoia with news articles about the girl whose body had been found the week before.

Now, with Thomas gone, Angela felt a sudden urge for the latest details of the case. She longed for anything to take her mind off the idea that Thomas could be having an affair. She hadn't seen or heard any updates about Samantha Rodgers since she had listened to the radio report the morning at the warehouse. She turned on the television, but with Thomas's late start this morning, all she found was the start of daytime television. The morning newscasts had ended more than an hour ago. She clicked on the radio next and tuned to 780AM for the latest news. Ten minutes of stock market talk and commercials passed before she decided to look for the newspaper.

The front stoop was empty and the driveway bare when she looked for the *Tribune*. She figured Thomas had already fetched it, and she checked the bathroom, a disgusting habit she'd never been able to break him of. When she was unable to locate the paper in the house, she decided to check the trash. She walked to the alley and lifted the lid to the trashcan. Inside, on top of black plastic Glad bags, rested an unread *Tribune* still wrapped in the plastic bag in which it was delivered. Angela rescued it from the trash and hurried inside.

The *Tribune* was filled with stories of The Thief and details about the only victim whose body had been found. Angela pulled at her eyelashes as she carefully read the articles, one at a time, and then delicately clipped them from the paper with a scissors to add to her growing file. She turned the page and started a new article that covered Samantha Rodgers and the shallow grave where her body was found. Angela's skin tingled as she read the story:

> *The body of Samantha Rodgers was discovered in a wooded area of Forest Glen, less than a mile from the main road. Deep bruising found on her neck, discovered during autopsy, suggests that she was strangled. The Chicago Police are asking for any information about the victim from the night she disappeared, and are leaning hard on Samantha Rodgers's parents' suggestion that on the night she went missing, Samantha was wearing a peridot-and-diamond necklace she had received for her graduation the month before. The police are approaching all city and suburban pawn shops to see if a necklace matching the parents' description will be found, hoping for the first lead in the summer's missing persons cases.*
>
> *The necklace in question carries an engraving of the victim's initials and birth date on the back: SR 7-29-57.*
>
> *Any information can be reported to the phone number below.*

Angela looked up from the paper. Her world narrowed in a migrainous aura of tunnel vision that captured only the utility door to the garage as she gazed through the kitchen window. She was on her feet in a flash, following the periscope of vision and heading out the back door.

CHAPTER 17
Chicago, October 26, 2019

*R*ORY WAS IN FULL BATTLE GEAR—GLASSES, BEANIE HAT, GRAY jacket, and lace-up combat boots. Her face burned crimson as she sat in her car in the parking lot. She took deep breaths as she thought of sitting across from her father's oldest client, a cold and calculating killer, pretending to hammer out the details of his release. An odd guilt came over her when she considered the notion that her dead father had some nefarious business relationship with this killer from 1979.

"Nothing can scare you unless you allow it to scare you." She took a few more calming breaths, and allowed the attack to escape her lungs with each exhale. When her hands were steady, and her lungs freely expanding and contracting without the hiccup rhythm of panic, Rory opened the car door, stood from the passenger seat, and sucked in the cool fall morning. She stood in front of Stateville Correctional Center in Crest Hill, Illinois. It was where The Thief had been housed for the past forty years.

She had her identification prepared, the paperwork filled out ahead of time, and a copy of Judge Boyle's orders to permit the impromptu visit. Still, processing moved slowly. She was finally called to the window to fill out additional visitation forms. A woman slid the partition window to the side and looked up from her computer.

"Name, please?"

"Rory Moore."

"Relationship to the inmate?"

"Attorney."

The woman typed on her computer for a moment.

"Name of the inmate?"

Rory looked at the file in her hands, read the name from the bottom flap.

"Thomas Mitchell."

CHICAGO
August 1979

*T*HE UTILITY DOOR TO THE BACK OF THE GARAGE WAS WIDE OPEN AS Angela pulled the picnic basket off the shelf. The wicker top rolled a few feet away when she dropped it, spinning on its edge like a coin as it twirled several times before coming to a rest. Angela had the necklace in her hand, dropping the case that held it to the ground, and was closely examining it. The green peridot and surrounding diamonds were dull this morning in the poorly lit garage, different from the morning when she had first discovered it. Back then, she had sat with the bright morning sun bringing the gemstone to life. So much was different now than had been that morning, like the light of her life had been drained from her, just like from the gemstones.

The tremor returned to her hands as she slowly turned the necklace over and strained her eyes to look for an engraving. She held the necklace up to the light that spilled through the window until she could clearly see the engraving on the back: *SR 7-29-57.*

Angela Mitchell's world ended that day in her garage. Some indecipherable correlation formed in her mind between the morning she had attempted to move the couch to the trash and today. Her life had been on a downward trajectory since then, and this morning, it had finally crashed in a fiery explosion.

She slowly looked back to the shelves in front of her and, without consciously knowing what she was doing, rummaged through other containers. She went through one box after the other until she came to a plastic carton that held Christmas decorations. She slid it from overhead, placed it on the garage floor, and lifted the lid. Inside were strings of Christmas lights tightly wound, sitting on top of an object that she could not immediately identify. Pulling the strings of lights from the box, Angela found a purse underneath. It was nothing she had ever owned. With a feeling of foreboding in the pit of her stomach and with trembling fingers, she unzipped the purse. Makeup and lipstick greeted her. A crumpled pack of Pall Malls and a lighter. A small wallet. She pulled the wallet from the purse as the cigarettes tumbled to the floor. She dropped the purse and turned the wallet over in her hands. She was light-headed. Her peripheral vision was blotched with dancing stars. She thumbed the driver's license out of the wallet and saw a picture of a blond-haired woman. Angela recognized her immediately as Clarissa Manning, the first victim who had gone missing in May. Angela had created an extensive biography on her, like she had on all the others.

Angela had no way of fully understanding the horrors she had stumbled onto in the storage room at the Kenosha warehouse, but early waves of comprehension began rolling onto the shores of her mind as she thought of the dual nooses and again about the news reports detailing the bruising on Samantha Rodgers's neck. She couldn't bring her mind to understand what might have transpired there.

As it all came to her, and while she stood with Clarissa Manning's ID card in one hand, Samantha Rodgers's necklace in the other, a rattling noise screamed for her attention. Angela's vision was still tunneled as she stared at the relics that belonged to the missing women. She finally had the answer to why she had been on edge all summer. She finally knew the reason why the long-dead obsessions and compulsions from her past had risen from the graves where she had buried them. As much as she tried to convince herself, it had nothing to do with the stranger from the alley, or with Bill Blackwell. Her sense of fear had been so acute this summer because she had been so close to the man responsible for taking the women.

The clattering noise continued until it finally pulled Angela back to the present. She stared wide-eyed at the back wall of the garage until her mind eventually processed the noise she was hearing. It was the rattle of the garage door opener overhead engaging the chains, the squeak of the springs as they twisted the door upward, and the rumble of Thomas's Ford truck approaching up the alley.

He was supposed to be in Indiana. He was supposed to be surveying a future job site. Angela looked down at her feet, the rushing of blood loud in her ears. There, on the garage floor, was the open plastic container, the lid slid to the side. Three strings of Christmas lights were haphazardly stacked next to it, and Clarissa Manning's purse, which had landed upside down, spewed its contents of makeup, lipstick, cigarette lighter, and loose change. The picnic basket and its cover, which had spun to a stop several feet away, lay there, too.

The rumble of Thomas's truck grew louder as the garage door continued to rise.

CHAPTER 18
Chicago, October 26, 2019

*R*ORY SAT IN THE BOOTH ACROSS FROM THOMAS MITCHELL. SHE knew from her father's file that he was sixty-eight years old, but the man across from her looked younger. Deep crevices ran from his nostrils, around his lips, and died somewhere near his chin. But otherwise, his face was chiseled and young-looking. If Rory didn't know better, she'd guess he was in his early fifties.

His expression was stoic when she sat in front of him, his handcuffed wrists resting on the table, his fingers folded as if in prayer, and an aura of patience emanating from him. He lifted the phone and placed it to his ear. Rory did the same.

"Mr. Mitchell, my name is Rory Moore."

"They said my attorney was here to see me."

"I'm sorry to inform you that Frank Moore passed away last month. I'm his daughter."

Rory noticed something in the man's eyes, whether it was emotion or simply contemplation was difficult to determine.

"Will this delay my release?"

"No. I've taken over the case and am handling the details."

"Are you a lawyer?"

Rory hesitated, just like when Judge Boyle asked her the same question.

"Yes," she finally said. "I worked occasionally with my father, and I've met with the judge who is overseeing your parole."

Thomas Mitchell said nothing, so Rory went on.

"The judge and my father were negotiating the terms of your parole. I'm familiar with the details."

Rory opened the file in front of her.

"You have some assets." She pulled a page from the stack. "Just over eight hundred thousand dollars remain in your account. If you're smart with your money, it should last for the rest of your life."

He nodded.

"My father had financial power of attorney. Those rights have transferred to me, and the judge has asked that I help you get established financially after your release. The world of banking has changed since you were a free man. The judge has asked that I help you with your finances for the first year and a half after your release."

"What about my living arrangements? I don't want to live in a halfway house," he said. "Frank was working on that for me."

"The judge has granted your request to live in the home located near Starved Rock. I see that you inherited the cabin from an uncle in 1994. My father placed it in a trust for you and it's been under management ever since as a rental property. The judge has ordered me, along with your social worker, Naomi Brown, and parole officer, Ezra Parker, to inspect the residence before your release."

"Fine," The Thief said. "Please make sure the heat is on."

Rory paused at his subtle attempt at humor.

"Have you been to this cabin before?"

"When I was a kid. I was surprised my uncle willed it to me. But I'm happy to have it, and Frank has kept it anonymous."

Rory had paged briefly through her father's work related to the inherited property. It made sense now that he had placed it in a trust to keep the owner nameless.

"There is a long list of requirements you'll be expected to follow during your first twelve months of release." Rory pulled another page from the folder. "You'll need to meet and speak regularly to your parole officer. You'll also be assigned a social worker, who will make sure you are getting settled. There is a list of doctors here that you will be required to see. An internist who will run regular drug testing, and a psychologist you will be required to meet with every other week. All of this is set up to help reintegrate you into society."

"There's not going to be any *reintegration.* I'll have folks trying to hunt me down. And if any of them find out where I'm living, it'll be the end of me. Frank anticipated this and took measures to assure my privacy. And for the same reason, I doubt it would be helpful to make me find work. No organization will want me, and I'll run into the same problem of people finding me. I have plenty of money to live a quiet life, which is what I intend to do."

"The judge has waived the work requirement based on your age, notoriety, and your financial means. Paperwork that covers all of these stipulations will be delivered to you for your signature. Once the papers are signed, the parole will move forward. Your release is scheduled for November third. Questions?"

"Yeah. What happened to Frank?"

Rory observed the man through the glass. The way he said her father's name felt personal.

"He had a heart attack."

"Damn shame."

Rory squinted her eyes behind her thick glasses. "You and my father seem to have had a close relationship."

"We did. He was my attorney, and other than the people on the inside, he was the only one I was regularly in contact with."

Rory wanted to ask what her father had done for Thomas Mitchell for forty years. It was more than appeal and parole hearings. She wanted to ask why this man had paid her father nearly $200,000 in retainer fees.

As if The Thief had read her mind, he said, "Listen, I'm sorry to hear about Frank. He was the closest thing I had to a friend. But I've got to concentrate on getting out of here, and keeping myself anonymous after I do. Can you help with this?"

His friend. Rory's phone vibrated in her back pocket. Then again, and again. Three notifications in a row. She offered Thomas Mitchell a forced smile, retrieved her phone from her pocket, and looked at the screen: **Rory. Very interested in talking with you about Angela Mitchell. I'm in Chicago and would love to meet, Catherine Blackwell.**

Rory had nearly forgotten about the message she left in the comments of Catherine Blackwell's Facebook page. She looked back to Thomas Mitchell. There was a woman still looking for justice forty years after this man had killed his wife. Rory's fingers itched with the urge to type a message back to Catherine Blackwell.

"Your parole is still scheduled for next week," Rory said, looking up from her phone. "Nothing's changed."

Thomas Mitchell nodded his head, hung up the phone, and pressed the call button underneath it. A moment later, a guard appeared and ushered him away.

CHICAGO
AUGUST 1979

*T*HOMAS PULLED HIS TRUCK INTO THE ALLEY AND PRESSED THE AUTO-matic garage door opener. As he approached the back of his home, he saw the top of the trashcan strewn into the middle of the alley. He stepped on the brake and shifted the Ford into park, then climbed out and retrieved the top. When he placed the lid back into place, he noticed that the newspaper he had deposited in the trash earlier in the day was gone. He rested a rock on top of the can and looked across the small backyard to the kitchen window, where he'd left Angela less than an hour ago. His senses were on fire since the night of her birthday when he'd found her in the garage. After twenty minutes on the Kennedy Expressway this morning, he felt something was wrong. He decided his trip to Indiana could wait. Things might be falling apart at home, and he had to deal with it.

Climbing back into his truck, he pulled into the garage and im-mediately noticed the boxes and cartons on the shelf were out of place. He knew this part of the garage well. It's where he hid his treasures. Now, as he stared at the shelving, he knew he'd made a mistake by leaving things unattended. Since she'd been through the boxes, who knew what she might have found?

He killed the truck's engine, climbed from the cab, and closed the truck's door. Thomas stood in front of the shelf and took in-ventory. He could tell that she had moved things around, but was unsure what, exactly, she had gotten into. As he started toward the utility door that led to the backyard, he noticed quarters, dimes, and pennies scattered across the floor. Turning back to the shelf, he reached for the clear plastic box that held three strings of Christmas lights and one of the girls' purses. He had placed it there immediately afterward, but hadn't disposed of it yet. It was difficult to get rid of their things. He liked to savor them for a time, until The Rush was gone. He should have kept the items at the warehouse, but there was a perverse pleasure in keeping their personal items so close to his home.

Pulling the box from the shelf, he opened the lid and found the three strings of lights wound in tight circles resting on top of the purse, just as he had left them. He leaned his waist against the box and pinned it to the shelf so his hands were free, then moved the lights and picked up the purse. Unzipping it, he poked around at the contents. Cigarettes and a lighter. Random makeup. He fingered the wallet and then lifted it out. It was a thin item, with a zipper that led to a small compartment for loose change, and slots for charge cards. Thomas looked down at the floor and the strewn quarters and dimes.

He turned the skinny wallet over and noticed an empty slot on the front where a driver's license would be slid for easy access. He thumbed through the pockets inside, and continued to poke around the purse but was unable to find the girl's ID card. He leaned his body slightly to his right, keeping the box pinned to the shelf, and peered through the curtains of the utility door to survey the back of his home. He could see into the empty kitchen.

His forehead wrinkled as he considered the possibility of his wife having discovered his secret. The implications would be disastrous. He dropped the purse back into the box, not bothering to rezip it. He dropped the wallet haphazardly on top of it, and then tossed the lights in. Sliding the box back onto the shelf, he next reached for the picnic basket and threw the lid to the ground. He ripped the tablecloth out of the basket and found it empty.

Dropping the basket onto the ground, Thomas exited the utility door of the garage, walked across the backyard, and turned the knob on the kitchen door. It opened.

"Angela," he yelled as he walked inside.

No answer.

"Angela?"

He heard a metallic thud in the basement and headed for the stairs. He took them quickly. When he reached the landing at the bottom, he saw a light in the laundry room. The dryer was running, and the lid to the washing machine was open as water filled the bin and Angela tossed clothes in.

He startled her when he approached and she let out a piercing shriek. Her body shook and she crumpled to the floor of the laundry room.

"Sorry," Thomas said. "You didn't answer when I called."

Angela looked up, running a hand through her hair.

"The washer and dryer were running. I didn't hear you."

"Sorry to startle you," he said, reaching down and helping her to her feet. He looked around the room, assessing the situation. "The back door was unlocked. I thought we talked about keeping the doors secured."

"Oh," Angela said. "I must have forgotten to lock it."

"Did you go out?"

"Yes. This morning. I took a bag of garbage out."

Thomas remembered the trashcan, the missing newspaper, and the top that had rolled into the middle of the alley.

"What are you doing home?" Angela asked.

The washing machine made a thundering sound and started gyrating as the barrel engaged and splashed water around. Angela noticed and closed the lid to muffle the sound. The dryer hummed and gave off heat.

"I decided to go tomorrow," Thomas said.

Angela nodded. He sensed her anxiety, a different kind than normal.

"Come upstairs," Angela said, picking up the empty laundry basket. "I'll make you some lunch."

Thomas watched her hurry across the basement and up the stairs. Alone in the laundry room, he looked around again. He sensed in his gut that something was wrong. He lifted the lid to the washing machine and saw the drum filled with water and the agitator twisting the submerged clothing back and forth into a frothy foam. He stood for another minute and listened to the sounds around him.

Finally his gaze came to rest on the dryer. He listened to it hum, and then identified what was wrong. It wasn't a noise that had piqued his suspicion, it was the absence of one. The dryer hummed quietly, but he heard nothing tumbling inside. No clanking of buttons and buckles on the metal interior. No thudding of wet clothes falling from top to bottom as the drum spun.

He reached down and opened the dryer door. Dry, hot air mushroomed out of the machine. When it passed, he looked into the dryer. It was empty.

CHICAGO
August 1979

*I*T WAS THURSDAY MORNING, THE DAY AFTER THOMAS HAD ARRIVED home unexpectedly and surprised her in the garage. Twenty-two hours since she saw Clarissa Manning's face staring back at her from the driver's license she had found hidden in the shelves of her garage. Less than one full day since she had identified the mysterious necklace she had found weeks ago as belonging to Samantha Rodgers. Were there other pieces of jewelry there, too, belonging to the other women whose biographies she had compiled? Angela had spent most of Wednesday night pretending to sleep while her mind imagined the women's possessions hiding on the garage shelves.

Like a slowly building pressure cooker, her paranoia grew each hour. She was convinced that Thomas knew about her discoveries. She had put the containers back on the garage shelf so haphazardly that he had to suspect she had been snooping through them. Thomas had canceled his trip to Indiana for today, and hadn't gone to work. His concern about Angela seeing the doctor had been replaced now by a different preoccupation—the garage. She watched him all morning through the kitchen window, pulling at her lashes and pinching her eyebrows. Thomas would appear every so often in the frame of the utility door when he walked from the back of the garage out to his truck in the alley, arms filled with boxes and cartons.

She ran through the moment when the garage door had started

opening the morning before. Somehow managing to get things back on the shelf, Angela had rushed into the kitchen and thought briefly of locking herself in the bathroom, to claim illness. Surely, she had been sick enough over the past couple of weeks for it to be a believable ruse. But she chose the basement and the laundry room instead. With the washer and dryer running she could pretend not to hear him come home, and then could feign being startled when he finally found her. It had provided her with an extra few minutes to hide Clarissa Manning's driver's license, which she had slipped down the front of her pants. Samantha Rodgers's necklace had gone into the washing machine, along with the clothes that had been on the floor. Her skin had bubbled with itch and burn when she left Thomas alone in the laundry room. He had stayed there for a minute or two after Angela retreated upstairs, and she had worried that he would reach into the foaming water and somehow retrieve the necklace.

Now, as she sat in the kitchen on Thursday morning, her mind frantically scrolled through her options. She needed to find a way out of the house and away from her husband. She contemplated her options as she sat in the kitchen and watched Thomas empty the garage. She stopped herself from her initial instinct to run—to run through the front door and never stop. But where would she go? To Catherine's? Certainly not. To the police? Possibly, she thought. But then she imagined the disparaging look in their eyes when Angela revealed her fantastic story. They would likely pack her into a squad car and drive her home and back to Thomas.

The phone rang. As Thomas loaded his truck with boxes, Angela pulled her gaze from the activities taking place outside. She walked over to the phone and lifted the receiver.

"Hello?"

"Mrs. Mitchell, this is Dr. Solomon. I've been trying to reach you."

She paused for a moment, upset with herself for having answered the phone.

"Mrs. Mitchell, are you there?"

"Yes," Angela said in a soft voice. "I'm sorry I haven't been able to call back."

"Mrs. Mitchell, I need you to stop taking the Valium I prescribed."

The bottle was empty. It wouldn't be a problem.

"Mrs. Mitchell?"

"I'm here."

"Stop taking the Valium and come back in to the office."

Dr. Solomon continued to talk, his voice static-filled and echoing as he explained to Angela the findings from his exam. Angela let the receiver fall to her shoulder as she released her grip on it. It bounced off her chest and hung from the wall mount, twirling in a circle. She thought she heard Dr. Solomon's voice again, asking if she was still there. Angela sunk to the floor, her back pressed against the wall. If the bottle of Valium was not empty, she'd have swallowed the rest of it.

CHICAGO
August 1979

SHE LAY AWAKE THURSDAY NIGHT, THE NEWLY EMPTIED GARAGE RUN-ning through her mind. All that was left were the only things that mattered—Samantha Rodgers's necklace and Clarissa Manning's driver's license—both of which Angela had hidden. Thomas had barely spoken to her since he found her in the laundry room, so she had no idea if he knew she'd found the relics.

In addition to the image of the now-barren garage shelves constantly blinking in her mind, Dr. Solomon's voice played over and over in her ears, like a record stuck and repeating. She hadn't slept the previous few nights and finally, with the bed empty next to her while Thomas continued his purging downstairs, fatigue overcame her and she drifted into a fitful trance.

Her sleep-deprived mind took her back to the hidden storage room in the Kenosha warehouse. She walked through the dingy, unlit space, the gray light of early morning barely brightening the windows high in the rafters. When she headed to the back of the warehouse, she twisted the handle on the storage room door and it creaked open. When the groaning door hinges quieted, Angela heard something else. It was a soft moaning. She stepped into the dark storage room and found Clarissa Manning hanging from one of the twin nooses. *Help me,* the missing girl said. She was holding a bundle of something in her arms. Angela walked closer to see what it was. As her eyesight adjusted to the darkened space, she saw an infant child wrapped in the green tarp that had been hanging in front of the door. As she reached for the bundle, the baby began to shriek.

Angela bolted upright in bed. She gasped for breath as if finally surfacing from minutes beneath water. Clarissa Manning's moans and soft pleas for help from her nightmare were replaced now by the growl of Thomas's truck. She threw the covers to the side and raced to the window. She saw Thomas pull his truck down the alley, the bed filled with boxes and cartons from the garage and the basement.

Angela quickly dressed. She knew she had only a small window of time. When she raced down the stairs, she saw that Thomas had been through every corner of the house. Angela had forgotten her file folder at Catherine's on Sunday morning, when she raced out of the house after Bill had come home. Now she was happy to have left the research file behind. If she had kept it hidden in the bedroom trunk, where she had always placed it when she was not working on it, Thomas would surely have discovered it. Angela badly wanted to bring that file with her, but knew there was no way to retrieve it. She had no time.

Clarissa Manning's driver's license had not been moved since she stuffed it down the front of her pants. She retrieved it now, and ran down the basement steps. When she reached the landing, she saw that Thomas had been through every inch of the space. Drawers were opened and the contents spewed haphazardly to the sides and onto the ground. Shelves were emptied, and Angela could hardly remember what had once filled them. An eerie chill came over her body as she imagined all the evidence she might have been living with for the past two years. She wondered how many more items had been stashed here, and whether she could have done anything to thwart Thomas's reign of terror, which she was sure had been going on for a decade. On the now-empty shelves may have been everything she needed to prove her theory. Still, though, she believed she had enough.

She ran to the washing machine and lifted the lid. The clothes she had put there the previous morning were flat and damp, the spin cycle having stuck them to the walls of the drum. She ripped one item after the other free until she heard a clanking within the machine. Angela reached in and found Samantha Rodgers's necklace. A slight bit of peace found her gut, now that she knew Thomas hadn't discovered it.

Back upstairs, she spent thirty desperate minutes jotting notes about her discoveries over the last week. Angela had passed the dark hours of night listening to Thomas rustle through the house, moving from the basement to the backyard and out to his truck as he emptied the house of evidence. She had listened, and prayed. Drifted between panic and fitful sleep, where she had dreamt of Clarissa Manning hanging from a noose. She fought against her urge to run and scream and cry. She had held her breath, and formulated a plan.

CHAPTER 19
Chicago, October 27, 2019

MEETING WITH NEW PEOPLE RANKED RIGHT UP THERE WITH ROOT canals. Rory did better when the stranger was otherworldly, a victim who needed Rory to reconstruct their death and discover what had happened to them. She had a harder time with the living. They interacted and questioned and judged. But the meeting with Catherine Blackwell presented an opportunity Rory would find nowhere else. The lure to talk with someone who had known Angela Mitchell was all consuming. Rory had an unexplainable urge to know everything about her.

It was noon when Rory walked up the steps of the bungalow house and rang the bell. Although she had never created a mental image of Catherine Blackwell, other than the grainy Facebook image, Rory was surprised to see a white-haired lady when the door opened. Rory guessed she was seventy, perhaps older. The math made sense if she was a friend to Angela Mitchell in 1979.

"Rory?" Catherine asked.

"Yes, Ms. Blackwell?"

"Call me Catherine. Come in."

Rory walked inside and followed the woman into the kitchen.

"Can I take your coat?"

Rory unconsciously had her fist tight on the top button, which was latched and secured at the base of her throat.

"No, thank you."

Rory managed to remove her beanie hat, but that was as far as she would go.

"Can I get you a coffee?"

"I'm okay."

Catherine poured herself a cup and they both sat at the kitchen table. Stacked on the table were several binders of information.

"I was very excited to receive your message," Catherine said. "I haven't had much traffic on my Facebook page lately."

"I was glad to find you," Rory said, pushing her glasses up her nose.

"I've become a bit of a sleuth in my old age," Catherine said. "And I'm proud to be a friend to the digital age rather than a stranger, as many people my age are. After I saw your comment on my Facebook page, I did some snooping. You have quite a reputation in the world of forensic investigation."

Rory nodded, averted her eyes, and reached again for the collar of her coat, making sure the top button was still secured. It made her feel safe and protected, anonymous somehow, even though she was anything but.

"Yes. I work for the Chicago Police Department as a special counsel, of sorts."

"And with the Murder Accountability Project," Catherine said with a smile. "Is that why you contacted me? Are the Chicago Police looking into Angela again?"

Rory paused. *Looking into her?*

"No, I'm afraid not. My curiosity about Angela Mitchell is mine alone." Rory shifted in her chair, leaned a little closer. "How did you know Angela? If you don't mind me asking."

Catherine smiled, setting her gaze on the steaming coffee. "We were dear friends. I mean, it was so long ago." She looked up. "Maybe I embellish our friendship when I think of it now. Perhaps I make more of it than it really was. But Angela meant a lot to me. She was a special woman, indeed."

"Special in what way?" Rory asked, although she believed she knew the answer.

"Angela was a beloved friend, but also a terribly troubled woman. She had a lot of . . . issues. Maybe that's why she and I were so close. She didn't have much of a support system. She was estranged from her parents, from what little she told me about them, and she had no other family to lean on. Angela was what we would now label autistic, but back then she was just horribly misunderstood by most. She was also an obsessive-compulsive. She suffered from debilitating bouts of paranoia. But despite it all, somehow she and I settled into a perfectly normal friendship that I cherished. During the summer of 1979, before she disappeared, she was going through another spate of her illness and I'm afraid . . ."

Rory waited a moment. "Afraid what?"

"I'm afraid I treated her no better than any of the people she tried to avoid."

"What happened?"

Catherine took a sip of coffee to steel herself. "I'm sure you are aware of the missing women from 1979."

Rory nodded. From what Lane had told her, she knew a brief amount about the women who went missing. None had been linked to Thomas Mitchell, despite wide speculation that he was responsible for their deaths.

"Angela had become consumed with the missing women that summer. She came up with a theory of who took them, and how he had killed them. But they were wild ideas, perhaps considered by some to be a conspiracy theory, of a decadelong string of missing women who had all succumbed to the same man. She had researched it all. She had reams of material and graphs and a detailed model of how it had all transpired. Similar women killed in similar ways, all in a tight location in and around the city."

Rory's breath caught in her throat. She thought about her work at the Murder Accountability Project, her and Lane's efforts to find similarities between homicides that might point to trends and serial killings. She thought of the cases that had been solved because of their algorithm. Angela Mitchell had been doing something similar before computers were widely used, before algorithms could be produced, before the Internet existed and put information at one's fingertips. The roots of Rory's curiosity about Angela Mitchell grew deeper, stretching into the folds of her mind.

"Here," Catherine said. "Take a look at her research."

Catherine pushed a three-ring binder across the table.

"This is everything Angela compiled that summer on the missing women, and all her theories on what happened to them."

Rory slowly pulled the binder in front of her and opened the cover. It was strange to see such a large volume of work with so much of it handwritten. There were many pages that looked to have been copied from books, the shadows of the old Xerox machine present on each page. But most of it was written by hand in neat print. Rory remembered the piggish writing from the detective's notes on the Camille Byrd case. Angela Mitchell's penmanship was immaculate.

Rory turned page after page that described the women who had disappeared in 1979, full biographies that must have taken hours to compile. She read each name, the details of their lives and disappearances sketched in her memory the way everything she looked at was imaged and categorized. Only the body of one woman featured in the biographies was ever found. Her name was Samantha Rodgers, and Angela had gone to long lengths to describe the woman.

Rory turned a page and came to a detailed drawing.

"What's this?"

Catherine leaned over the table to get a better look.

"Oh," she said. "That was one of Angela's final theories. She told me she found that contraption at Thomas's warehouse, hidden in a back room. Angela believed it was how he killed the women, hanging them in some fashion. I'm afraid that was all too much for me."

Rory analyzed the bizarre drawing that depicted two nooses juxtaposed to one another, the rope between them winding through a triple pulley system that took on the shape of an M and looked barbaric.

"And I'm sad to admit," Catherine continued, "that when Angela showed me all of this just before she disappeared, I turned my back on her. I told Angela her theories were over the top. That she couldn't possibly be right. I told her that the summer and the missing women had gotten the best of her, and that she was on the wrong track. I tried to convince her that she was in no danger. But then . . ." Catherine looked away from Rory, down into her coffee again. Her voice was lower when she finally spoke. "Then she was gone."

Rory didn't recognize what was happening at first, and then she noticed that Catherine Blackwell had begun to cry. Rory stirred with anxiety. She was incapable of comforting strangers.

"There, there," Rory heard herself say, wondering where the words came from or what on earth they meant. Rory cleared her throat and continued on. "Why do you have all of Angela's notes?"

"Just before she went missing, she left them at my house—whether she did it accidentally or on purpose, I've never known for sure."

"Why didn't you give them to the police?"

"Because the police were never going to charge Thomas with anything but Angela's murder. That was clear from the start."

"But this drawing." Rory pointed to the binder. "Didn't the police find this device at Thomas's warehouse?"

"His warehouse burned to the ground. He made sure there was nothing to find."

Rory took one last look at Angela Mitchell's notes before she closed the binder. "I'm curious about the Facebook page. You call it *Justice for Angela* and ask for anyone with information to come forward. What exactly are you looking for all these years later?"

Catherine collected herself and looked up at Rory. "Answers," she said, wiping her eyes with a tissue. "I've been looking for answers for decades. The Facebook page is just a more public way for me to do it."

"But that's what I'm having trouble understanding. What *kind* of answers? There was a trial, and a conviction."

Catherine smiled. It was more a disappointed look than it was a kind gesture. "That trial provided no closure. It provided the City of Chicago and all its frightened residents with peace of mind. But it answered no questions about Angela Mitchell. It's been forty years, and I still want to know what happened to her."

Rory stared at Catherine Blackwell, narrowed her eyes, and cocked her head just a bit. "Her husband killed her."

"Oh," Catherine said, shaking her head. "I'm afraid that's just not true. See, there's something you need to know about Angela."

Rory waited. "What's that?"

"She was fiercely intelligent. Much too smart for Thomas to have killed her. Angela disappeared on her own accord. I turned my back on her just before she left, and I've never forgiven myself for it. I hope someday to tell her how sorry I am for how I treated her."

Rory leaned closer, resting her elbows on the kitchen table. "You think Angela is still alive?"

Catherine nodded. "I know she is. And I pray you'll help me find her."

CHICAGO
August 1979

*I*T WAS APPROACHING MIDNIGHT WHEN THOMAS MITCHELL PULLED INTO the parking lot of his Kenosha warehouse. The long industrial road that led to his secluded lot had always made for perfect cover. During the day, he could see a car approaching as soon as it turned down the smoky road and threw dust into the air. At night, headlights announced another's presence as clearly as a lighthouse spotlight. And if someone attempted a stealth approach, the gravel road would betray the vehicle with loud crunches well ahead of their arrival.

Until recently, though, he had never been concerned with such things. He had covered his tracks well, and had a nice distance between the locations of the bodies and his warehouse. But he'd made a grave error by underestimating his wife. Mostly, he overlooked her aptitude for suspicion. Now he needed to take precautions while he considered the best way to deal with her. It was a risk to leave her alone in the house, but he had no choice but to visit the warehouse. The unknown, of course, was how much Angela had found, and what, exactly, she knew. The safest assumption was that she knew everything, even though this was impossible.

He thought briefly of the previous night when he emptied the house. He considered taking her here to the warehouse to end things properly, but several obstacles stood in the way of that decision. The greatest of which would be that he'd have to report his wife missing. She would be added to the list of victims claimed by the man the police called The Thief, and the pressure on him would be uncomfortable. Part of him was enthralled with pretending to be stricken by the horror gripping the city this summer. But the logistics of that move were complicated, and Thomas had decided, instead, to take a different route. He had hauled everything he collected from the garage shelves and the basement crawl space—a decade of memorabilia, much of which he didn't remember—into his warehouse and to the storage room in the back.

He had precautions set in place in case things started falling apart, or if he ever made a mistake. He never thought the threat would come from inside his own home, and the dilemma had put him in a crunch. His wife was typically a very predictable person. He never had trouble manipulating her emotions, or controlling her movements. He was sure with time he could learn everything she had discovered, and mold it in a way that would convince her that she had made a great mistake. But to do that required time, and he wasn't sure how much of that he had.

When the bed of his truck was empty, he crawled under each of his cement trucks and punctured the gas tanks. The smell of fuel was pungent when he locked the doors ten minutes later. As he drove down the dusty road and out of the complex, he saw in the rearview mirror the subtle glow of flames starting to rise from the warehouse.

CHICAGO
August 1979

*T*HE PACKAGE WAS DROPPED SATURDAY MORNING, ALONG WITH A large stack of mail, on the reception desk at the front of the police station. It sat unattended for two hours before the clerk got around to sorting the pile. The package—an oversized, thick-padded manila envelope—was finally placed in the detectives' bin, where it sat for another hour. Just after lunch, one of the detectives picked up the envelope and inspected it. There was a name and a return address in the upper left corner.

Belching from fast food and soda, he brought it to his desk, sat down, and tore open the package. Peering inside first, he eventually dumped the contents onto his desk. Across the desktop blotter spilled a photo ID, a necklace of diamonds and green gemstone, newspaper clippings, and a handwritten letter. The detective slowly inspected the necklace, then stopped when he saw the name on the driver's license. When he finally got around to reading the newspaper article and letter, he quickly picked up his desk phone and dialed. It was Saturday afternoon and the staff was thin.

"Hey, boss," the detective said. "Sorry to bother you on a weekend, but I got something you need to see."

Two hours later, calls had been made, facts had been checked, and at three o'clock on Saturday afternoon, the detectives dropped everything back into the envelope, slipped their arms into suit coats, and headed out of the precinct offices.

CHICAGO
August 1979

*T*WO DAYS AFTER THE WAREHOUSE BURNED TO THE GROUND, THOMAS
Mitchell was gravely concerned. He was inundated with police reports, insurance claims, employees and clients inquiring about
being paid, and outstanding jobs waiting for completion. He had
anticipated all of it, and knew there was no other way. But the
planned commotion was not what had him out of sorts. He'd come
home in the early hours of morning after torching his warehouse
with the stale smell of whiskey on his breath from his stop at the
bar, and had passed out on the couch.

When he woke late Saturday morning, he had a long list of er-
rands to run. He first noticed the unmarked squad car parked
across the street that afternoon. When he made a run to the insurance adjustor's office, he saw the same car in his rearview mirror.
He had other places to go, but didn't dare drag the tail anywhere
that was unsafe. When he pulled back into his garage hours later,
he walked to the front room and peeled the curtains to the side to
see the car back in its spot, parked across the street.

By evening, he started making calls because it was what a concerned husband was supposed to do. He called Catherine Blackwell, and even resorted to calling Angela's parents. No one had
heard from her, which he knew would be the response. But what he
wanted was a record of his concern so that if anyone looked, they'd
see his desperate attempts to find his wife.

It was nine o'clock at night when he had exhausted his options, and considered that the next logical step would be to call the police. He swallowed hard at the thought. He had taken care of the warehouse; the garage and basement were empty. Despite his precautions, he had a strong sense that things were falling apart, and that he might have to put his final safety effort into place: run.

He had money stashed for that exact reason, but before he had a chance to seriously consider this last option, there was a knock on the front door. He looked around his empty house, then slowly walked to the foyer and opened the door. Two men in suits stood on his porch. The humid summer night layered their foreheads with perspiration.

"Thomas Mitchell?"

"Yes?"

The man pulled a badge from his waist and held it in front of Thomas's face.

"Chicago Police. We'd like to speak with your wife."

A grave look came over Thomas's face, and he tried hard to morph his distress of self-preservation into something that might be mistaken for spousal concern. He cleared his throat.

"I'm afraid I haven't heard from her all day."

CHAPTER 20
Chicago, October 27, 2019

*T*HEY WERE STILL SEATED AT CATHERINE BLACKWELL'S KITCHEN TABLE. Catherine had poured herself another coffee. Rory had declined again.

"You see, outside of a standard Google search," Catherine said, "I'm afraid I don't make a very good detective. It's been forty years and I know as much about what happened to Angela now as I did back then. The Facebook page was my effort to include others in my search for Angela, which was why I was so excited to hear from you."

"I'm not sure I'd be able to help you," Rory said.

It was a ridiculous statement and Rory knew it as soon as the words floated from her lips. Rory Moore was the perfect person to help Catherine find answers. She reconstructed deaths for a living. She pieced together bits of evidence that had been overlooked by everyone else. She pored through information and found answers where everyone else saw only questions. If Angela Mitchell were alive, Rory was better equipped to find her than anyone else.

"Then why did you contact me?" Catherine asked.

Rory adjusted her glasses. "I heard about the case," she lied. "It's been in the news lately, with Thomas Mitchell's upcoming parole. I was curious. That's all. I'm sorry to have raised your hopes, but I'm not the one to help you, and . . ."

Rory stopped herself, then spoke again.

"Catherine, I don't mean to be dismissive. But have you considered that perhaps the reason you've found no answers for forty years is because there are no answers to find? Have you considered that Thomas Mitchell actually *did* kill Angela, as he was charged?"

"Many times, dear. Many, many times over the years. But there's been one thing that's always convinced me otherwise. One thing that's made me sure she's still alive."

"What's that?"

"A couple of years after Angela went missing, a man came poking around. He contacted me to ask questions about Angela. Seemed to know a lot about me and my relationship with Angela."

"After the trial? This man came around after the conviction?"

"Yes," Catherine said. From the stack of binders, she pulled a leather-bound folder in front of her and turned the pages. "I recorded everything back then. Oh, where is it?" She turned a few more pages. "Yes. Here it is. On November 23, 1981, I was visited by someone who claimed to be looking into the death of Angela Mitchell."

Rory paused, working it out in her head.

"If this man came after the trial was over, what was he looking for?"

"He never came right out and said it, but I knew what was happening. He believed Angela was alive, and he was looking for her."

A flutter went through Rory's chest. "What did you tell him?"

"Nothing. I refused to speak with him. I knew what was going on, and I wasn't going to help in any way."

Rory squinted her eyes. "What was going on?"

"Thomas was looking for Angela. If he could find her, his sentence would be overturned and he'd be a free man, despite the many other women he killed. The women Angela had discovered. The women she became obsessed with. Thomas hired this man to find Angela, I'm sure of it. And ever since that moment, I've known she was alive. She's been hiding for forty years."

Rory became dizzy. A spinning light-headedness meant to fog her mind, a defense mechanism, perhaps. But her thoughts were clear and she knew the answer to her question before she formed it.

"What was his name?" she asked quickly.

"Who?"

"The man. The man who came asking questions. Do you know his name?"

"Yes, I recorded everything," Catherine said, looking at the page in front of her. She ran her finger down the print, stopping near the bottom and pausing a moment before looking back at Rory.

"His name was Frank Moore."

PART II

THE RECONSTRUCTION

CHICAGO
November 1981

*F*RANK MOORE WAS TWO YEARS REMOVED FROM HIS STINT AT THE PUB-
lic defender's office in Cook County when he signed on at Garrison
Ford. The public defender's gig was a rite of passage for most criminal defense attorneys, a way to rapidly acquire a large number of
cases, learn the law, get in front of judges, and endure the spoils of
wild courtroom failures. It was a part of every great defender's
coming of age, a painful post–law school education necessary to
forge a successful career defending criminals. Frank's record over
the first two years of his career had been good enough to land him
a job at Garrison Ford, one of Chicago's largest and most accomplished criminal defense firms. He joined in the summer of 1979
with grand visions, monumental goals, and a true passion for pro-
tecting the rights of those who sought his help. Had someone told
Frank Moore back then that he'd spend most of his career running
a one-man shop, far from the spotlight of Garrison Ford's high-
profile cases, he'd have never believed them. He was young and
hungry and filled with fire. Nothing was going to get in his way.
That is, until he was assigned to the case that would change his life
forever.

The summer of '79 had been plagued by the disappearances of
six women, and the city was on edge. When the police found their
man, Frank's phone rang. His boss, a partner in the firm, needed
his help on a sensitive case. A man named Thomas Mitchell, who
had notoriously been dubbed The Thief, had hired Garrison Ford

to defend him against the charge of killing his wife. For a high-profile firm, it didn't get much better. Frank Moore, young and bright and ambitious, would do the scut work of research and briefs. He jumped at the opportunity.

Over the following two years, between the summer of 1979 and the fall of 1981, the case took nasty and insurmountable turns. In the end, Garrison Ford had presented a failed defense of Thomas Mitchell, and The Thief was sentenced to sixty years for the murder of his wife. After the trial, Frank Moore became lead counsel on Thomas Mitchell's appeals. It was during the appeals process, when Frank met often with his client to discuss strategy, he first started to believe Thomas Mitchell's wife might be alive.

"I've filed the notice of appeal," Frank said. "Next I'll finish my brief and submit it in the next week or ten days."

"And the brief goes after her?" Thomas Mitchell asked.

They were seated in a private interview room at Stateville Correctional Center, which was reserved for privileged attorney-client meetings. Frank was on one side of the table, and his client—handcuffed and orange jumpsuited—on the other. Frank knew it was possible that someone from the prison was listening to their conversation, but not likely. And he didn't really care.

"It goes after how the defense obtained the alleged evidence against you. It goes after the judge's decision to allow that evidence to be presented in court."

"Good. Go after the judge and go after the evidence, but go after her, too. She was having a nervous breakdown when she did this to me. She was swallowing Valium at three times the rate it had been prescribed. Plus, mentally, she was not all there."

"We have a lot of ammunition, Thomas. My first brief will be based mostly on the legality of the evidence presented against you, the complete circumstantiality of it all, and the argument that none of it should have been allowed in court. If our initial appeal is denied, and there is a very good chance it will be, then our next appeal will include details about your wife's mental state when she disappeared. Remember, the appeals process allows us to continue to the federal level through the writ of habeas corpus, if needed. And there's a lot of work to be done on the state level before we even consider that route. Hopefully, someone in their right mind within the appeals court makes the sound and just decision about this. So I'll make a strong opening argument in this initial appeal to the state. But we'll save details about your wife for later, if we need them, including the fact that you were convicted of second-degree murder without the prosecution producing a body."

"They can't produce a body, because there *is* no body. Where are you on that? Any progress?"

Frank gathered some papers and placed them into his bag. Pulled out a different stack and looked at it. "Her parents were a dead end. They hadn't seen her for many years before she disappeared. Only a few times since she turned eighteen, they told me."

"Could you read them?" Thomas asked. "You didn't get a sense that they were lying to you?"

"They weren't lying."

"She had to have help. A woman like Angela, she doesn't just go off on her own. She'd be too scared. Sometimes she couldn't bring herself to leave the house. Now I'm supposed to believe she up and vanished all on her own. No, someone helped her. Someone is *still* helping her. Her parents are the most likely ones. Did you tell them you were looking for her?"

"Thomas"—Frank put his elbows on the table and leaned closer to his client—"They were very upset. They believe, like the rest of the country, that Angela is dead. I didn't tell them who I was or that I thought their daughter was still alive. I made up a story about the possibility of a civil suit."

"Maybe you should have told them what you're really after."

"That's not the right approach. They believe their daughter is dead, I'm not going to fill them with false hope that she's alive."

"It's *not* false. She's alive."

Frank nodded his head. "But I'm not the one to tell them that. I'll conduct my search for her the way I think is best."

"Did you talk with Catherine?"

"Catherine Blackwell, your business partner's wife. Yes. I visited her a couple of weeks ago. She's still very distraught at the mention of you or Angela. We didn't have a fruitful conversation."

"Do you believe me?"

Frank stared at his client—convicted of killing his wife, accused of killing many more—and paused too long before he answered. "I'm looking for her, aren't I? If I didn't believe you, do you think I'd be spending all my time on this? And by the way, I've got to start billing for my time."

"I've got money."

"It's going to be expensive."

"I'll pay you whatever it costs to find her. But I want you to do this quietly. Don't involve your firm. I'll pay you separately."

"I haven't even told my wife what I'm doing. Do you think I'm about to tell the partners at Garrison Ford? On the record, you and I are working on your appeals. Off the record, you're retaining my services independently to look into a personal matter, settle your debts, handle your finances, negotiate your way out of the business you still technically co-own, deal with your property, et cetera. I'll write up the paperwork."

"What's next?" The Thief asked.

"I'll file the notice of appeal this week."

"No. What next with your search for her?"

"Oh," Frank said, collecting his papers to leave. "The psychiatric facility where she spent her teen years."

CHAPTER 21
Chicago, October 28, 2019

*L*ANE PHILLIPS STOKED THE DYING EMBERS AND BROUGHT THE OR-
ange glowing logs back to life. He stacked two more splinters of
wood on top, watched the flames grow, and sat on the couch, where
his laptop was open. Rory was next to him, her own computer on
her lap as she typed away. Fall had come quickly, descending on
them from the heavens as cold Canadian air swept across the
Midwest to send temperatures into the forties. It felt too soon to
turn on the heat, so they opted for their first fire of the season.

"So your father was forever tied to this man, and now you
are, too?"

"Not forever," Rory said. "But for at least eighteen months. I'll
represent him at the final hearing, review all the stipulations one
more time, and hand him off to his parole officer. The judge ordered me to look after his finances with monthly reports for a year
and a half, since he's got a solid nest egg stashed away, and my father was listed as the financial power of attorney. So I'll make sure
he doesn't go broke. Then he's on his own."

"And why the order to go out to Starved Rock?"

"The judge waived the requirement to live in a halfway house
due to his notoriety. He inherited a cabin near Starved Rock in the
nineties from an uncle. My father put it in a trust and handed it off
to a management company. The property has been a vacation
rental for all these years. He's going to live there, so the judge ordered me to tag along with the social worker and the parole officer

to have a look at the place ahead of the release. Make sure it meets all the requirements."

"I'm going with you," Lane said.

Rory hadn't told Lane about her meeting with Catherine Blackwell. She allowed him to believe her nervousness had started with her visit to Stateville Correctional Center. It was a logical conclusion, as compared to the real source of Rory's distress—that her father had been trying to find Angela Mitchell before he died. And more troubling than the discovery itself was what it was doing to Rory. That walled-off place in her mind had been disturbed, the once-calm waters clouded now with muck and filth. The only way to restore clarity was to figure out what her father had found. The only way to tame those waters back to peace, and to quiet that place in her mind, was to look for Angela herself. To ignore this urge was to stoke the flames of a sickness she had managed to control for many years. She knew the best way to extinguish the impulse was to nurture it, like Aunt Greta had taught her as a child when Rory defused her fanatical impulses by mastering the detailed craft of restoring china dolls. The burning question now, though, was if Rory would be reconstructing the woman's death, or following the footsteps of a woman who was still very much alive.

"Fine," Rory said. "Come with me." She looked up from her laptop and offered a rare glimpse of emotion. "Thanks. I didn't want to go alone."

A pang of guilt prickled her neck for keeping her secret from Lane. The man had done nothing more than love her—and all of her flaws—for the better part of a decade. Didn't he deserve to hear this part of her life? Perhaps so, but she couldn't bring herself to tell him. Rory pointed to Lane's computer, then looked back to her own.

"Let's go, we're way behind. What have you got?"

Lane continued to stare for a moment, as if he sensed something more she wasn't saying. Rory felt his stare, but kept her attention on the laptop.

"Okay," Lane said, giving in and looking at his own computer monitor. He scrolled through the pages. "I've been watching an area outside of Detroit, southeast portion of the city and into the adjoining counties. It's been coming up on the algorithm. Several hits in just the last four months. There have been twelve homicides in the last two years where the victims have been homeless women or prostitutes, all African-American. Little or no family support, a few who were only identified at the morgue through fingerprinting and matching to the Michigan fingerprint identification program of convicted criminals. Basically, no one knew they had been killed. No family, no friends."

Rory was typing on her computer. "Easy targets with little risk."

"Correct," Lane said.

"How did the algorithm pick them up?"

"Manner of death."

Each week, Lane and Rory ran through trends picked up by the algorithm Lane had created. It took into account several different factors about crimes reported from across the country, looking for trends and similarities. Doing so allowed them to recognize commonalities between homicides in a particular geographic region. When enough markers and tags showed up in the same location, Lane and Rory were alerted. Then they jumped in and started digging. To date, the Murder Accountability Project had identified twelve serial killers—defined as a single person having committed at least three homicides—across America in which arrests were made. Many more hot spots were trending, where local police were following up on leads. Tonight's meeting was a weekly occurrence where Rory and Lane pointed out marks that were trending on the software. Sometimes it was a cluster of homicides in a tightly focused location, or a group of homicides carried out with the same suspected weapon, or on the same type of victim. It might be how a body was disposed of. It could be the occupation of the victim. The algorithm tracked over five thousand indicators looking for similarities.

When they could make a strong enough case, Rory and Lane took their findings to the authorities in that area. With Lane's reputation as a forensic psychologist and criminal profiler for the FBI's Behavioral Science Unit, and Rory's credentials as a reconstructionist who pieced together the very findings the algorithm looked for, they made the perfect team. Police departments listened to their conclusions, and many had started using Lane's software to track homicides on their own.

"All of them were killed by some sort of blunt-force trauma—blows to the side of the head—and then the bodies were disposed of in Dumpsters."

They were in the process of logging the names of the twelve Detroit victims, and cataloguing their findings, when the doorbell rang. Rory looked at her watch. It was almost ten o'clock. She walked to the front door and peered through the peephole. Ron Davidson stood on her porch.

"Shit," she said before pulling the door open. "Hey, Ron."

"Gray," he said in a measured tone. "You're not returning my calls again."

Rory exhaled loudly. "Sorry. I've been busy with this . . . thing. For my dad."

"I've heard all about it since you asked me for those old records." He leaned closer to the screen door. "Christ, Gray. Your dad repped this guy?"

Rory nodded. "Looks like it, yeah."

"Did the boxes from 1979 have what you needed?"

"Yes. Or . . . I'm not sure. I haven't been through them all yet." Her hand habitually moved to her face to adjust her glasses, but she realized she wasn't wearing them. She never did when she was alone with Lane. "Thanks for coming through on those."

"No problem. I owed you for taking Camille Byrd's case."

The two stood without speaking for a moment, Detective Davidson on the front porch and Rory inside behind the screen door.

"Can I come in?" Ron asked.

"Yeah, sorry. Of course," Rory said, opening the door.

She led her boss into the living room, where Lane was still tapping away on his computer across from the roaring fire.

"Lane," Rory said. "Ron's here, we've got to talk."

Lane looked up. "Ron, how are you?"

"Doing good, Doc."

The two shook hands.

"Sorry to interrupt," Ron said. "I'll just be a minute."

"No worries," Lane said.

"In here," Rory said, walking Detective Davidson past the darkened den, where all her dolls stood on the shadowed shelves, and into her office. In addition to the three boxes from 1979 that rested by her desk, the contents of which were spread across the surface, Camille Byrd's photograph also hung from the corkboard with the few scant notes Rory had made nearly two weeks ago about the autopsy findings.

"Walter Byrd contacted me," Ron said. "He says he hasn't heard from you. He said he called a few times, but never got a call back. Sounds familiar."

"I don't have anything to tell him yet."

"Then tell him *that,* Rory. But tell him *something.*"

"I feel like crap, Ron. I agreed to take the reconstruction, then my father died, and I've been tied up in dissolving his law firm and . . . everything else I ran into. I haven't put many hours on the case."

"I'm sorry for the timing, Rory. I know you've got a lot on your plate."

Rory looked over at her desk and saw the remnants of her research from the 1979 case strewn across the surface. She remembered sitting at the desk a few nights before, stumbling across her father's notes and wondering what he had been doing for Thomas Mitchell throughout all the years he represented the man. Now she knew.

"I'll get back to Camille Byrd. I promise."

"Have you looked into it at all?"

"Just a glance," Rory said, remembering the night she'd paged through the medical examiner's report, the image of Camille's bruised and damaged throat sparking in her mind. Rory glanced over at the picture of Camille Byrd on the corkboard. She felt the spidery tentacles of guilt crawl up her back. She had dreamt of Camille Byrd two nights earlier, coming across her body as it lay in Grant Park. Rory had tried to apologize for ignoring the case, but the girl was dead and cold in her dream when Rory shook her. As she stared now at the photo and into the dead girl's eyes, Rory felt the urge to hide behind her thick-rimmed glasses, turn up the collar of her coat, and look away.

"I'll put some hours on it."

"When?"

"Soon, I promise."

Her phone rang from her back pocket. Rory held up a finger.

"Sorry." She retrieved her phone and checked the number. Although not in her list of contacts, Rory immediately recognized the number. It had been burned into her memory the way everything else was, but this particular phone number held a greater significance than simply her remarkable memory. The last time she received a call from this extension, she had learned that her father was dead. Was it irony, Rory wondered, that she had also been with Ron Davidson when she had accepted the last call?

"Celia," Rory said to her father's administrative assistant. "Is something wrong?"

"Oh, hello," Celia said, caught off guard. "No, nothing's wrong. Well, I'm not sure. I have to see you. I have something of your father's that I'm not sure what to do with. Can we meet this week?"

Rory spun through her schedule. She had to make the trip out to Thomas Mitchell's cabin, meet with Judge Boyle and the parole board for the final hearing, finish the legal paperwork to get her newest and only client out of jail—which was scheduled to happen in one week, get his finances in order, and now dedicate some time to Camille Byrd's reconstruction. All of this while putting off the burning desire to start her own search for Angela Mitchell and figure out what had happened to her.

"I'm swamped at the moment, Celia," Rory said, knowing that her father's law firm was all but shut down and wrapped up besides the Thomas Mitchell affair. "Can we put it off for a couple of weeks?"

There was a pause before the soft voice answered: "I really need to see you, Rory."

She thought she heard quiet weeping. Rory remembered Celia's tears dripping onto her neck when the woman had embraced her at her father's law office.

"Yes," Rory said. "Then we'll meet this week. I'll call you tomorrow to find the best time."

She heard more sniffling and ended the call without waiting for confirmation. She placed the phone in her back pocket and looked at her boss.

"Give me another week, Ron. In the meantime, I'll call Mr. Byrd and give him an update."

The detective nodded. "Okay. But I need something soon, Rory. Something new. Anything."

"I'll have something to you by next week," she said.

CHICAGO
November 1981

*F*RANK MOORE HAD TRACKED HER GENEALOGY, THE BEST HE COULD figure. If Angela Mitchell were alive, she would likely rely on friends or family. This was his hope, anyway. Because the other possibility—that she had disappeared on her own—presented an insurmountable obstacle he'd never be able to scale. How would he find her if she had simply vanished? What if she had left the state to hide in a corner of the country where no one would look? Based on what Frank knew about the woman, this was a very conceivable possibility.

Angela Mitchell had been a loner her whole life, moving from her parents' custody as a child, to an extended stint at a juvenile psychiatric hospital in downstate Illinois that lasted until she was released at age eighteen. From there, Frank's research got murky. Her parents had been out of the picture since she became a legal adult, and Frank's trip down to St. Louis to visit them had been fruitless. Angela Mitchell's parents hadn't seen or heard from her in years prior to her disappearance. They hadn't even known she married. The next time she showed up on Frank's sketchy timeline was when she met Thomas Mitchell in Chicago, had a short courtship, and then married. She had no close friends besides a woman named Catherine Blackwell, who was the wife of Thomas's former business partner. Frank's journey to the Blackwell residence had been unsuccessful, a little strange, and ultimately a waste of time and energy.

Through archival information he found at the library and some names given to him by Angela's parents, Frank had made a list of distant relatives to call on. These were cousins, and siblings of her parents, and cousins of her parents, and other further removed folks that had at one time or another been part of Angela's life before she met Thomas Mitchell.

For the past three months, Frank had been looking for any hint that his client's wife was still alive, as Thomas Mitchell swore she was. A twenty-eight-year-old associate, Frank was anxious to prove himself at Garrison Ford. He filled his days by slogging through research and briefs, and occasionally making an appearance in court to assist the partner to whom he was assigned. He spent his nights hunting down a woman who was likely dead and buried. Newly married, with a nurse for a wife who worked the afternoon shift at the hospital, he had the time to look. He was happy being paid to chase a ghost. But God almighty, he could only imagine what would happen if he actually found her. His client would be free, the conviction overturned, and Frank's stock at Garrison Ford would rise quickly. Perhaps he'd make partner before forty.

The latest lead was written on a scrap of paper—a name and address—and stuck with Scotch Tape to his dashboard. The rural road, an hour and a half west of the city, was empty. Frank couldn't imagine there ever being much traffic this far out in the sticks, and he drove freely as the sun set in front of him. Cornfields stretched out on either side of the road, as far as he could see. The once-tall stalks were now cropped down to nothing. Large bales of hay, spun in tight spirals, studded the field in random patterns.

He came to a T in the road, checked his map, and turned left. After another three miles, he eventually saw the top of the two-story building rising above the otherwise-flat terrain. The campus sprawled out over many acres. In the middle of nowhere, the white structure looked like a prison. Frank was sure it felt that way to many of its patients. He turned into the parking lot and pulled past the sign indicating that he had arrived at BAYER GROUP JUVENILE PSYCHIATRIC FACILITY. He found a spot and parked. Inside, he signed in.

"Which resident are you visiting?" the receptionist asked.

"No resident," Frank said, standing in his wrinkled suit after making the long drive from the Garrison Ford offices. "I'm here to see Dr. Jefferson."

"Do you have an appointment?"

"Yes. I called earlier in the week."

"Let me find him," the receptionist said.

Frank paced the waiting room for five minutes until the door opened.

"Mr. Moore?"

Frank turned around to see a thin man with tiny glasses and a long white coat.

"Dale Jefferson, we spoke on the phone."

"Yes," Frank said, walking over and shaking hands. "Thanks for taking a meeting."

"Sorry it's not under better circumstances," Dr. Jefferson said. "Come back to my office."

Frank followed the doctor into the psychiatric facility, through a long white corridor, and into his office. The space was decorated like a living room—a couch, coffee table, and two end chairs. A wall of built-in shelving held volumes of textbooks. Dr. Jefferson sat in one of the chairs and motioned for Frank to take a spot on the couch. A file was resting on the coffee table and Dr. Jefferson picked it up as he sat.

"It's a terrible shame about Angela. I was unaware of the situation at first because the news media never used her maiden name. And, sadly, Thomas Mitchell has gotten more attention than any of his victims. Society is more interested in The Thief than the lives he stole."

Frank was not here to debate the psychology of society, and wasn't about to mention that his client was convicted of killing only one woman, not a slew of women. In fact, Frank hadn't mentioned his association with Thomas Mitchell to anyone he had encountered during his months-long search for Angela. The court of public opinion had pinned all the missing women from the summer of 1979 on Thomas Mitchell, and Frank knew he needed to hide his motives for why he was asking about a woman who had supposedly been killed more than two years ago.

"Yes," Frank finally said. "It's a shame."

"You said Angela's family is looking into a civil lawsuit?"

"Yes," Frank said, crossing his legs. A poker player might see this as a nervous reaction to hide his lie. "I'm looking into matters myself to see if a civil suit is possible, given the circumstances."

"You'll excuse me," Dr. Jefferson said. "The man must be very troubled, but if they're not going to put him to death for what he did, then I say lock him up for life and drain him of all his resources."

"Well," Frank said, clearing his throat, "I'm going to see what I can do."

"Do you represent Angela's parents?"

Frank paused briefly. "Yes."

"From what I remember, they didn't have a wonderful relationship with Angela. Always terrible to see fractured relations between parents and child. And now, never to be repaired."

"Yes. It's a shame," Frank said again.

"Do you have children, Mr. Moore?"

"I'm just married. Maybe in a year or two my wife and I will try."

Dr. Jefferson held up the file. "What can I help you with?"

"Civil suits can be nasty, so I want to find out as much about Angela as possible. I know she spent time here during her teen years, and I'm wondering if I could ask a few questions."

"Of course."

Frank removed a piece of paper from his breast pocket. "Angela came here in 1967 when she was seventeen years old."

"That's correct."

"How long was Angela here?"

"Seven months. She left on her eighteenth birthday. I'm afraid we didn't help Angela as much as we, or her parents, had hoped."

"So, once she became an adult, she left on her own?"

"Yes. Bayer Group is a juvenile facility. We only treat youths who are younger than eighteen and under a parent's or guardian's supervision. Once they become legal adults, they stay only if they choose to do so. Angela did not."

"And what was Angela admitted for?"

Dr. Jefferson read from the file.

"'Oppositional defiant disorder, social anxiety, and obsessive-compulsive disorder.' She was also autistic, which complicated her treatment."

"So, when Angela turned eighteen and you could no longer legally keep her here, her parents picked her up? Do you know what happened to Angela after her time here?"

"It wasn't her parents," Dr. Jefferson said. "Like I mentioned, that relationship was fractured. During Angela's time here, I felt like we were making such poor progress that I suggested to her parents that perhaps Angela should be discharged and return when she had an attitude that might be more receptive to accepting help. Her parents were against discharging her. I'm afraid at that point they had reached the end of their patience with her."

Frank sat forward on the couch. "So what? They dumped her here?"

Dr. Jefferson shrugged. "I wouldn't put it that way. They wanted to get Angela help, and they felt unable to help her on their own."

"So she turns eighteen. You can't keep her here. Where did she go? Back with her parents?"

Dr. Jefferson shook his head. "No. Angela was released of her own accord. She was legal at that point."

"Yes, but she was just eighteen, with no job, no money, and, I presume, no transportation. Where did she go? She just walked out into the cornfields?"

"One of our counselors tried following up for a few weeks, but never heard back from her. The last address we had for her was in Peoria, Illinois."

"What was in Peoria?"

"The best I remember, a friend of Angela's lived there. The friend signed in the day Angela was discharged. Helped her pack her things. According to our records, Angela left with her."

"Do you have a name for this woman?" Frank asked quickly, then paused to control his excitement. This was the first real lead he'd come across while searching for anyone who might be connected to Angela Mitchell during her adult years. "If she's a relative, we may be able to add her name to the civil suit."

"Of course," Dr. Jefferson said, paging through the file until he removed a single slip of paper and pushed it in front of Frank. "Last name was Schreiber. She was one of our on-call nurses. Not sure this is the correct address anymore. That was a number of years ago."

CHAPTER 22
Chicago, October 29, 2019

*T*HEY DROVE TOGETHER AND FOLLOWED THE CAR IN FRONT OF THEM, which held the social worker and the parole officer. Thomas Mitchell had inherited the cabin in 1994 when his uncle died. Rory had tracked the property the best she could from her father's paperwork. The uncle had died of pancreatic cancer and had willed the cabin to his nephew. Rory's father had placed the cabin into a trust. A rental company had taken good care of the place, and according to the financial documents she found in the file, the property had provided a nice source of income over the years. It was a two-bedroom A-frame just outside of Starved Rock State Park, about an hour from the city.

Located so close to the park and the Illinois River, the cabin had been easy to rent over the years. The rental income had been self-sustaining and allowed the management company to stay current with upkeep. Rory's father had dismissed the management company the previous year, and had carefully documented his monthly trips to keep the cabin updated, surely anticipating his client's arrival.

When they reached the outskirts of Starved Rock, the social worker slowed in front of her. Rory assumed she was consulting her GPS. The lead car took off again, and Rory followed it through winding roads on the north side of the park. They traveled across bridges, where short waterfalls fell over bluffs and where evergreen pines rose up into the clear October sky. Had she not been on a

journey to see the future home of a suspected serial killer, the setting would be majestic.

After fifteen minutes of slow going, stopping at each intersection
before deciding which direction to turn, Rory and Lane arrived at
the entrance to a long dirt driveway canopied tightly by foliage that
had started to morph to fall colors. A mailbox stood isolated, just to
the side of the drive, and Rory figured she could check off at least
one of the judge's requests. If anyone wanted to send The Thief a
letter, he'd receive it via the United States Postal Service.

She turned onto the driveway and followed the social worker
along the uneven path for a hundred yards. The cocooned driveway eventually opened to a clearing in which stood a cedar-sided
A-frame cabin. The piece of land was impressive. Rory's mind
imagined an aerial view of the property, which was cut into a
densely forested area. The clearing where the cabin stood was five
acres of grass and gravel and clay that butted up against the thick
forest around it. The end of the driveway led in a circle around the
cabin. As Rory drove the loop around, she spotted the river
through the trees off to her right. A path was cut in the forest, and
a set of stairs led down to a dock that ran out into the water.

"Well," Lane said from the passenger seat, staring out his window, "you can't argue that this is anything but the perfect place for
a suspected serial killer to hide for the rest of his life."

Rory shook her head. "And I was thinking how beautiful this
place had been for the families that rented it all these years."

"No you weren't. You wouldn't reconstruct deaths for a living if
you were really thinking that."

Rory pulled around the cabin and parked. She grabbed her
thick-rimmed glasses from the dashboard, put them on her face,
and pulled her beanie hat down her forehead. "Yeah, you're right,"
she said, opening the car door. "This place is creepy as hell. Be
right back."

Rory climbed from the car and met Naomi Brown, the social
worker, at the front of the cabin, inspecting the residence as she
did. Rory had the key, which she had found in her father's office.

"Have you been to your client's home before?" Naomi asked.

"He's not my client, exactly," Rory said, shaking her head and adjusting her glasses. "No, I haven't seen the place."

The social worker looked at Rory for a moment. It was the confused look Rory often received and always hated.

Rory twirled her finger in the air and pointed at the cabin. "Let's get this out of the way."

"There is a list of requirements," Naomi said. "Including a functioning landline, a current U.S. Postal Service address, and other items. It's mostly a formality, but since the judge is agreeing to this unique living arrangement, we need to check all the boxes."

"Then let's check them," Rory said as she climbed the steps to the front porch. The wooden boards creaked under her weight. She inserted the key in the door and pushed it open. Ezra Parker, the parole officer, snapped photos of the outside before entering. Inside, they found a well-kept home furnished the way any rental property might be, with a couch and chairs positioned around a stone fireplace in the front room. A kitchen was off to the left, and another room for dining. A screened-in porch on the back of the home offered a view of the sprawling acres that led to the forest, through which the river was visible and reflecting the October sky. Stairs led upstairs to two bedrooms.

The group took thirty minutes to inspect the place. Naomi Brown checked all the boxes to show that the home met the judge's requirements. Ezra Parker snapped all the required photos.

"Until your client acquires an automobile," Naomi said, "there is a convenience store half a mile down the road."

Rory nodded. She had a sudden desire to leave the place, realizing that her authority over Thomas Mitchell's finances would likely require her to help him with purchases, such as a car. As they headed to the front door, they noticed the red footprints they had all tracked in from outside. Rory looked down at her combat boots, noticing for the first time that they were covered in a crimson dust.

"Sorry about that," Naomi said. "We should have removed our shoes."

"What the hell is it?" Rory asked, lifting her foot to examine the bottom of her boot.

"Red clay," Ezra said. "It's common around Starved Rock. The soil is saturated with it. It gets everywhere. Your car will be a mess, too."

Rory looked at the bloodred footprints.

"Time to go," she said. "I'll call someone to clean the cabin before his release."

CHICAGO
November 1981

*T*HREE DAYS OF PHONE CALLS HAD GONE UNANSWERED BEFORE FRANK decided to make the drive out to Peoria and have a look himself. Angela Mitchell had been discharged from Bayer Group Juvenile Psychiatric Facility in 1968, thirteen years ago, and it was very possible that whoever had once lived at the address Dr. Jefferson provided no longer did so today. But since it was his first legitimate discovery he'd come across while looking for any trace of Angela Mitchell in her adult life, prior to marrying Thomas Mitchell, it was worth the drive.

He made the trip on Saturday morning when traffic out of the city was light and the drive time was just over two hours. He drove past acres of harvested cornfields—not very different from his drive out to Bayer Group the other day. Tractors sat parked in the middle of the fields, and silos rose up occasionally on the otherwise-flat horizon. When he turned onto a long stretch of two-lane road, address numbers were stenciled on roadside mailboxes situated next to long, stretching driveways that led to isolated homes nestled on large plots of land, each property far from its neighbors. He found the address that was listed in Angela Mitchell's file.

The driveway was winding as he turned onto it. Dogs appeared from behind the house as he pulled his car to the end of the drive, barking and following the car as he came to a stop. Frank slowly opened the door. Two German shepherds greeted him and barked for his attention, both jostling to position their heads under his hand. He obliged by petting them while he stared at the farm-house.

The front door opened and a woman walked onto the porch. She stared down at him. Frank held up his hand in an amicable wave and walked toward her. The dogs barked and followed, jumping and leaning into his legs.

"They won't hurt ya," the woman said from the porch. "Leave the man alone! Go on, get in the backyard!"

The dogs barked and abandoned their playful assault and disappeared behind the house. Frank walked to the foot of the porch stairs.

"Ms. Schreiber? Do I have the name right?"

As Frank approached, he got a better look at the woman, who he guessed was in her late fifties or early sixties.

"Yeah, that's me. What can I help ya with?" she asked. "You selling encyclopedias or vacuum cleaners or some such?"

"No," Frank said with a laugh. "My name is Frank Moore, I'm an attorney. I'm here to ask a few questions about Angela Mitchell. Or Angela Barron, to use her maiden name. I believe you knew her?"

Frank saw the woman's face go slack. Her jaw loosened and her mouth opened. Her eyes widened as if Frank had pulled a gun from his waistband and pointed it at her. She took a step backward, her free hand reaching for the door handle.

Frank lifted his hands. "I'm just here to talk."

"I got nothing to say. Now get off my property or I'll call the police."

"I'm not here to cause any trouble, ma'am. I'm looking into a civil lawsuit that might help Angela's family."

"I want you to leave my property." Her eyes were wide and feral. "Right now!"

The woman's demands turned the scene quickly into something Frank had not anticipated.

"Okay," Frank said, reaching into his pocket and pulling out his business card. "If you decide you want to talk about Angela, give me a call. My number is on this card."

"Tubs! Harold!"

At the sound of their names, the dogs barreled from behind the house. This time, their demeanor was aggressive. Their playful yelps had morphed to growls. Frank dropped his business card as he backpedaled. The dogs nipped at his ankles as he hurried to his car, and then they bared their teeth with vicious snaps, once he had locked himself inside. His forehead was slick with perspiration as he started the engine and glanced back to the front porch. The woman was gone, but Frank saw the curtains in the front window bend slightly.

The white speck of his business card caught his eye. It was lying on the ground where he had dropped it. He pulled a U-turn and headed up the long drive and away from the barking dogs. He knew he had discovered something, but Frank Moore had no idea what it was.

CHAPTER 23
Chicago, October 29, 2019

*T*HE CHINA DOLL RESTED ON THE PASSENGER SEAT AS RORY DROVE south out of the city. She took the Kennedy Expressway until it turned into I-94, then followed I-80 east for a short spurt to exit at Calumet Avenue. She pulled into the town of Munster, Indiana, fifty minutes after she left her house in Chicago. Three Floyds Brewery was long closed when she turned into the parking lot. The last time she'd been to the brewery was in May for Dark Lord Day, a ticketed twelve-hour event where stout lovers got the only chance of the year to buy their favorite beer. Rory attended because it was one of the rare public events she enjoyed, because beer flowed liberally, and Lane had expressed interest. She didn't go for the reason everyone else did—to stock up on Dark Lord, although she did that, too. For most regular folks, when their Dark Lord supply was gone, they had to wait until the next year to find more. Rory, thankfully, was not a member of the regular folk.

She grabbed the doll from the passenger seat and stepped out of the car. Her breath was visible in the chilled night air. She pulled her beanie hat low on her head, adjusted her glasses, and started toward the building. The parking lot was lit by a single yellow halogen bulb at the top of the tall post in the middle of the parking area. As she walked along the blacktop, the golden glow of the halogen mixed with her still-red footprints to create an orange trail away from her car. Rory noticed the strange footprints and stomped her combat boots to rid them of the last of the red clay that remained from Starved Rock earlier in the day. The memory of the bloodred prints she had tracked through the cabin gave her a shiver. Hence, the trip to Munster to settle her nerves. Her fridge at home was empty.

She walked to the side of the brewery and knocked on a gray metal door. It opened almost immediately.

"Rory the Doll Lady," a large man said. His thick beard dribbled down to his chest and was striped with gray. He wore a *3 Floyds Brewing Co.* ball cap. "You almost made it six months."

Rory had left Dark Lord Day in May with what most would consider a year's worth of stout. But she had been on hiatus for most of that time, and her alcohol consumption always increased when she was on a break. And the most recent developments in her life had caused her to prematurely run through the rest.

"Kip," Rory said. "Always nice to see you." She held up the doll. "Simon and Halbig. It's German, rare, and in pristine condition."

The large man took the doll and inspected it like he knew what he was looking at. He stroked his long beard.

"Can I find this at Walmart?"

"Not a chance."

"Taylor's been begging for one. She heard about the doll I gave Becky over the holidays."

Rory knew Kip had handfuls of grandchildren. Always looking to one-up his rival grandparents at birthdays and Christmastime, restored china dolls had been his go-to gift for the past two or three years. They were rare and expensive and could not be one-upped by his competition. Rory wasn't sure what she'd do when Kip ticked off all his granddaughters to charm with her rare dolls. She'd have to ration her Dark Lord like everyone else. Until then, she bartered.

"Retail?" Kip asked.

Rory shrugged. "Probably four hundred."

"And what are you asking?"

"Two cases."

"Straight up?" Kip asked.

"I'm feeling generous."

Kip stroked his beard once more while he looked at the Simon & Halbig doll. "You got papers on it?"

"Come on," Rory said, reaching into the pocket of her gray coat and producing the original papers describing the doll. She'd picked it up the previous year at auction for next to nothing. It had been in terrible condition with multiple fractures running through the porcelain and clumps of missing hair. Rory had expertly managed the fractures, erasing them to near invisibility. She relied on Aunt Greta to come up with a solution for the bald patches on the skull, which, of course, the old lady did. When Rory handed the doll over tonight, it looked brand-new. Had she returned to the same auction hall where she found it, unloading it would bring a payday far north of $400.

Kip nodded as he took the papers. "Be right out."

A few minutes later, they walked across the parking lot. Kip pushed a dolly with two cases of stout stacked on it. He loaded them into Rory's car and closed the trunk. Rory climbed behind the wheel and started the engine. She rolled down the window when Kip knocked.

"You walk through a pumpkin patch on your way here?" Kip asked, looking at the orange, lunarlike footprints around the car.

"Not a pumpkin patch," Rory said, pushing her glasses up her nose. "But a real frickin' mess, that's for sure." She attempted a smile. "It's why I'm here at midnight, let's just leave it at that."

"Yeah. When I got your call, I figured you were in bad need of a fix."

"It's beer, Kip. Not heroin."

"A fix is a fix."

Kip reached into his coat pocket and pulled out a bottle of Dark Lord, frosted from having come straight out of the cooler. He produced a Swiss Army knife from his other pocket. The Dark Lord emblem was inscribed across the front of it. Peeling it open, the double-side blade shined on one side with the sharpness of a scalpel. The other side sported a bottle opener. Kip popped the cap and handed it to Rory through the window.

"Watch yourself on I-80. Goddamn state troopers got eagle eyes."

Rory smiled and took the ice-cold bottle. "Thanks, Kip. I'll see you in May."

"Here," he said, handing her the Swiss Army knife as well. "I know that doll's worth more than a couple cases of beer."

Rory nodded her thanks, then pulled out of the brewery's parking lot and onto Indiana Parkway. A few minutes later, she was on the highway with her cruise control set at one mile per hour slower than the posted speed limit. She sipped her Dark Lord and enjoyed the ride back to the city.

Rory found herself parked in front of her father's house. It was close to one in the morning. She was becoming unhealthily fixated on the woman from 1979. Angela Mitchell had somehow reached back across the years to grab hold of some part of Rory's consciousness. Like a tuning fork that has been tapped, the vibration from the mystery surrounding the woman was at once barely audible but yet impossible to ignore.

At first, she failed to understand why Angela Mitchell had such a hold on her. Or, at least, Rory wouldn't admit it. To do so required self-reflection, and the acknowledgment of her own flaws and idiosyncrasies. Baring her soul had always been difficult, even if she were doing so only to herself. The connection had started when Rory learned that Angela was autistic. The link had strengthened when Rory read the descriptions that painted Angela as an introverted woman on the outskirts of society, someone who never truly fit in and who had few, if any, close relationships in her life. A woman who had been too scared to go to the authorities even when she suspected her husband was a killer. Since she had learned that Catherine Blackwell believed Angela Mitchell could still be alive, Rory's mind was in overdrive. That her father had once searched for her, and perhaps had spent much of his life looking, had produced an unhealthy obsession with Angela Mitchell. From the low vibration in her mind, a single question formed: What did her father find? It was too much for Rory to neatly pack away, compartmentalize, and forget about. Rory knew she would use all her skills and talent to reconstruct Angela's whereabouts.

She climbed from her car and strapped her backpack over her shoulder. Opening the trunk, she grabbed a second Dark Lord from one of the cases and then used her key to enter her childhood home. A wave of emotions suddenly washed over her. Rory couldn't remember the last time she cried. In fact, she was unsure if she had ever experienced the emotion during her adult life. She didn't think so, and wasn't about to start now just from walking across the threshold to her childhood. Her father was gone. He had carried with him a great secret. It was enough for her to be curious. Crying would produce nothing useful.

She closed the door behind her, walked into her father's office, and sat behind his desk. She used Kip's Swiss Army knife to pop the top on her stout, and looked around the darkened room. Rory's greatest gift was her ability to piece together cold cases, to pore over the facts and discover things other investigators missed until a picture of the crime—and sometimes the perpetrator—became clear in her mind. Her understanding of a killer's thinking and motive came from examining the carnage he left behind. The frustration with attempting to reconstruct anything about Angela Mitchell lay in the fact that there had been nothing left behind. Thomas Mitchell left no carnage, and this made Rory wonder about the man's guilt. Was it possible, she asked herself, that he had spent forty years in jail for a crime he didn't commit? The more puzzling dilemma was whether he had spent decades in jail for a crime that had never happened.

She clicked on the desk lamp in her father's office and pulled Lane Phillips's thesis from her backpack. He had written it for his dissertation more than a decade ago. It was a dark and ominous look into the minds of convicted killers. A tour de force that came from Lane's two-year crusade, during which he personally interviewed more than one hundred convicted serial killers around the world. The thesis still echoed in the hallways of the FBI, even though Lane had long ago moved on from his time as a profiler there. It was also Rory's go-to reference material when she needed to remind herself how to think like a killer, a useful technique when trying to piece together a crime. Rory took a sip of Dark Lord and turned to the cover page: *Some Choose Darkness* By Lane Phillips.

She'd read the thesis many times, and was always drawn to the same section. She turned to it now. The heading always put a flutter in her chest: "Why Killers Kill."

She read Lane's discernments on what made a person choose to end another's life: the rationalizing that occurred, the blocking of emotion, the pouring of societal norms and moral obligations into a black hole of the mind. This concept got back to the core of his thesis: At some point in every killer's existence, a choice is made. Some choose darkness, others are chosen by it.

Rory finished her beer while she sat in her dead father's darkened office. She looked around her childhood home, the quiet of the empty rooms allowing her mind to form the questions that gnawed at her. She thought about Angela Mitchell. She wondered if the mysterious woman had chosen darkness all those years ago, or if darkness had chosen her.

CHICAGO
November 1981

*F*RANK MOORE CONTINUED TO KEEP HIS HUNT FOR THE GHOST OF Angela Mitchell to himself, sharing none of his investigation with his bosses at Garrison Ford. And he hadn't yet mentioned anything to his wife. He had been named lead counsel for Thomas Mitchell's appeals, a task he was handling with efficiency and skill. Frank had kept private the fact that the man had hired him to look for his dead wife. He had received the request with confusion and suspicion, but since his bizarre encounter at the farmhouse in Peoria, and perhaps for the first time, Frank considered that Angela Mitchell might actually be alive.

He sat at his desk at Garrison Ford, the phone to his ear. Next to him was the thick folder of research. It held all the information he had collected thus far on Angela Mitchell, her troubled adolescence, her stint at Bayer Group Juvenile Psychiatric Facility when she was seventeen years old, and Frank's conversation with Dr. Jefferson. The file ended with the address of the farmhouse in Peoria and the name of the woman who had driven Angela from Bayer Group the day she discharged herself on her eighteenth birthday—Margaret Schreiber.

He spent a week researching the woman. His phone calls to the county and the literature he had managed to obtain from public records told him that she had owned the home for eleven years. She held a mortgage and was current on her taxes. She was a certified nurse-midwife at the local hospital in Peoria. Over the past few days, Frank had pulled permits from public county records and nursing licenses from the Illinois Department of Professional Regulation. He made phony phone calls to inquire about the hospital's services, and had pieced together an impressive biography of Margaret Schreiber.

"She left Bayer Group on her eighteenth birthday," Frank said into the phone. "I found the woman who picked her up."

"It wasn't her parents?" Thomas Mitchell asked in a static-filled voice from prison.

"No. She signed herself out, but a woman named Margaret Schreiber helped her. It's my only lead so far. The only non–family member whom I can link to her before she met you. I'm running with it for now."

"Have you talked with her?"

"Briefly," Frank said.

"Did you ask about Angela?"

"I mentioned her."

"And? You think she knows something?"

Frank remembered Margaret Schreiber as she backpedaled through the front door of her farmhouse. He remembered the fear in her eyes. He remembered the curtains as they shifted slightly when the woman peeked through the window as he drove away. She was hiding something, and Frank had a good idea what it was.

"I'm not sure," he finally said. "But when I know more, I'll be in touch."

Frank hung up the phone and logged the fifteen-minute call to the Thomas Mitchell file and tacked it onto the appeals billing. His secretary walked into his office.

"I'm heading to lunch," she said. "Here are your messages from the morning." She held yellow slips of paper in her hand. "Your wife called. She's going to work early and won't see you tonight. Howard Garrison stopped by, wants you to come see him. And a strange message from someone who wouldn't give her name. She said, hold on . . . it was a bit strange."

Frank felt a numbness run through him as the secretary shuffled the paper slips.

"Here it is. She said . . ." Frank's secretary looked up from the message to stare at him with raised eyebrows. "'Sorry about the dogs'? And she'd like to talk with you as soon as possible." The secretary handed him the message. "You know what that's all about?"

"Long story," Frank said, standing quickly and hurrying around his desk. "I'll call my wife later. Tell Mr. Garrison I got hung up with something. I'll see him tomorrow."

"She wouldn't leave a phone number," the secretary said as Frank hurried out of the office.

"That's okay. I don't need one."

He jogged out of his office, chasing the ghost of a woman who disappeared two years ago.

CHAPTER 24
Chicago, October 30, 2019

*A*FTER RORY'S MOTHER, MARLA, DIED SIX YEARS EARLIER, HER FATHER had threatened to downsize to a condo, but could never bring himself to do it. Instead, he kept the three-bedroom house, where Rory was raised, and lived in the too-large space in order to keep the memory of his wife alive. It dawned on Rory the night before that with her father gone, she'd have to empty the place like she had done the law office, box everything up, and stick a FOR SALE sign in the front lawn. After too many Dark Lords, she had lain on the sofa with a strong beer buzz. She contemplated the sad and unenviable task of clearing out her childhood home of all its memories to allow a different family to start the process of painting a new story over the ones that were here now. She had contemplated it all while using the alcohol to numb her senses. Eventually she dozed off and was gone to the world.

Rory woke now in her father's office. Sunlight skewed through the window and across her face, causing her to shield her eyes as she woke. A dull headache greeted her as she sat up on the couch and rubbed her temples. Her father had died in this room. It was where Celia had found him, and Rory felt some cathartic sense of peace for having stayed here through the night. Maybe she offered her father's spirit a night of company. Maybe she was still drunk on Dark Lord.

The empty bottles of stout sat on her father's desk, and the computer exposed the last of her voyeuristic attempt to discover what her father had learned about Angela Mitchell before his death. If he had found anything at all, he didn't put it onto his computer. She cleared the bottles from the desk, sat again in the chair where her father had died, and used her phone to find the websites of three moving companies, the numbers of which she jotted on a sticky note. There were a number of storage facilities in the area, and she picked a few at random. She spent thirty minutes making calls and arranging times. When she was finished, she shut down the computer and looked around the room. Her father's office appeared different in the morning light than it had in the dark hours of the previous night. She noticed the cabinet door at the bottom of the desk was opened a crack, and saw the knob to a safe peeking from the crevice between the edge of the door and the frame of the desk. Rory pulled the door open.

The safe was built into the desk, and she immediately spun the dial, trying common combinations of numbers. They all failed. She spun through her birth date, then her mother's and father's. When she finally tried her parents' wedding anniversary, the door swung open. Crouching down below the desk, Rory peered into the vault of the small safe. A thick folder sat on the shelf. She retrieved it and placed it on the desk. She opened the cover and found Thomas Mitchell's parole letters dating back two decades, all marked *Denied*. Her father's appeal letters were attached to each denial. When Rory made it to the bottom of the stack, she found a letter from the parole board that suggested great progress by Frank Moore's client, and a changing in the board members' thinking. Two more letters praised the evolution and rehabilitation of Thomas Mitchell, and then, at the bottom of the stack, the parole letter marked *Approved*.

Rory paged back through the stack, glancing at the dates on top of each letter, her mind registering and cataloguing each month, day, and year. Her father had been part of all of the hearings and appeals dating back to the 1980s. She stacked the appeal letters and parole board correspondence to the side. The next stack of papers was handwritten letters from Thomas Mitchell. The penmanship was perfect block, all-caps letters that looked as though they were traced from the print of an old-fashioned typewriter. Rory recalled the detectives' chicken scratch from the many reports she had read throughout her career. Thomas Mitchell's writing was in stark contrast, evidence of a man with nothing but time in front of him. There was no urgency to his work. There was no reason to rush. His writing was deliberate, each letter a perfect match to the one preceding it. As Rory skimmed the page, she noticed the repetitive way the man composed his A's. He used no crosshatch, and the letter looked simply like an inverted V. The character jumped from the page in every word where it was present:

I, THOMAS MITCHELL, ELECT MY ATTORNEY, FRANK MOORE, TO BE PRESENT AND TO SPEAK ON MY BEHALF ON THE MATTER OF MY LATEST PAROLE HEARING.

The unique symbol gave Rory a nauseous feeling, as if the missing crosshatch represented a sinister deletion of something more significant in the man's soul. She pushed the letters to the side and pulled the last pile of papers in front of her. The stack was a rubber-banded collection on top of which was her father's writing: *Angela Mitchell.*

Rory's breath caught in her throat. Chronicled in the pages was what appeared to be her father's research into the life of Angela Mitchell, her family, friends, and acquaintances. A long list of names, with check marks and notes next to each one. She recognized Catherine Blackwell's name. She moved her finger down the page, reading each name.

"Your friend said I might find you here."

The voice startled her, and the breath Rory held in her throat came out with a yelp. She looked up to see Celia standing in the doorway.

Rory put her hand over her chest. "Christ, Celia. You scared the hell out of me."

"Sorry. I knocked, no one answered. But I saw your car outside."

Rory stacked the papers together. "What are you doing here, Celia?"

"You never called me back. I went to your house this morning. Your friend said to look for you here."

Rory vaguely remembered a drunken call to Lane the night before while she snooped through her father's computer.

"Sorry," Rory said. "I've just had so much going on."

Rory recognized something in Celia's expression.

"Is something the matter?"

"I'm afraid your father has left me with a burden I can't handle," Celia said, holding a small object in her hand. "He gave me this a long time ago. Told me to keep it to myself."

Rory squinted her eyes; her contact lenses were dry from having slept in them and she couldn't make out the object in Celia's hand.

"What is it?"

"It's the key to his safe-deposit box."

CHICAGO
November 1981

*F*RANK STOPPED HIS CAR AT THE EDGE OF THE LONG DRIVEWAY. THE farmhouse stood in the distance. It was late afternoon and the shadows of maple trees stretched across the property. He turned the wheel and advanced up the extended drive. The dogs appeared from behind the house to chase his car, hopping at the excitement of a visitor. Frank worried that they would sense his fear from the last time he was here, when he had barely made it to the safety of his car as they tried to rip him to shreds.

He wasn't about to open the door, but he shut off the engine and waited while the dogs barked and announced his presence. After a minute, the woman appeared on the front porch and shouted at the dogs, and they promptly ran to the back of the house. Frank stood slowly from his car.

"C'mon inside," the woman said.

Frank walked up the steps and onto the creaky front porch. The woman opened the screen door and Frank followed her inside. They entered the sitting room off the foyer. A large bay window looked out over the fields behind the property. The woman appeared older, now that Frank had a good look at her, perhaps a bit haggard, as if life had treated her badly. She ran a hand through her coarse gray hair as she sat on the sofa.

Frank was prepared for small talk, but didn't need to be. He had his story prepared, but wouldn't use it.

"Why are you asking about Angela?"

The directness of the question caught Frank by surprise, and he felt the sudden need to tell the truth. For months, he'd lied about what he was doing. For months, he'd been deceptive as he tried to find any useful thread that might lead to the whereabouts of a woman he was rapidly believing might be alive. But for some unexplained reason, the woman in front of him now seemed as though she'd be impervious to his stories. "I've been hired to see if Angela is . . ."

Frank struggled with his words for a moment.

"Is what?"

"Is still alive."

The woman shook her head. "She warned me that he'd come looking for her."

A tremble went through him. A buzzing deep in his soul. "Who warned you?"

The woman looked at him. A dead stare that was unrelenting.

"Angela."

Frank felt as though he were falling. The air drained from his lungs, and when he spoke again, his voice was soft and weak.

"She warned you that *who* would come looking for her?"

The woman's voice was equally frail when she answered.

"Thomas. She said he'd never stop looking for her."

CHAPTER 25
Chicago, October 30, 2019

"WHERE DID YOU FIND IT?" RORY ASKED, LOOKING AT THE KEY IN Celia's hand.

Rory had been through every square inch of her father's law office. It was empty.

"I loved your father," Celia said in a voice congested from crying. "We loved each other, Rory. We didn't tell you, because Frank thought you'd be upset that we were together."

Rory sat up in the chair, reached to adjust her glasses before realizing they were on the coffee table next to the couch, where she had slept. Her beanie hat was there, too. As she stood from her father's chair, she did so barefoot, her combat boots in a heap next to the table. All Rory's protective gear was gone as she listened to Celia confess to a relationship with her father.

"It was a year or so after your mother passed. Frank worried that you'd think we were together before that. But we never were, Rory. I would never do that. Your father was so sad after Marla passed. My own husband had died years before, and we just found each other and fell in love."

"Okay," Rory said, holding up her hands. "I don't really want to know any more, Celia. Not right now."

Her head ached from too much Dark Lard, but through the pounding, Rory pieced things together. The relationship explained Celia's wild emotions at the funeral, and her near-debilitating, tear-dripping embrace when Rory met her to start the process of dissolving the law office. A profound sadness came over her as Rory considered the last few years of her father's life. He had gone through a deep and agonizing depression after Rory's mother had passed. And during the last year, Rory had sensed that her father had been overly stressed. Perhaps it was because he had found happiness with another woman, but couldn't share his newfound joy with his daughter. Rory had always been his to protect, and her father had gone to great lengths throughout his life to make sure Rory was never hurt by anything he did. Now Rory had discovered a part of his life she wished she could have enjoyed with him. The crying she worked so hard to prevent last night nearly came to her now before she managed to stop her eyes from welling with tears.

"I'm sorry to tell you this way, Rory. I've struggled with it ever since Frank died. I even thought about never telling you. And perhaps that would have been the easiest solution, except for this."

Celia walked over and pushed the key across the desk. "Your father had a safe-deposit box. He told me that if anything ever happened to him, I was supposed to take what was in the box and keep it to myself."

Rory composed herself, picked up the key. "What's in it?"

"I have no idea. I think money, but I don't feel right keeping it. Frank promised that he'd always take care of me . . . you know, financially. But if he left money behind, it belongs to you."

Rory picked up the key and ran her fingers over the grooves on the blade. An eerie feeling ran up her sternum and through her neck to cause her ears to ring. The hair follicles on her head tingled. She looked at the stack of papers she had just discovered in her father's safe and knew it was not money he wanted Celia to hide.

Rory parked her car in the bank's parking lot just before nine o'clock. Celia sat next to her in the passenger seat. The Dark Lord headache still gripped her temples and her mouth was cotton dry. She was adorned in her protective armor—hat, glasses, gray jacket, and Madden Girl Eloisee combat boots.

On the ride over from her father's house, Celia explained that a year after they started dating, Frank had asked her to sign papers that put her on the safe-deposit box as a registered holder. Celia had never asked about the contents of the box; she only knew that it had caused Frank much distress when he asked Celia to watch over them. As they waited in the car, Rory took a quick sideways glance through the edge of her glasses and noticed Celia staring at her. The woman was anxious to talk about her relationship with Rory's father. Rory was anxious for a Diet Coke and some privacy. Mercifully, a bank employee unlocked the front doors just as the car's digital clock blinked to 9:00 A.M.

Rory pointed through the windshield. "Bank's open."

They each climbed from the car and made it across the lot. Inside, they rode the elevator to the bottom floor and approached the reception desk. A woman smiled at them. Rory allowed Celia to take the lead.

"We need access to Box 411."

"Are you both registered holders?" the woman asked.

"No," Celia said. "Just me."

"Only registered holders are allowed into the vault, but you're welcome to wait in the reception area just outside."

"That's perfect," Rory said. "Thank you."

Celia handed over her ID and signed a card. The bank employee made a copy, checked Celia's signature to the one on file, and retrieved the master key from a locked cabinet on the back wall. The woman disappeared briefly as she walked around the corner, then opened the door to where Celia and Rory waited.

"Right this way," the woman said.

They walked to the other side of the floor where thick metal bars separated the reception area from the vault of safe-deposit boxes. The gate had been opened earlier in the morning, as had the vault door beyond. The woman pointed to a waiting area with tall, round tables. Rory walked over and watched Celia walk with the woman past the gates and into the vault. A few minutes later, Celia reappeared with a thin metal box in her hands.

The woman smiled. "Let me know when you're finished."

Celia placed the box onto the surface of the tall table. "I'll leave you alone," she said to Rory.

Rory nodded, kept her gaze on the box. When she was alone in the room, she lifted the lid and stared at the contents. There were just a few pages inside. She lifted the first packet, which was her father's last will and testament. She turned the pages slowly, found nothing out of sorts, and placed it to the side. When she examined the next document in the box, the room began spinning. Slowly at first, but faster with each passing moment. She placed her hands on the table to steady herself as she lifted the page and read it.

The room rotated with such ferocity that Rory reached for her temple as she studied the page, knocking her glasses to the floor. She took the last article from the bottom of the box, another single document, stumbled backward until she collided with the wall. Her beanie hat fell from her sweaty scalp and she sunk to the floor as she read.

CHICAGO
November 1981

"ANGELA WARNED YOU THAT HER HUSBAND WOULD COME LOOK-
ing for her?" Frank asked.

The woman stayed silent.

"Angela is alive?"

Margaret looked away from him, out the window and to the vast
expanse of land behind the house. "How did you find me?"

Frank accepted the dodge without pushback. He knew he was on
the cusp of a monumental discovery. "You were listed on the Bayer
Group's log as the one who picked Angela up on her eighteenth
birthday when she left the psychiatric hospital."

"Damn it," she said. "We thought long and hard about any trail
that might lead to me. Anything that might link us to one another.
We thought we were safe."

She pulled her gaze from the window. "So now I know *how* you
found me. But I need to know *why* you're looking. Did he send you?"

Frank swallowed hard. A sinister sense of dread hung in the
room, and his connection to Thomas Mitchell never felt so wrong.

"There are some people who . . . believe Angela is still alive. That
she disappeared to get away from her husband. The police were
convinced he killed her, and the district attorney mounted a good-
enough case to convict him. But I'm wondering if they were all
wrong."

"Did he send you?" she asked again.

He felt a seismic shift in what he was trying to accomplish. His

journey had been set to help his client, but now he felt as though
he were putting lives at risk. Frank nodded.

"Yes," he finally said. "Thomas Mitchell hired me to find his
wife."

The woman's eyes widened with fear. "You mustn't ever tell
him what you've discovered. Do you understand? He must never
find me."

"Were they wrong?" Frank asked. "Were the police and the prosecution wrong? Did Thomas Mitchell kill his wife?"

"No," Margaret said. "But he killed so many other women."

"Where is Angela?"

"He killed all those women, just like she said. And she told me
he would come looking for her. She told me he'd hire people to
find her. It took two years, but Angela was correct."

Frank kept to himself that he had already discussed this lead
with his client, something he now regretted. Some part of him felt
that doing so was a grave mistake.

"Tell me what happened," he said. "I can help you. If you need
help, I promise I'll find a way."

From another room, far off in the farmhouse, there was a
squeal. Frank looked out into the hallway when he heard it. It came
again and again. Louder and louder. Crying.

"Come with me," the woman said.

She stood from the couch, walked into the foyer, and started up
the stairs. Frank noticed the perspiration beading down from his
temples. He followed the woman to the base of the stairs. An odd
premonition came over him that if he continued up the staircase,
his life would never be the same. But the lure of Angela Mitchell,
the ghost he had been chasing, was too great to prevent his steps.
He heard the floorboards creak under his feet as he followed the
woman up the stairs. With each stride, the cries grew louder. More
than cries now, they were shrieks.

At the top of the landing, the gray-haired woman turned and entered a room. Frank paused when he reached the last step, then
looked down the long staircase he had just ascended. The wooden
railing and the rungs within it blurred in his vision. The foyer
below, and the front door, and the dying afternoon sunlight pour-

ing through the window, all swirled together in a distorted image. He still had time. The opportunity was still in front of him. He could race down the stairs and to his car. He could drive away from this farmhouse and never come back. He could tell his client it was a dead end. He could lie.

In the end, though, he didn't run. Instead, he turned and walked to the open doorway through which the woman had disappeared. A baby carriage stood in the corner. The small child standing in the crib, red-faced and angry, was the source of the crying. The screams were so visceral now that Frank had the urge to cover his ears, but curiosity pulled him into the room. When he walked through the threshold, the cries subsided as the gray-haired woman lifted the baby into her arms.

As Frank entered the room, a strange sensation came over him. It felt as though a thousand sets of eyes were watching him. Then he realized why. Three of the four walls in the nursery contained built-in shelves. Each shelf was lined with antique china dolls in perfect rows, three on each shelf. They looked immaculate as they glowed under the lighting with their unblinking eyes focused on him.

"He mustn't ever find her," the woman said.

PART III

THE FARMHOUSE

CHICAGO
May 1982

*F*RANK MOORE TURNED HIS CAR ONTO THE COUNTY ROAD AND ACCEL-erated down the long stretch of two-lane highway flanked by freshly planted cornfields. His wife sat next to him in the passenger seat. The sun was behind them this Saturday morning and cast a slanted shadow of their car onto the road in front of them. It had rained for most of the month of April, but so far May was doing a splendid job of ushering spring along, bringing sunshine and flowers. For Frank and Marla Moore, the season brought hope as well.

"How did you find this family?" Marla asked.

"It's a long story," Frank said. "But I've been searching since we heard the wait list was so long. I received a phone call last week."

"You met them without me?"

"Just to make sure it was legitimate. You've been through so much already with . . ." Frank's voice trailed off. He wanted to avoid talking about the miscarriages. They always sent Marla into bouts of depression, and today was meant to be a joyous day, even if it was filled with deceit.

"I've heard stories of people being scammed for money when they don't go through a formal agency," Frank said. "I wanted to make sure this was on the up-and-up before I got you excited."

"Is it?"

Frank paused. "Yeah, it's legit."

"You're sure about this?" she asked.

Frank looked at his wife. "I'm sure."

Frank saw Marla smile for the first time in months. An hour later, they pulled to the edge of the farmhouse. A waist-high, white painted wooden fence surrounded the property and went on for acres.

"Are you ready?" he asked.

"Is this real?"

Frank nodded his head slowly. "It is."

He turned into the driveway and coasted along the gravel until he stopped the car in the same spot he always did. Six months had passed since the first time he came to this house. He'd lost count of the number of visits he'd made since he first stumbled onto his discovery. He wished he had more time to figure it all out, but no matter how long he waited, the blueprint to their plan would never be perfect. It would be dangerous. It might even be disastrous. But perfect? Not a chance in hell.

He'd never kept a secret from Marla in the short few years that they had been married, and he'd gone into his relationship with the idea of never keeping anything from her. But life sometimes delivers unforeseen opportunities. Unexpected callings that make certain transgressions palatable in the grand scheme of it all, when life asks of you more than you ever thought you could give.

The dogs knew him now. They were playful and relaxed as they hopped next to him as he walked to the porch with his wife's hand in his own.

The door opened and the woman smiled.

"Marla?"

Frank's wife swallowed hard and nodded. "Margaret?"

"Oh, dear, no. No one but my grandmother ever called me Margaret. Please call me Greta." She pushed the screen door open. "Come on in. I can't wait for you to meet her."

CHAPTER 26
Chicago, October 30, 2019

*R*ORY CARRIED THE KESTNER DOLL INTO THE NURSING HOME. SHE found Greta sitting in her chair. It was the first time in weeks, since before her father had died, Rory had seen her out of bed. A strange feeling washed over her when she stared at her aunt. A lifetime of memories flashed in her mind—images of long weekends spent at the farmhouse, passing the days restoring the china dolls with Greta. The satisfaction Rory felt when Greta allowed her to place a finished doll on the shelf in the room upstairs was like nothing else she had ever experienced. An obsessive-compulsive disorder, diagnosed when Rory was six years old, had threatened her childhood. But somehow, in the room upstairs at Aunt Greta's farmhouse, Rory was able to tend to the needs of her mind.

Working on the dolls purged all the tenuous demands of her brain. Rory's habits, and the mandate for perfection, not only went by without judgment or worry when she worked with her aunt, but the time Rory spent in that room upstairs *demanded* all the redundant and meticulous acts that were an unwanted nuisance during the rest of her life. As soon as Rory discovered this outlet, the rest of her days were untouched by the requests of her mind. In adulthood, Rory began her own collection and applied to it the craft Greta had taught her. When Greta's health began to fail, she made it clear that the upstairs room in the farmhouse belonged to Rory, and that she alone was in charge of watching over the collection. Those dolls now lined the shelves in Rory's den.

But her childhood felt different now. Nothing seemed the same since Rory had opened that safe-deposit box to find a birth certificate listing Greta as her birth mother, and documents showing Frank and Marla Moore as her adoptive parents. Rory understood so little and wanted so many answers.

"Hey, old lady," Rory said.

Greta glanced at Rory before looking back at the muted television.

"I tried to save you. There was too much blood."

Rory took a deep breath, angry with herself for the sudden frustration she felt toward Greta. A moment of pause reminded Rory that Greta could no more control the random thoughts that popped into her mind and were spewed from her mouth than Rory could control a sneeze.

"He's coming. You told me. But there's too much blood."

"Okay," Rory said. "It's okay."

"He'll come for you. But we have to stop the bleeding."

Rory closed her eyes briefly. She hadn't asked anything of Greta for many years. In fact, their roles had been reversed over the course of their lives. Greta, once the caretaker who settled Rory's anxiety, was now the patient, and it was Rory who calmed her great-aunt during bouts of unrest such as this. The fact that Rory wanted answers tonight that only Greta could provide was not an excuse to abandon her when she was in distress. Rory took a cleansing breath and walked to the side of the chair. She knew the best remedy for Greta's turmoil. It was the same one that had saved Rory as a child.

"We've got to finish this Kestner," Rory said. "The owner is getting impatient. You promised me one more coat would do it."

Greta blinked at the sight of the doll, as if the Kestner pulled her across the years, away from the tortured memories of the past and back to the present. She gestured for the doll. Rory kept her eyes on the woman she had known as her great-aunt for her entire life. Up until her dead father's lover had given her a key to a safe-deposit box that told her otherwise. She eventually took Camille Byrd's Kestner doll out of the box and laid it carefully on Greta's lap. From the closet, Rory wheeled the art kit she had brought a few nights before, set the pastel paints on the rolling table, and pulled it over to Greta's side.

"In sunlight," Rory said, pointing to the doll's left cheek, "the hues match perfectly. But incandescent brings out the flaws, and fluorescent bleaches it out."

"One more coat," Greta said. "And I'll polish the undamaged side to bring it all together."

Rory sat on the edge of the bed and watched her work. The sight of Greta restoring a doll transported Rory back to the farmhouse, to the long summer days and quiet nights. She spent every summer of her childhood at Greta's place. During the school year, if a bout of obsession took hold of her, Rory's parents would pull her from school early on Friday for a long weekend at the farmhouse. There was no better remedy for her OCD and anxiety than a visit to the country and the restorations that waited there. Now, as Rory sat staring at Greta, the relaxed feelings she usually experienced while restoring a doll were replaced instead with thousands of questions.

"Are you working?" Greta asked, pulling Rory back from her thoughts.

"Yes," she said.

"Tell me."

Rory paused. She hadn't had a meaningful conversation with Greta in weeks. Tonight, though, presented a rare window of lucidity, where her aunt was interactive and coherent.

"That Kestner. It belongs to a dead girl."

The brush in Greta's hand stopped. She looked at Rory.

"She was killed last year. Her father asked me to look into it."

"What happened to her?"

Rory blinked several times, aware again of how badly she had neglected the case. A small part of her was concerned that Ron Davidson would be disappointed in her. A bigger part worried about Walter Byrd, who had put his faith in Rory to find justice for his daughter. But mostly, Rory's heart ached for Camille Byrd, whose spirit waited for Rory to come for it, find it, and help it to a place of proper rest. Take it from its frozen grave in Grant Park and lay it carefully where it belonged so the girl could find peace.

Rory remembered another dream she'd had about the dead girl. Of walking through Grant Park and trying unsuccessfully to wake her as Rory shook Camille's cold shoulder as she lay lifeless on the grassy knoll. Rory refocused her eyes, returning from the wandering abyss of her thoughts. Greta was staring at her.

"I don't know yet."

Greta stared at her for a minute, then went back to work. An hour later, Greta finished polishing and coloring the cheek and forehead. She dusted the face one last time until the Kestner doll, once damaged and in disrepair, looked flawless.

"Greta," Rory said. "It's absolutely perfect." She remembered the deep fissure that had run through the left eye socket when she first examined the doll at the library. When Rory laid the doll horizontally, the left eye closed in perfect unison with the right. The cheeks matched one another, and the fracture that had started at the hairline and run down to the chin was gone.

"As close as we'll get. The girl's father will be happy with what you've done."

"What *you've* done as well."

Greta looked back to the doll. Rory watched her, concerned that she had suddenly fallen into a lost moment and that her mind would be gone for the rest of the visit. The abrupt changes in demeanor happened so often now that Rory was no longer shocked by them—Greta, present and alert one moment, gone the next.

But instead of staring off into a void of dementia, Greta spoke as she examined the doll.

"It reminds me of when you were young," Greta said.

Rory nodded. "Me too."

Greta smiled. "Sometimes those summers seem like yesterday."

"Greta," Rory said, standing from the edge of the bed and moving closer. "Why did my parents bring me to your place so often? Why did I spend every summer of my childhood at the farmhouse?"

A long stretch of silence followed before Greta pulled her gaze from the Kestner doll and looked at Rory. "You were a nervous child, but found peace at my house."

Rory couldn't argue this fact. All the anxiety that surrounded her days, the angst that rose like early-morning fog off a lake, faded away when she was at Greta's farmhouse. But Rory now understood there was another reason for her time there.

"Was the time I spent with you an *arrangement,* Greta? Something you worked out with Frank and Marla?"

Greta blinked, but didn't answer. She brought her gaze back to the doll in her lap.

"I found the papers, Greta. Dad had a safe-deposit box where he kept them. My birth certificate. The adoption papers."

Rory stared at Aunt Greta for a full minute without talking, allowing the confession of her discovery to settle between them. She wanted to press for answers. Wanted to hear the truth from the only person left living who could provide it. But Rory saw Greta's eyes retreating to that faraway place, perhaps intentionally. More likely, though, just the result of the small stretch of coherence having spent its worth before the dementia pulled Greta's mind back to oblivion.

As she watched Greta, Rory sensed a longing from the woman she had known her whole life. A woman who had saved Rory's childhood from what might have been years of torment and ridicule. A woman she had always thought of as her great-aunt, but whose identity now had been jumbled in Rory's perception, like a fully set dining table once perfect and ordered being tipped on its side. The pieces suddenly too muddled to sort. Rory saw it in her eyes, a sense of sorrow that the restoration of the Kestner doll was over. It had been a channel to the past. To the summers and weekends when a young girl developed a lifelong friendship and unbreakable bond with a middle-aged woman she knew as her aunt.

"I wish I could have saved you as easily as Rory and I save the dolls," Greta said, her eyes now vacant and set on the television.

"I *am* Rory." She crouched next to the chair. "Greta? Can you hear me?"

"Yes, we'll hide you. He'll come, like you said. I tried to save you, but there was too much blood."

Rory closed her eyes briefly. Greta was gone. The visit was over. She stood up, lifted the doll from Greta's lap, and carefully laid it in the box.

CHICAGO
May 1982

FRANK AND MARLA SAT NEXT TO EACH OTHER ON THE COUCH. THE VIS-
itations had taken place every weekend for the past month, with
Frank and Marla making the trips out to Peoria each Saturday and
Sunday to spend the days at Greta Schreiber's farmhouse, getting
to know the child. The girl was asleep now. Marla had just finished
reading *Goodnight Moon* while the child lay in her arms. It was a ritual she was starting to love, Frank could see. Marla hadn't wanted
to put the child down, and only released her when Greta suggested
they talk about the future.

Frank knew the first part of his plan was working. His wife was
becoming emotionally attached to the little girl. It was a critical
part of his strategy. The bedrock, in fact, that needed to be laid in
order for it all to work. Now, as the child slept, Frank was about to
present the proposal to his wife. The specifics of which, Frank was
sure, would sound simultaneously too good to be true and too out-
rageous to be possible.

"For this to work," Frank said to Greta, "Marla needs to know
everything. If we're going to pull this off, there can be no secrets.
We'll help in any way possible, you have my word. I know much of
the story, but not all of it. I want my wife to know everything. Please
start from the beginning so we're all on the same page."

Greta nodded. Her hair seemed to have whitened a shade since
Frank first stepped foot on the farmhouse property the previous
fall. Clearly, the stress she was carrying on her shoulders was crush-
ing her.

"I'm a nurse," Greta said. She was speaking to Marla, as Frank had previously heard this portion of the story. "I work for the hospital here in town as a midwife. I make house calls to assist patients who have chosen to undergo a more natural childbirth in the home. I also counsel young women at Bayer Group."

Frank turned to Marla. "Bayer Group Juvenile Psychiatric Facility."

Frank watched Marla nod, as if any of this made sense to her. He knew her mind was fixated on the child and the possibility that she would be theirs.

"I work with the girls at Bayer Group who were pregnant, or who had once been pregnant. I counsel them on what to expect. I've been doing it for many years, and it was during my time at Bayer Group that I met Angela. She was seventeen then."

Marla looked away from the bassinet. "Who?"

"Angela Mitchell," Frank said.

Marla looked at her husband. Her eyes were squinted and her forehead wrinkled. "The girl who was killed a few years ago? The girl from the summer of 1979?"

Frank nodded. "Yes."

Marla cocked her head. "Your firm represents Thomas Mitchell," Marla said. "You're working on his appeals."

"Yes," Frank said, taking Marla's hand. "I told you we needed to understand the full story before we move forward. That's why we're here."

Frank took a second to stare at his wife, making sure she was on board for what was about to transpire. Finally she nodded. They both looked at Greta.

"Angela was at Bayer Group for several months when she was seventeen years old. This was in 1967." Greta shook her head. "Hard to believe that was fifteen years ago. Whenever I went to Bayer Group to counsel my patients, I noticed this introverted girl off in the corner by herself. One day, I approached her, not as a nurse or as a counselor, just out of concern. I was hoping to make this young woman feel not so alone."

"Hi," Greta said as she sat across from the quiet girl she always saw sitting alone.

The girl didn't look at her, or acknowledge her presence in any way.

"I'm Greta. I'm a nurse here."

This caused the girl to glance quickly in her direction and then back to her lap.

"I'm not taking the medication," the girl said. "I don't care who you are or how nice you pretend to be."

"Oh, I'm not a psychiatric nurse. I work with some of the girls here, talking with them about the future."

Greta leaned a little closer.

"Are they giving you medication you don't want?"

"Yes," the girl said.

Greta looked around the rec room. The television was playing and a couple of girls were on the couch in front of it. No one else was in the room.

"What are they giving you? Maybe I could talk with someone?"

The girl looked at her. Greta saw fear in her eyes, and a glimmer of hope, too, at the idea that Greta may be able to help.

"Lithium. All it does is make me sleep and cause wild dreams. Sometimes the dreams even come while I'm awake."

"That's called hallucinating, and it's a common side effect of lithium." Greta scooted her chair closer. "Have you told your doctor about it?"

"Yes, but he doesn't care. They just want me to sleep and stay sedated."

"When you say 'they,' who are you talking about?"

"My parents and the doctors." The girl looked at Greta. "Will you help me? No one in here will help me."

Greta reached down and took the girl's hand. Greta felt her recoil, but after a moment, the girl squeezed back.

"What's your name, dear?"

"Angela."

"I'm going to help you, Angela. I'll find a way to help you."

CHAPTER 27
Chicago, November 1, 2019

*R*ORY SAT IN HER OFFICE WITH CAMILLE BYRD'S PHOTO LOOKING down on her from the corkboard. On the desk in front of her were the documents she had recovered from her father's safe-deposit box. She stared at the adoption papers until her vision blurred. Her mind was beginning to strain in the unhealthy way Rory always worked to avoid. The redundant considerations that prevented clear thinking had started to descend on her, and like a cornered animal, she fought back at them. She knew the consequences of succumbing to them. She pushed the torment aside and swiped the adoption papers to the floor. Then she went back to the pages she had found in her father's desk safe and rifled through the parole board's letters. She read through years of appeals made by her father when he was a young attorney with Garrison Ford, arguments that poked holes in the prosecution's case that her father argued was built solely on circumstantial evidence. She read her father's scathing description of Angela Mitchell as an overmedicated autistic woman who struggled socially and who did not have a firm grasp on reality. Rory tried to convince herself that the pages in front of her were merely her father's attempt to fulfill the oath he took to protect all those who sought his help. But something about the research told a different story.

It was subtle, what was coming to the surface of her attention. Elusive enough that Rory was sure no one else would see it. There was a change in tone. Rory picked up on it as she read through her father's appeal letters. The tenor of the arguments changed throughout the years, even if the content and facts within the letters remained the same. Perhaps, Rory thought, after years of failure, her father had lost a bit of passion trying to defend Thomas Mitchell. Perhaps, after two decades of redundancy, he had given up hope that any appeal would make a difference. But Rory couldn't stop herself from thinking that maybe something else was happening. That perhaps her father's letters held a different motive. That maybe her father never wanted Thomas Mitchell out of jail.

She poured another Dark Lord and continued to read.

CHICAGO
May 1982

*T*HE CHILD REMAINED SLEEPING AS GRETA CONTINUED HER STORY about Angela Mitchell and how the two had come to know each other. Frank and Marla Moore listened from the couch as Greta poured coffee.

"I slipped Angela my phone number that day we first met in the corner of the rec room at Bayer Group. She was alone in the world with no one, not even her parents, to turn to. I had to help her. I spoke with both her doctor and the director of Bayer Group. My boss at the hospital back then was close with the medical director over there, and with some pushing, I was able to get Angela's parents more involved and have the lithium stopped. It took a few weeks, and during the whole process, I met regularly with Angela. Not in any formal manner, just as . . . I guess you'd call us friends."

Greta sat on the couch and sipped her coffee. She looked at Frank. "And that's how you found me. Because of my friendship with Angela. When she turned eighteen, Bayer Group could no longer keep her unless she chose to stay. She did not. She called me to pick her up. I pressed her to contact her parents, but that relationship was too fractured to repair. So I obliged. She signed herself out of Bayer Group, but my name was on the log that day as the one who picked her up. The best I can tell, it was our only mistake. I brought Angela here to the farmhouse. She stayed for a year, working and saving money until she had enough to move on. When she was nineteen, she left for the city. That was 1968. She found a job and was managing on her own. She called every so often. Even called to tell me she had met a man," Greta said. "Unfortunately, that man was Thomas Mitchell."

She took another sip of coffee.

Marla and Frank were sitting on the edge of the couch. Marla was listening intently, and Frank sensed that she was working to make the final connection.

"So you and Angela stayed in touch?" Frank asked to move the conversation along.

"Not really," Greta said. "For a while we did. For a few years, she'd call every once in a while to tell me how she was doing. She told me her parents had moved to St. Louis, that she had found a job, that she had her own apartment. I was very encouraging, and I always invited her out to the farmhouse if she wanted a visit. But then she met Thomas, and after that she stopped calling. Years went by and I didn't hear a thing from her."

Greta paused again to sip her coffee. She replaced the cup on the saucer and looked back at Frank and Marla.

"Then, in the summer of 1979, I saw the news reports."

"That Angela had disappeared?" Marla asked.

"Yes. My heart broke when I saw her face on the television. And when the news came out that her husband was the man responsible for all those missing women from that summer, I felt that I had failed Angela. I had worked so hard to help her when I first found her sitting at the table all alone at Bayer Group. We had become close during the year she spent here. But then, I just let her leave. I let her walk off into the world. When I heard what happened to her, I was stricken with guilt that I hadn't done more to guide her life. For those two days my heart ached in a way I'd never experienced."

"For what two days?" Marla asked.

Greta looked at Frank. He nodded. Frank Moore needed his wife to hear it all.

* * *

Greta Schreiber sat at the workbench in the room upstairs. The wall shelves were decorated with porcelain china dolls arranged in perfect rows. She had started a new project two days before, just after news spread about the most recent events in Chicago. Angela, the girl she had befriended at Bayer Group years earlier, and who had spent an entire year at the farmhouse when she was eighteen years old, had gone missing and was suspected to be the latest victim of the man authorities called The Thief. The startling revelation that this man was Angela's husband had sent Greta pacing the kitchen for the better part of the night. But now, the damaged doll in front of her was providing the distraction she needed. The hairline fracture, which ran across the crown of the skull, down over the ear, and to the base of the jaw, required just enough attention that for as long as she worked on it, she didn't think of the young girl she once knew.

A noise pulled her concentration away from the restoration. She heard an automobile's wheels crunching over the gravel of the long driveway that led from the main road to the farmhouse. Greta stood from the workbench and walked over to the window, peeling the curtains to the side. She saw a silver sedan pulling slowly down the drive, a gray cloud of dust floating behind it. Tubs and Harold barked and jumped alongside the approaching vehicle.

She stayed at the window while she watched the car approach, and only when it stopped with no sign of the driver leaving the vehicle did Greta turn from the window and head down the stairs. A moment later, she opened the front door and walked onto the porch. The car was parked at the front of her lot, the driver sitting behind the wheel. The windshield reflected the blue sky and maple trees to prevent a clear look at the person behind the wheel. Greta waited until finally the driver's-side door opened. A thin woman climbed from the car, a hooded sweatshirt drooping from her frail frame. She lifted both hands to her head and pulled the hood down.

"Sweet Jesus," Greta said, bounding from the porch and down the steps. When she reached the woman, she hugged her tightly.

The woman whispered into Greta's ear.

"I need your help."

Greta backed away, taking Angela's face in her hands. She had the appearance of an alopecia patient. Her eyebrows were missing, and the lashes on her lids were present only in random clusters. Scratch marks climbed her neck and stretched beyond the collar of her sweatshirt. Greta remembered a similar appearance from when she had first met Angela at Bayer Group, but today's version was severely pronounced.

"We need to call the police. People think you're dead."

"No. We can't call the police. We can't call anyone. He can never find us. Promise me, Greta. Promise you'll never let him find us."

CHAPTER 28
Chicago, November 1, 2019

*R*ORY PUSHED THE APPEALS LETTERS TO THE SIDE AND PULLED IN front of her the stack with Angela Mitchell's name scrawled across the top. The pages chronicled her father's search for the woman after she disappeared in 1979. Rory had been reading these pages the morning Celia found her in her father's office. She had been scanning the names of the people her father contacted during his search when Celia showed up with the safe-deposit box's key.

Rory forced the rest of it from her mind—the idea that her father was subtly trying to keep Thomas Mitchell in jail—and concentrated only on that which was in front of her. There was something ominous about seeing proof that her father had been searching for Angela Mitchell. Catherine Blackwell's notes left little doubt that it was true, but some part of Rory refused to believe it. Now, as she sat staring at her late father's notes that recorded his search for Angela, she could no longer deny it. The woman was out there somewhere.

Rory read about her father's trip to St. Louis to talk with Angela's parents. She read about his visit to Catherine Blackwell's house on the north side of Chicago. She read about his trip to a psychiatric hospital where Angela had been treated when she was a teenager. Rory pored through her father's investigation into the whereabouts of Angela Mitchell with a rabid thirst for details, turning the pages with fervor and frenzy until she came to the name of a nurse—the nurse who had driven Angela Mitchell away from the hospital on her eighteenth birthday. Rory's vision funneled until a strange kaleidoscope of images danced in front of her when she saw the woman's name: *Margaret Schreiber.*

She had trouble breathing, her lungs heavy with panic and confusion, unable to expand or contract. Her father had been searching for Angela Mitchell, retracing her life and following her past to a juvenile psychiatric hospital—where she had been befriended by the woman Rory had believed her whole life to be her great-aunt, but whose identity had been blurred by the adoption papers and birth certificates. None of it registered in Rory's mind. Her confusion could be chalked up to denial, but she knew it was more than that. She had been trained to see things others did not. To root through details of cases and reconstruct a picture of events that was invisible to others. But discovering a connection between Greta and Angela sent her mind spiraling. A deep ache started below her sternum and rose like bubbling lava from the crater of a long-dormant volcano. Rory couldn't remember the last panic attack she'd had. It would have been as a child. It would have been before she found the healing outlet in the upstairs room of Greta's farmhouse.

She swallowed the rest of her Dark Lord, hoping the fluid would physically wash away the rising fear, and that the alcohol would dull her senses. She ran to the refrigerator and popped the top on another beer, stood in the darkened kitchen and raised the bottle to her mouth. In a few swallows it was half gone. Dizzy, she stumbled to her den and clicked on the lights. She stared at the china dolls that lined the shelves. The room was a replica of the farmhouse and she hoped the sight of the restored dolls would dampen the panic that coursed through her body.

Rory needed to occupy her mind with something other than thoughts of Greta and her parents and how they might be linked to Angela Mitchell. Having just completed the restoration of Camille Byrd's doll, she had no current projects to work on. She opened the chest that sat in the corner and pulled out a doll she had purchased at auction. It was tattered and ruined and would take a great deal of skill and concentration to restore. Rory sat at her workbench and tried to analyze the damage, but her mind would not take the bait. The usual lure of the doll's needs was trumped tonight by the discovery that Greta had known Angela. Her go-to method of skirting a panic attack was failing.

She left the den, grabbed another Dark Lord, and ran out to her car. She pulled from the curb with her headlights bringing to life the dark and empty Chicago streets. She drove without thinking. She knew the address from the file. It was on the north side. She took side streets and tried to control her speed. She was in no condition to be behind the wheel, both from too many Dark Lords and because she was not in her right mind. Twenty minutes later, she pulled past the bungalow where Angela Mitchell had lived in 1979. The houses were close together, and the entire block was silent and dark, with only front-porch lights shining in the darkness.

Rory stared at the front of the house for a few minutes, sensing the strong connection she had felt since first learning about Angela Mitchell. A relationship had formed, like with the subjects of the crimes she reconstructed, between her and Angela. Rory felt an obligation to find the woman. To let her know that there was someone who understood her struggles and her pain.

Pulling past the house, she turned the corner and crept into the alley behind the home. A chain-link fence protected the small backyard of Angela Mitchell's previous residence. A detached garage opened into the alley. Rory stood from her car and walked in front of it. She stared at the back of the home. She wondered what had transpired here all those years ago, and how it was connected to all the people in her life.

The car's headlights cast her shadow along the pavement of the alley, her legs forming an inverted V. As Rory stared at her shadow, she sensed something inside her, something tugging for her attention. She could not place the feeling or determine why the sight of her shadow gave her such a chill until she realized that the headlights threw a silhouette on the ground in the exact same way Thomas Mitchell designed his A's in his perfect block penmanship with no crosshatch—Λ. Then it occurred to her. As she stood in the dark alley and stared at her shadow, she realized that she had not only come to Angela's home, but to Thomas Mitchell's as well. The revelation hollowed her chest and gave resurgence to her hyperventilating lungs. But it was impossible for Rory to understand the real reason for her clairvoyance. She was standing in the exact same spot where Angela Mitchell stood forty years earlier, just as determined to uncover what had happened to the women who went missing that summer as Rory was today.

The back-porch light came on and caught her attention. Then the kitchen window flashed with light from inside. The rear door opened.

"Can I help you with something?" a man yelled from the door frame. "Or maybe I should call the cops and see if they can help? Or maybe I'll come out there and utilize my Second Amendment rights for someone trespassing on my property."

Jolted by the sudden confrontation, Rory turned and hurried back into her car. Her shadow darting and then disappearing.

"Get the hell out of here!" she heard the man yell as she climbed behind the wheel. She pulled out of the alley, sideswiping a trash-can in the process.

CHICAGO
May 1982

*F*RANK AND MARLA REMAINED ON THE COUCH AS GRETA TOLD HER story. Marla leaned forward when she asked her next question.

"Angela Mitchell was never killed by her husband?"

"No," Greta said. "But he would have killed her if she hadn't left."

Marla took a quick glance at her husband, then back to Greta. "What happened to her?"

Greta hesitated.

"Where is she, Greta? And what does it have to do with our adoption?"

Greta shook her head, looked over at Frank as well.

Frank nodded. "We need to know everything, Greta. I made a promise to help you, but we both have to hear the whole story."

Greta took another sip of coffee and then gently replaced the cup on the saucer. "After Angela told me, I knew there was no turning back."

Two days after Angela appeared in her driveway, Greta drove to the reservoir that sat a mile from the farmhouse. Angela followed in her own car. They waited until dusk, until the summer sky was brushed lavender and the clouds caught the remnants of the setting sun on their underbellies and blushed a cherry red. It was just dark enough to provide cover, but light enough to guide their actions. Greta parked a hundred yards from the reservoir, and then climbed into the passenger seat of Angela's car for the last leg of the journey. Angela pulled her car over the long grass and to the edge of the drop-off that led to the water. They both got out.

Greta looked around to make sure they were alone; then she reached through the driver's-side window to make sure the car was in neutral. They positioned themselves behind the rear bumper, dug their heels into the ground, and pushed. When the front wheels crested the bank, gravity took over. Greta and Angela watched as the car careened into the reservoir and disappeared beneath the water. They waited for ten minutes as the water bubbled while the car released trapped air from below. When it became too dark to see the disturbance on the surface, they walked to Greta's car.

On the way back to the farmhouse, Greta looked over at Angela.

"How far along are you?"

"I'm not sure."

"Have you been vomiting?"

"Yes," Angela said, "for a couple of weeks. I thought it was nerves until the doctor called."

"Okay," Greta said. "Probably a month or two. That means you're due in the spring. We'll have no problem delivering in my house. I've done it dozens of times. Our issue will be keeping you and the baby hidden. We'll have to file the proper documentation. And even if we skip that process, eventually there will be school registration and life in general. I can keep you hidden. For a while, anyway. Everyone thinks you're dead. But after you deliver, we'll have to figure out a long-term plan. Hiding a child is nearly impossible."

"He can never know he has a child, Greta. Promise me you'll find a way."

Greta nodded her head slowly. She had no idea how she could agree to something so impossible, but still she said, "I promise."

CHAPTER 29
Chicago, November 1, 2019

*R*ORY PULLED HER CAR TO THE FRONT OF HER HOUSE, THE passenger-side wheel hopping the curb as she did so. She stumbled up the stairs, keyed the front door, and headed up to her bedroom. She hadn't experienced such a powerful attack since childhood, and she understood the devastating effects they could have if she failed to stifle it. She fell into bed. Rising above the white noise in her mind—above the revelation that her parents had hidden her adoption, beyond the notion that Aunt Greta was not the person she had always believed her to be, and louder than the incessant whispers that she was due in front of Judge Boyle and the parole board with Thomas Mitchell tomorrow—were the unrelenting calls from Angela Mitchell.

Atop the panic was the lure of a mysterious woman who was somehow linked to all the people Rory had loved in her life. It was a pull Rory could not ignore. It reminded her of her childhood, when a similar sensation had taken hold of her. She folded the pillow over her head and pressed it to her ears to quiet the whispers that came from within.

Rory worked to control her breathing. She closed her eyes and cleared her thoughts. There was a process—a way to manage the attacks. She tried to remember the tricks. The breathing exercises that always brought her to a proverbial fork in the road. In one direction was a restless night during which her mind would not cease, with wild and relentless thoughts keeping her awake. In the other direction was the calming lure of sleep and the charm of shutting down her brain, allowing dreams to run effortlessly through the folds of her mind.

She worked for thirty minutes on her breathing, pushing all other thoughts from her mind other than an image of her lungs expanding and contracting. Finally she skirted onto this other road, the peaceful road, and soon her breathing was deep and rhythmic.

Rory woke in the bedroom of the old farmhouse.

It happened every so often. A few times every summer. Aunt Greta would put her to bed, tuck her in, and shut off the lights.

"Remember," Aunt Greta would say, standing in the doorway. "Nothing can scare you unless you allow it to scare you."

Greta would close the bedroom door and Rory would fall peacefully to sleep, the way she always did during her stays at the farmhouse, where the angst and worry had never been able to find her. Rory would typically sleep straight through until morning. But tonight was one of the times she woke in the small hours of night, her body filled with energy that put a buzz in her chest and in her head and in her fingers and toes. She literally vibrated with vigor, overcome with an awesome desire to explore. The sensation had her tossing and turning in bed. The first few times she had encountered this phenomenon Rory fought against it. She kicked the covers and reset the pillows until sunlight filled the window frame the next morning, spilling around the blinds to finally push away the urge to wander into the night and discover the source of her unrest.

Rory was careful never to mention this feeling of angst to anyone. Her parents sent her to Aunt Greta's farmhouse to escape the anxiety she felt during the rest of her life—to dispel it, really—and if they knew about these rare bouts of midnight disquiet, they might decide that Rory's visits to Aunt Greta's were no longer serving their purpose. She loved her long weekends and summers in this peaceful place, so Rory kept the odd nights of sleeplessness a secret. That, and because describing the middle-of-the-night sensation as anxiety wasn't quite right. Rory felt no worry when these spells of wakefulness came to her at the farmhouse, only the temptation of the unknown and the call for her to climb from bed and explore its meaning.

She was ten years old the night she decided to give in to the lure. When Rory woke, fully alert and without a trace of grogginess, the bedside clock told her it was 2:04 A.M. Her chest vibrated with the familiar curiosity she had come to know after many summers at her aunt's farmhouse. Throwing the covers aside, she climbed from bed, pulled by an invisible need. She opened her bedroom door and endured the whine of the hinges. She crept silently past Aunt Greta's bedroom, beyond the second doorway that led to the workshop, where the restored dolls stood in perfect rows on the shelves, and down the stairs. She opened the back door and slipped out into the night. The stars shimmered down on her from the heavens, obscured occasionally by thin sheets of shadowed clouds traced silver by the moon. Far off in the distance, a lightning storm ignited the horizon with off-and-on flickers of brightness, delivering a low rumble of thunder minutes later.

Standing on the back porch, Rory gave in to the pull in her chest. Her feet followed like a magnet drawn to a giant slab of faraway metal. She walked without effort through the field behind the house, found the low, two-rung wooden fence at the edge of the property, and followed it, her hand gliding over its smooth surface as she walked. Near the back of the property, where the fence cornered and turned at a ninety-degree angle, Rory found what was summoning her. On the ground, she saw the flowers she had watched Aunt Greta collect earlier in the day.

Every morning, Rory observed Greta gather flowers from the garden. It was Rory's job to bundle them with twist ties. Rory always asked Greta about the flowers, and she had asked that day as well. She questioned what Greta did with them each day, and where they ended up. Rory's inquisitions were met with vague answers. Tonight, however, she found them. The roses had been placed on the ground in a gentle heap, isolated and alone in the back corner of the property.

Another lightning strike appeared far off on the horizon, adding just enough light to the gray glow of the moon to bring to life the cherry petals. Rory crouched down and removed a rose from the bunch, lifted it to her nose, and inhaled the sweetness. The buzzing in her chest dissipated, and a soothing calm came over her. The feeling of tranquility had always drawn her back to her great-aunt's farmhouse. Tonight, under the tarnished glow of the moon, she harnessed that serenity in a single rose placed to her nose.

When another lightning strike brightened the area, Rory bent down and gently replaced the rose on the pile, then turned and ran back through the gray night until she reached the house. She climbed into bed. Sleep came instantly. Throughout the rest of her childhood, and for all the remaining summers that Rory stayed at Greta's farmhouse, the mysterious middle-of-the-night insomnia never again found her.

CHICAGO
May 1982

"*I*'M GOING TO QUIT MY JOB," FRANK SAID. "I NEED TO LEAVE Garrison Ford."

"To get away from him?" Marla asked. Her eyes were red-rimmed from crying.

"No. To take him with me. I need to keep Thomas Mitchell as close as possible if this is going to work. I need to be the only one he hires to look for Angela. The only one he trusts."

"He'll never stop looking," Greta said. "Angela was adamant about that. If it's not Frank, then it will be someone else."

"I need to control the information he receives," Frank continued. "He needs to believe I'm making progress. I'll find something to feed him for a while, but ultimately my search will come up empty. I'll make him believe me. What's important is for him to think I'm looking for her. As long as he believes this, he won't look himself. He won't employ anyone else. The man trusts me, and I plan to build and keep that trust."

"For how long?"

"For her entire life," Frank said.

Marla looked off. Her eyes wandered to the stairs, and Frank knew she was thinking of the child sleeping in her crib.

"What will we do for money, Frank? How will we support ourselves?"

"I'll hang my own shingle. I've got enough experience to go off on my own. And he's willing to pay me for my services."

"Thomas Mitchell?"

"Yes. He needs an attorney to file his appeals and handle his finances. And he'll pay me on the side to continue my search. He'll
be my first client."

"Frank," Marla said. "It's just . . . not what I imagined."

"Please," Greta said, looking at Marla. "I need your help. We
need your help. You're the perfect couple to love this child. Imagine what sort of life she might have if the truth is ever discovered.
Imagine if the public discovers that Thomas has a child from the
wife he was imprisoned for killing. And how could she ever live a
normal life, knowing her father killed a string of women?"

Marla began crying again. All three of them had been pulled
into an impossible situation. All three thought of the child sleeping
peacefully in her crib. An innocent child who deserved none of
what waited for her. Marla slowly shifted her gaze to Greta.

"Where is she? Where's Angela?"

Greta let out a long breath, and then it was she who began to cry.
"I tried to save her. There was too much blood."

*Something was wrong. The bleeding was intense and constant as Greta
examined Angela's pelvis. Preeclampsia had forced bed rest for the past few
weeks, and spotting had gotten Greta concerned. But Angela had insisted
Greta treat her without involving a physician. It was too risky, she had argued. And Greta couldn't disagree that with Angela's face on the news during Thomas's trial, she would be immediately recognized. So Greta had
treated the blood pressure issues, forced bed rest, and monitored her like a
hawk. But Angela had woken tonight, her water having broken. She was
hemorrhaging badly. Now she was in the throes of delivery.*

"Push, Angela. Push."

"I can't," Angela said.

*She was covered in sweat as she lay on the bed. A surgical gown hung in
front of her to block the view of her lower half. Greta's head was only inter-
mittently visible as she worked to deliver the baby.*

"I know it hurts, but you have to push, Angela!"

"No. I can't. I just can't."

*"Okay," Greta said, shaking her head. "We're going to the hospital, sweet-
heart. Something is wrong. You're bleeding too much."*

"No! We can't go to the hospital. He'll be set free. And he'll know about the baby. Please!"

Greta looked back down. The hemorrhaging had intensified. She swallowed down the fear that rose in her throat, then nodded her head. She worried about the baby, but more so about Angela. Her home, despite the equipment she had gathered over the past few months, was simply not equipped to handle such complications. Greta was not equipped, either.

"Then I need you to push. Do you hear me?"

Angela did. She pushed and pushed.

PART IV

THE CHOICE

CHAPTER 30
Chicago, November 2, 2019

THE COURTROOM HEARING WAS A FORMALITY, COMPLETELY UNNECESsary, and the last place Rory wanted to be this morning. Still reeling from her panic attack, mildly hungover, and with her mind squarely preoccupied with the enigmatic dream she'd had the night before, she was desperate to get to the nursing home and ask Greta about her connection to Angela Mitchell. But Frank Moore had agreed to this hearing months ago as a way to provide a final voice to the board members, who were allowing this man to walk free two decades before his sentence was complete. Present with Rory in the courtroom were the six members of the parole board, a designated representative from the district attorney's office, who looked like he was straight out of law school, and a court clerk, as well as Naomi Brown and Ezra Parker, the social worker and parole officer who had accompanied Rory to the Starved Rock cabin. They all wore some form of appropriate attire for a courtroom, except Rory.

She looked more like the parolee than his attorney, dressed as she was in gray jeans and a dark T-shirt. She couldn't get away with wearing her beanie hat in court, so she allowed her wavy brunette hair to fall to either side of her face like barely parted window curtains. She made sure her glasses were in place, and when she walked into the courtroom, her combat boots rattled and drew everyone's attention. She had warned Judge Boyle that she was not meant for a courtroom. The stares would normally have sent her

into a state of panic, but she spent most of her angst during the
height of her attack the previous night when she drunkenly drove to
Angela Mitchell's old house. It had once been Thomas Mitchell's
house as well, she thought just as the side door of the courtroom
opened and two bailiffs appeared. They led Thomas Mitchell into
court and sat him next to Rory. Judge Boyle materialized through a
different door and took his spot on the bench.

"Good morning," the judge said, his voice echoing through the
nearly empty courtroom. "This will be a brief hearing."

The judge kept his gaze on the papers in front of him and never
looked up to see those present in his courtroom. He appeared to
be as excited about this morning's proceedings as Rory.

"Ms. Moore, I've brought the board up on the latest circumstances of the passing of Mr. Mitchell's previous attorney, and that
as his new representative you've agreed to all the previous stipulations."

They covered again the living arrangements, regular check-ins
with the parole officer, restriction on drugs and alcohol, drug testing, and on and on.

"Yes, sir. Yes, ma'am," Thomas said whenever a member of the
board addressed him.

The formalities took fifteen minutes. Once everyone was satisfied, the judge shuffled some papers.

"Mr. Mitchell, your release tomorrow will be tricky," Judge Boyle
said. "There is intense media attention surrounding the exact details, and Ms. Moore and I have discussed the importance of you
staying anonymous. The press release lists a ten A.M. release. I'd
like to keep that as the formal time listed, but release you instead at
four-thirty A.M. It will still be dark. The warden has agreed to this,
and to an east-side exit. I think this will be the best way to keep
things discreet and allow you to get to your residence without notice."

Unstated, but agreed upon long ago, was that his attorney would
be the one driving him from jail. He had no one else in his life.
And now, Thomas Mitchell no longer had Frank Moore.

Judge Boyle looked at Rory. "Transportation has been arranged?"
Rory nodded.

"Mr. Mitchell. You've been an exemplary inmate. The state hereby agrees to your release at four-thirty tomorrow morning, November third. I hope you make much of your life from this point forward. Good luck to you."

"Thank you, Your Honor," Thomas said.

The judge banged his gavel and was up and gone, his robe drifting like a cape in the wind.

Thomas looked at the board members, bowed his head. "Thank you."

He was gracious and kind. A perfect gentleman. Rehabilitated and ready to integrate back into society.

CHAPTER 31
Chicago, November 3, 2019

WITH LANE NEXT TO HER IN BED, RORY WATCHED THE BEDSIDE clock tick, tick, tick, minute after minute, until it reached three o'clock. She hadn't slept, hadn't even closed her eyes. She had considered a middle-of-the-night visit to see Aunt Greta. Greta would typically have been the perfect person to calm Rory's nerves about sitting alone in her car with Thomas Mitchell, but Rory knew that the next time she saw Greta, she needed to take advantage of whatever small window of opportunity presented itself to ask about Angela. She would need to be clear and concise, and to do this, Rory needed to gather her wits. During the dark hours of night, as Lane slept next to her, she decided to tackle the obstacle of delivering Thomas Mitchell to the Starved Rock cabin before seeing Greta. At 3:15 A.M., she pushed the covers to the side and climbed from bed.

The warm flow of water crashed over her head. She spent more time in the shower than usual before she finally shut off the spigot and readied herself for what was coming. Twenty minutes later, she was dressed in her usual battle gear. She laced up her combat boots and was about to head out the front door and into the darkness when she saw Lane dressed and waiting in the darned front room. He sat with crossed legs and his arm draped over the back of the couch, staring into the black fireplace.

"What are you doing?"

Lane turned at the sound of her voice.

"Not a chance I'm letting you go by yourself."

"Lane—" Rory started to say, but he was already up and out the door. A few seconds later, she heard her car door slam.

"Thank God," she whispered to herself.

At four-fifteen, they pulled to the east gate at Stateville Correctional Center in Crest Hill, Illinois, and waited. The headlights illuminated the chain-link fencing. At precisely 4:30 A.M., the side door opened and spilled yellow light into the predawn darkness. Figures appeared, silhouetted by the brightness inside the building that cast their shadows in front of them like long, slender ghosts. The scene brought Rory briefly back to the other night, when she stood in the alley behind Angela's previous home—Thomas Mitchell's home—and stepped in front of her car's headlight to cause her shadow to creep out in front of her.

The chain-link fencing parted as the figures approached, and when the group reached the edge of the enclosure, only one of them continued on. Rory's sternum ached as Thomas Mitchell walked through the darkness, opened the door, and climbed into the backseat.

The ride to Starved Rock took just over an hour. There was no conversation in the dark car, only the hum of highway as they sped along I-80 guided by the brightness of the headlamps. She took the appropriate exit and navigated the side streets with the aid of Lane's GPS, eventually slowing when she approached the nearly hidden driveway that led to the secluded cabin.

"Wow," Thomas said from the backseat. He was staring through the side window. The first glimmers of dawn were on the horizon, ushering away the dark night and replacing it with a soft blue. "It's been a long time."

Rory didn't know if he was talking about the cabin or the sunrise. She didn't ask, just turned onto the drive. The car rocked as she steered along the canopied drive, finally emerging into the clearing where the A-frame cabin sat in the teal glow of morning. She put the car into park when she reached the end of the driveway, turned and draped her right arm across the front seats so that her hand was touching Lane's shoulder.

She handed a key over the seat.

"I only found one key in my father's office."

Thomas took it and climbed from the rear of the vehicle. He carried with him a zipped plastic bag the guards had provided. It represented everything he owned in the world. Rory stood from the driver's seat, popped the trunk, and removed a small backpack. They both approached the front porch.

"There's no food," Rory said.

Her father would have probably stocked the fridge. Rory never considered it.

"But there's a convenience store about half a mile down the main road."

Thomas nodded. "I remember."

She handed him an envelope of money she had withdrawn from his account using the password set up by her father.

"Here's some cash to get you started. There's also an ATM card in there with access to one of your accounts. Pass code is on a sticky note. Are you familiar with ATMs?"

He nodded. "We had a card system inside. I'll figure it out."

"ATM machine is at the convenience store. Food and clothes will be your first necessities." She handed him the backpack. "I put this together for you. It'll do until we can get you a vehicle. But you'll need a driver's license first. We'll have to work on all that. You think you can survive on a week's worth of clothing and the convenience store for a few days while I work out the details?"

"I'll manage. Thank you."

He keyed the front door and stepped inside. After a quick look around, he was back in the doorway. "Thanks for the lift."

"Answer the phone if it rings. Your parole officer will be calling today to give you instructions. His name is Ezra Parker. You're required to check in with him every day."

"Will do."

"Here's his card. Keep it by the phone."

He took the card from her hand.

"Got it."

Rory nodded. "We'll talk soon."

It was getting brighter as she walked back to the car, the sun's yellow glimmer through the trees made Rory feel as if she had emerged from a dangerous journey.

At just after 8:00 A.M., Rory and Lane pulled to the curb outside her house. Her nerves were frayed, she was sleep deprived, and the adrenaline rush was on a steep decline. She was exhausted when she walked across the front lawn and up the steps to her porch. Lane put his arm around her. With her father gone and Greta too elderly to embrace her, there was only one person left in her life whose touch she enjoyed. She put her head on his shoulder and they climbed the stairs to her front stoop.

"I'll make coffee?" Rory asked.

"You don't drink coffee."

"I'll open a couple Diet Cokes."

"No," Lane said. "I've got a class this morning. I'm already late. You should get some sleep. You were up all night."

"I have to see Aunt Greta."

"Now?"

"Something's come up. I have to talk with her."

"Get some sleep. I have a faculty dinner tonight. I'm giving the keynote address. But I'll try to skip out afterward and come see you."

She let him kiss her.

"Okay?" Lane asked.

Rory nodded. Her eyes were droopy with fatigue. "Okay."

She turned and entered the house. After the door was closed, Lane looked down at the porch, which was covered in ruddy dust. He noticed the trail of bloodred footprints from Rory's boots. They led from the street, across the front lawn, and up to the patio.

CHAPTER 32
Starved Rock, Illinois, November 3, 2019

*T*HOMAS MITCHELL CLOSED THE DOOR TO THE CABIN AND WATCHED through the window as Frank Moore's daughter drove the circular path around the cottage and disappeared into the forested drive from which they had come. Once she was gone, he looked around his new home, checking each room. He walked back out onto the front porch and into the dawning morning. It was the first time in forty years that he witnessed a sunrise. He sucked in the scent of the pine trees, his brain tricking him at first into believing he smelled the usual antiseptic bleach that had greeted him for the last many decades. But no, he tasted only the fresh scents of morning, of freedom, of opportunity.

So much had transpired at this place. He had history here, at his uncle's cabin tucked away in the woods. And there was more to come. The final chapter of his life was about to be written here. He planned to find her. To bring her here, the way he should have done years before.

He took just a moment to enjoy the rising sun before he went back into the cabin and sat on the couch. Across the coffee table, he spread the contents of the plastic bag the guard had given him when he stood at the precipice of the open gate at Stateville Correctional Center. The trinkets and possessions he had accumulated during his life in prison had been left in his jail cell. He knew the guards had pocketed the knickknacks to sell to rabid fans. The Thief still had a following. But all that mattered to him were his papers. The tedious and meticulous notes he had taken over the years. They were a verbatim list of everything he had ever spoken about to Frank Moore. Every lead the attorney had ever brought him during the search for his wife. Every person Frank had contacted. Years of plotting had boiled the list down to an essential few. Thomas knew where to start. He planned to waste no time. Forty years of waiting were about to end.

Hours later, the sun was high above and his white skin burned under the unfamiliar rays. His shirt was soaked through with perspiration as he stepped onto the shovel for the thousandth time. The mound of dirt had grown thigh-high and it took a good stride down to reach the bottom of the hole. He spent another hour widening it, and another squaring off the corners. It had been so long since he'd dug a grave that he nearly forgot the thrill it brought. It meant The Rush was coming.

The anticipation surged through him. He swiped his forearm across his face to clear the sweat; then he speared the shovel into the earth again. And again. And again.

CHAPTER 33
Chicago, November 3, 2019

A BUZZING WOKE RORY FROM A DREAMLESS SLEEP. THE BEDROOM WINdows displayed a fading chestnut sky as night fell. The combination of her first panic attack in nearly three decades, more than twenty-four hours without sleep, and the tormented task of driving Thomas Mitchell from jail had resulted in total exhaustion. She was disorientated when she woke. The buzzing came again. She searched for the source until she heard it once more and finally recognized that her phone was vibrating. She grabbed it from her bedside table, expecting to see Lane's number. Instead, though, it was someone else. The series of numbers immediately registered. Dragging the slider to the right, she placed the phone to her ear.

"Mr. Byrd?"

"Yes, hi. Rory?"

Rory waited, still groggy and suddenly aware that she sounded so.

"Sorry. Did I wake you?"

"No," she said. There was a long pause as Rory stood from bed and walked to the window. It was past 5:00 P.M. and the sun had set. She realized that she'd slept the entire day.

"Hello?"

"Yes," Rory said. "I'm here."

"I was calling to get an update about the case. To see if you've made any progress."

Rory blinked the sleep from her eyes. "I'm afraid not. I mean, I haven't gotten to it yet. But I promise I will. In the meantime, I've finished Camille's doll. I just need to make some last alterations. I'll call you next week and we'll arrange to meet."

There was another pause. "That would be fine."

Rory ended the call. She checked her text messages, but found none. She tried Lane, but got no answer. His class had ended hours ago. He was probably on his way to dinner. He wouldn't be back for another few hours. She climbed back into bed to wait for him. She needed to close her eyes for just a moment. When she did, it took only seconds for sleep to take her again.

CHAPTER 34
Chicago, November 3, 2019

*C*ATHERINE BLACKWELL FINISHED THE TEN O'CLOCK NEWS AND SHUT off the television. The lead story had been the release of Thomas Mitchell, aka The Thief, from Stateville Correctional Center earlier in the day. With no footage of the release, reporters speculated that he had been discharged early in the morning under cover of darkness. That, or there had been a delay. Authorities and prison spokespeople offered no updates, and likely would not until the following morning. Still, reporters stood vigil outside the correction center, hoping to break the news if The Thief ended up walking from behind the prison walls into the hot lights of their cameras.

What a shame, Catherine thought. *What a terrible shame.*

She walked into the kitchen, removed a glass container of milk from the refrigerator, and poured it into the bowl on the ground. The sound of the cap suctioning off the jar brought her cat roaming from under the bed in the other room to lap at the cool milk. Catherine went to the sink and placed the empty bottle into the garbage bag, tied it tightly, and carried it to the back door. The cat was immediately on her heels.

"You want to explore, don't you?" Catherine said. "Come on."

She opened the back door and the cat ran out into the night. Catherine walked to the alley behind her house and lifted the top to the large plastic garbage can to drop the bag inside. The cat was at her side again.

"Not feeling adventurous tonight? Go find a mouse."

But the cat was unusually needy this evening, not wanting to leave Catherine's side. Catherine sensed something ominous as she stood in the alley. The cat hissed into the night.

"What's wrong? What do you see out there?"

The cat hissed once more before darting from Catherine's side, swallowed quickly by the black night. As Catherine squinted into the darkness, feet shuffled behind her. She turned quickly, startled. Their eyes met and she let out a short scream, which was quickly stifled by his hand.

CHAPTER 35
Chicago, November 3, 2019

GRETA SCHREIBER LAY IN BED, EYES CLOSED AND IN A WILD STATE OF dementia. Her mind flashed with images from the past. Quick bursts of colorful mirages from a previous life.

"Where is she?" a voice came from the darkness.

"I tried to save you," Greta said. "There was too much blood."

The farmhouse flickered in her mind. The makeshift delivery room. Angela lying on the bed. The blood. The doubt. The terror.

A grave worry filled Greta's chest, now like it had that day.

"Where is she?" the voice asked again.

"We have to go to the hospital," Greta said. "Something's wrong. There's too much blood."

"I'll ask one more time," the voice said from the darkness. "You picked her up from the psychiatric hospital. I know she came to you for help. Where is she now?"

Greta opened her eyes. The farmhouse disappeared, replaced by a hospital room, a blue glowing television, and a looming figure standing over her bed. The figure leaned closer so that his face was inches from hers.

"Where. Is. She."

Greta blinked. Her mind cleared. She knew the face in front of her. She'd seen him on the news all those years ago. He was older now than when she had watched updates of his conviction on television while Angela sat next to her. Older than the photos that had appeared in the papers. But she was sure it was him. It was not a surprise that he was here, nor was this day unexpected. Frank had worried about it for years and had voiced his concern to Greta many times.

"Last time," the man said. "Where is—"

"Nowhere." Greta's voice was gravelly and inaudible.

The man leaned closer so that his ear was close to her lips. The blue glow of the television disappeared from Greta's vision when the man bent over her.

"Again," he said.

"Nowhere you'll ever find her. Nowhere you'll ever go."

The blue light came back as the man stood up. Then it quickly disappeared again. Greta felt the pillow press against her face. She kept her arms at her sides and never tried to resist. Her mind drifted off.

I tried to save you. There was too much blood.

CHAPTER 36
Chicago, November 4, 2019

*I*T HAD BEEN MORE THAN FORTY-EIGHT HOURS SINCE HER PANIC ATTACK and Rory was starting to feel her body balance itself. The sleep had helped, and now she was ready to face the source of her angst. Greta was linked to Angela Mitchell, and Rory had finally made it to the nursing home to ask her about it. Camille Byrd's Kestner doll lay in its box on the passenger seat. It would be good ammunition for when Rory asked Greta the tough questions she had planned. Rory would not let her off the hook today. Today she needed answers. She needed to understand the mysterious veil that had fallen over her life, a web that connected everyone she loved to a woman who supposedly died forty years ago.

As she pulled into the lot, Rory saw red flashing lights from an ambulance and fire truck that were parked in the turnabout in front of the building. Greta had been a resident here long enough that red lights and sirens were routine for Rory. Throughout nearly every resident's tenure, they suffered some sort of medical crisis that required a trip to the hospital. Emergency vehicles parked out front were a daily ritual.

Rory walked in front of the fire truck, whose engine was roaring. In the lobby, she scribbled her name into the visitor log and paused as she went through the process of printing Greta's name and room number, and then signing her own along the narrow line. Rory had gone through the routine so many times over the years that the practice had attached itself to the image of her aging great-aunt sitting in her room and staring at the blue light of the television. But something caught her attention as she stared at the visitor log today. A vague, subconscious intuition made her hesitate as she penned her name. Before she had a chance to decipher the premonition, Greta's nurse appeared in the corner of Rory's eye. She was walking in a hurried fashion, an urgency to her pace. Rory looked up from the sign-in sheet, dropped the pen to the floor. Things slowed. The rushing nurse took on an underwater motion, her hair flowing behind her in slow motion.

Rory felt the woman take her hand, her eyes dripping with sympathy.

"I'm afraid your aunt has passed, Rory."

Rory blinked as the world caught up and began again in real time. The noises of the lobby came back to her. The people moved around her with normal gaits and at a normal speed. The framed picture on the lobby wall blinked red with the flashing lights outside.

"She was perfectly happy when she went to sleep last night," the nurse said. "We found her this morning. She passed overnight. Peacefully and with no distress."

Rory stood still and offered no reply, the Kestner doll secured under her arm.

"Would you like to see her?"

Rory nodded. She would.

CHAPTER 37
Chicago, November 4, 2019

*R*ORY LAY IN BED, SHE COULDN'T SHAKE THE IMAGE OF THE ZIPPER pulling the gap in the body bag together, Aunt Greta's face disappearing. With it, a part of Rory vanished, too. She had fought against it when Celia called a month ago to tell Rory that her father was dead. And she battled to prevent it when she walked into her childhood home and was assaulted by memories of a life gone by. She tried to resist again tonight, but had no chance of stopping the tears this time. She cried like she never remembered doing as a child, and had certainly never done as an adult.

It wasn't that Rory Moore didn't feel the emotions of pain or sadness, she did. But those things affected *her* differently than they affected *most*. Those sensations altered her mood and changed her thinking. They pulled her back from interactions and made her want to hide from the world. They made her want to be alone. Rarely, however, did pain cause the socially accepted form of bereavement—hysterical crying. Tonight was one of those rare occasions. Rory lay on her side, head sunk in the pillow, and wept.

So many things were gone. Greta had been Rory's last living relative. Besides Lane Phillips, Rory loved no one else in this world. But the anguish she felt now carried another significance. In addition to the end of her lineage, gone, too, was Rory's chance for answers about the adoption papers. About Frank and Marla Moore. About her summers at the farmhouse. About her true relationship to Greta. And about Greta's link to Angela Mitchell. Ever since

Rory started reconstructing her death, the mysterious woman seemed to be tied to everything in Rory's life. It was a connection that felt otherworldly, stronger than the usual relationship Rory developed with the victims of the crimes she reconstructed. And so it was that on the night Greta died, she could think of nothing but Angela Mitchell.

Regret was her companion as Rory closed her eyes, seasoning the tears that ran down her cheeks to soak the pillow. Soon sleep was pulling her. She surrendered easily to it, because within the slumber was something else: the familiar lure she had known as a child, the temptation that had drawn her from bed and ushered her to the prairie behind the farmhouse, where she once found peace. Tonight, though, as her eyes fluttered under her lids, she recognized that it was someone different that pulled her mind. Still, it was irresistible.

It was dark and quiet when Rory walked into Grant Park. The Chicago skyline shined in the distance, intermittent windows lit yellow in the skyscrapers that were set against a black sky. Rory squinted against the darkness. She walked past Buckingham Fountain and to the cobblestone path flanked by birch trees until she came to the clearing where Camille Byrd's body had been found nearly two years prior. The girl was there now, sitting alone in the grassy knoll. The halogen bulb of a lamppost highlighted her body. A brick wall in the background caught her shadow. She looked tranquil with her legs crossed in a yoga pose, a blanket cloaked over her shoulders. The girl lifted a hand when Rory appeared, a gentle wave that filled Rory's heart simultaneously with peace and sorrow.

Camille held something in her lap, and as Rory walked onto the grass and approached the girl, she got a better look at what it was. The Kestner doll was splayed over the girl's crossed legs. Camille ran her hand over the doll's knotted hair. Rory squinted in the darkness and saw the jagged fracture down the left side of the doll's face, the eye socket split open like a chestnut.

"I'm sorry I've neglected your case," Rory said. "I'm sorry I've ignored you."

The girl smiled. It was a radiant smile that put a serene mood over the area where someone had dumped her body. There was no anger or disappointment in her eyes.

"You haven't ignored me," Camille said. "You've thought of me more than anyone else."

"I promise to get to your case. I promise to find the person who did this to you."

"I know you'll come back to me."

Rory took a step closer. The Kestner looked as ruined as the day Walter Byrd had given it to her.

"You become close with the people whose deaths you reconstruct. You always have. It's the way you figure things out that no one else can. And you'll solve your own riddle as well. All the answers are in front of you. All the things that are troubling you. All the things that make no sense . . ." Camille ran her hand over the doll's face. "The truth is easy to miss, even when it's right in front of us."

Camille shifted the doll in her arms, stared into its eyes.

"You and Greta did such a great job on her."

At the mention of her name, Rory's mind ignited with images of Greta as she babbled with dementia each time Rory walked into her room, confused and overwhelmed by Rory's presence.

"I tried to save you. There was too much blood."

Rory remembered the fear in Greta's eyes each time she visited. The distress that lasted a few desperate seconds until Greta snapped back from the tortured memories of her past.

"I wish I could have saved you as easily as Rory and I save the dolls."

The world began to spin as Rory remembered the mysterious pull that had taken hold of her as a ten-year-old girl, the one that ushered her to the prairie behind the farmhouse. Everything blurred around her as she thought of the roses heaped in a pile on the ground, of their sweet scent that filled her body when she placed them to her nose, of the peace that came to her.

As quickly as the spinning started, the world stopped. Rory found herself alone. Camille Byrd was gone. In her place on the grassy knoll was a bundle of roses and the Kestner doll, restored to perfection.

Greta's voice echoed in her ears:

"I tried to save you. There was too much blood."

"There's too much blood. We have to go to the hospital."

"He's coming. You told me. He'll come for you."

Then Camille Byrd's voice:

"The truth is easy to miss, even when it's right in front of us."

As Rory stood in the grassy knoll of Grant Park, it all made sense. The connection she felt to Angela Mitchell and all the similarities that linked them, her father's appeal letters that screamed to Rory an ulterior motive about never wanting Thomas Mitchell out of jail, Greta's connection to Angela, her career as a midwife, the adoption to Frank and Marla Moore, her father's stress during the final year of his life as he could no longer stop Thomas Mitchell's release from jail.

And something else that tugged at her. It was so close to surfacing, but the harder she reached into the far recesses of her mind to retrieve it, the more she stirred in bed. Rory moaned now as she tried to pull herself from sleep. As Rory tried to run, she heard Camille Byrd's voice. When she turned, the girl was back on the grass, standing with the blanket cloaked over her shoulders. The yellow halogen painted Camille's shadow on the wall behind her, and the image triggered Rory's mind. She understood what had been bothering her, and she knew it was Camille who had helped her epiphany.

"Thank you for restoring my doll. It means everything to my father."

When Rory looked, the Kestner was flawless as it rested in Camille's arms. The girl waved again and then Rory ran and ran.

CHAPTER 38
Chicago, November 5, 2019

S HE WOKE WITH A JOLT, KICKING HERSELF AWAKE. THE SHEETS WERE tangled around her legs and it took her a moment to free them. Covered in sweat, she felt her heart thundering as she remembered her dream. When she replayed the image of Camille Byrd's shadow cast on the brick wall, Rory jumped from bed. She stepped into a pair of jeans, pulled on a T-shirt, and sunk her feet into her combat boots. She draped her beanie hat over her head as she crashed through the front door and climbed into her car.

At just past midnight, there was no traffic and she reached the nursing home in fifteen minutes. She sped into the turnabout, where the ambulance and fire truck had been parked the day before, left her car running and the driver's-side door open as she ran into the building.

Rory had made many midnight trips to the nursing home over the years, and knew the place would be asleep. There was a young man tending the front desk when Rory rattled into the lobby in her combat boots.

"Hi," the man whispered in a voice meant to display the serenity of the place at such an hour. "Are you here to see a resident?"

"I need to see the visitor log from yesterday."

"Do you need to sign in?"

"No, I just need to look through the log from yesterday."

"Are you looking for a specific resident?"

Rory took a breath. She could play this one of two ways. Force the issue by threatening to have Ron Davidson of the CPD down here in a matter of minutes to find the log for her—or play the sympathy card. She chose the latter.

"My aunt passed yesterday. Her dear friend came to see her just before she died, and I've forgotten her name. I'm sure she signed in, and I was hoping to recognize her name."

"Oh." The young man was immediately defenseless. "Of course."

He opened a drawer behind the desk and pulled out a thick three-ring binder. He placed it on the counter, spun it so that it was upright for Rory, and opened the cover. Bound neatly into the rings were the year of visitor log sign-in sheets. Yesterday's was on top. Rory placed her finger on the first line of the page and quickly skimmed down the names until she saw it.

Her fierce mind flashed with images of Thomas Mitchell's penmanship from reading the letters he had written to her father. The Thief's writing had been meticulous, all caps, and in perfect rows despite the lineless paper on which it was printed. Rory remembered the unique way in which he wrote his *A*'s as inverted *V*'s.

The character had jumped from the page in every word where it was present. The unusual symbol filled her vision now as she remembered the font. The nursing home began to spin, just like in her dream. She remembered Camille Byrd's image from her dream, when the girl stood and the halogen light painted her shadow on the brick wall. It reminded Rory of the night she stood in the alley behind Angela Mitchell's house, her legs forming the same inverted V. Rory remembered, too, the eerie sensation that had come over her that night. She had felt it again yesterday when she signed the visitor log—a premonition she had been unable to place. It had screamed for her attention just before the nurse appeared out of the corner of her eye, hurrying toward her to break the news about Greta. Now, measured and with a gentle push from Camille Byrd, Rory was able to comprehend it. Thomas Mitchell's penmanship was present on the page in front of her. The same inverted *V*'s.

The person who had come to see the resident in room 121 had written Greta's name in perfect block, all-caps letters: *MARGARET SCHREIBER.*

CHAPTER 39
Starved Rock, Illinois, November 5, 2019

*I*T WAS APPROACHING 2:00 A.M. WHEN RORY TOOK THE HIGHWAY EXIT. I-80 had been empty, but for the rare set of isolated headlights, and now she found herself truly alone as she took the sleepy country roads that led toward Starved Rock State Park and the cabin that waited in the woods. She'd driven the route twice before, and this third outing came from memory. She didn't hesitate at the forks, didn't contemplate the T's. She knew the way. The route had burned itself into her memory the way everything else did. The same way all the details of her life were stored and categorized.

Rory wasn't always aware of the things her mind noticed or picked up on, and could not readily comprehend the enormous volume of material her memory logged. But since her dream, since finding Camille Byrd's spirit nestled in the grassy knoll in Grant Park, all the cryptic elements of her childhood and the farmhouse—of Aunt Greta and her parents, of her visits to the nursing home and the dolls she restored, of Greta's seemingly random mutterings, of the mysterious pull that had once drawn her to the back property of the farmhouse as a young child, of the instant attraction she felt toward Angela Mitchell, and of the nearly identical symptoms they shared of social anxiety and obsessive compulsion—all came to her with vivid clarity. She knew what it all meant. She had finally grasped that elusive element of her existence that had been out of reach for so long, and it had taken nothing more than a push from the spirit of a dead girl who waited for her help.

"The truth is easy to miss, even when it's right in front of us."

Rory's epiphany had brought her to this place tonight. She was at the precipice of darkness, and her soul felt tainted by it. She was unsure if it was possible to correct this mutation at the core of her existence, but anger drove her to try. She made the final turn of her journey. Her headlamps were the only source of light in the otherwise-black night. Until she turned them off. Then only the moon was present, and it offered little guidance. She pulled her car to the side of the road, crunched over the gravel, and turned off the engine. Two hundred yards ahead was the canopied driveway that led to Thomas Mitchell's cabin.

She picked up her phone for the hundredth time, stared at the lit display. She'd had Lane's number plugged in and ready to connect multiple times throughout the drive to Starved Rock, but had stopped herself from calling. The same for Ron Davidson's number, which she had also pulled up during the hour drive. To call either of the men in her life would have prevented her from doing what she was about to do. Rory decided that only one man would be part of her life tonight—the one who had played a silent and unknown role in her existence. The man who had, perhaps, formed her character. The one who had taken from her more than she could reclaim tonight.

As she climbed from her car and eased the door closed, she wondered if extinguishing the source of a fire could stifle the flames that blazed in adjacent structures? The silence of the night overwhelmed her ability to answer her own question as she headed toward the canopied drive. Halfway between her parked car and the cabin's driveway, Rory found a path that led into the forest. She clicked to life the flashlight on her cell phone and followed the trail. Two hundred yards later, she heard the gentle gurgling of water and knew the river was up ahead. When she came to the clearing, the river bled to either side and reflected the moon off its surface like a mystical snake slithering through the night. She followed the riverbank for another two hundred yards until she found the dock she had seen during her first visit to the cabin with the parole officer, Ezra Parker, and the social worker, Naomi Brown. There was a long stretch of neglected stairs that led from the water's edge up the steep embankment. She took them cautiously, one at a time, as her sternum began to throb and her head became flush with blood.

At the top of the stairs, she saw the cabin sitting in the middle of five acres. The square clearing was surrounded by forest. As she slowly set off for the structure, the moon cast a faint shadow next to her. It was her only companion.

CHAPTER 40
Starved Rock, Illinois, November 5, 2019

S HE APPROACHED FROM THE REAR. THE WINDOWS OF THE CABIN WERE dark, the sort of darkness that made Rory think she was looking into a black hole. Rory slowly navigated her way from the edge of the forest and across the long stretch of grass behind the cabin. She crept without the aid of her flashlight. The grass beneath her boots felt level and her steps were unchallenged. But as she came to within fifty yards of the cabin, she took a step but found no earth beneath her. She stumbled forward, falling a full three feet until her feet finally hit the ground. By then, it was too late to right herself. She crashed face-first onto the ground, the damp odor of soil heavy in her nostrils.

She lay still for a moment, attempting to gain her bearings. She felt for her phone, which was thrown from her hand on impact. When she found it, she turned on the flashlight. As she looked around, it was clear that she was in a freshly dug hole. Above her, a mound of dirt sat in the dark. Climbing to her knees, Rory slowly stood from the pit, the top of which was up to her waist. Her breathing was labored when she looked back to the cabin. It remained dark and quiet.

She climbed from the hole, shut off her cell phone, and started off again toward the cabin. When she came to the gravel drive that encircled the cottage, she remembered bending her car around its curves two mornings before. She followed it again now to the front of the cabin and reached into the pocket of her coat to feel for the only weapon she thought to bring—the Swiss Army knife Kip had given her.

She peeled open the blade as she crossed the gravel, her combat boots crunching over the rocks and the red clay that covered the ground. Her first stride onto the stairs caused the porch to creak under her weight. In the dead of night, it may have been a cannon shot. After a moment of pause, Rory continued to the next step, and then the next, until she was standing at the front door of the cabin. To pause now would be to lose her nerve. She grasped the handle and twisted. The door opened without protest, the hinges squeaking softly as the handle floated from her grip. She waited thirty seconds, felt a tremor rattling her fingers. Darkness welcomed her as she stepped inside.

Her mind pulled up the blueprint of the floor plan from her only other time in the cabin, back when she came here with the social worker and parole officer. Despite the darkness, she knew there were three rooms on the first floor—front room, kitchen, and a porch at the back of the house. The stairs to the left of the front door led to two bedrooms and a hall bath. He would be upstairs. He would be sleeping. Just like Greta had likely been when he entered her room.

She started up the stairs, the blade vibrating in her grip.

The bedrooms were empty. The beds were bare, absent of sheets or blankets. Rory descended the stairs, clicked on her phone's flashlight, and splayed it across the front room. On the coffee table were papers scattered in a cluttered mess. She lifted one of the pages and saw his meticulous block penmanship chronicling his years-long search for his wife. An eerie stimulus simmered just below her sternum. Unable to help herself, Rory sat on the couch, placed the Swiss Army knife on the table, and flipped through the pages. It would have been easy for her to become lost in the words, to surrender to the call to reconstruct his path over the years and see how far his research had taken him. And she might have succumbed to this temptation had she not come across the handwritten map.

Written in his distinct block lettering, the inverted Vs jumped out at her everywhere they appeared. She tried to understand what she was reading. It looked to be a plat of survey for the cabin and the land on which it sat. Architectural renderings of the property and its boundaries. On the formal diagram, rectangular boxes had been drawn by hand. They were organized in a grid formation and covered the open area behind the cabin. In each of the boxes, a name was written. Rory immediately recognized the names as the women who had gone missing in 1979. She dropped the survey to the ground when she realized she was holding a map of a makeshift graveyard, and that she had likely just pulled herself from a freshly dug grave.

CHAPTER 41
Starved Rock, Illinois, November 5, 2019

S HE STOOD IN THE FRONT ROOM OF THE CABIN, THE PLAT OF SURVEY and the graveyard map at her feet, and her body temperature quickly on the rise. She felt the perspiration on the back of her neck, and recognized her inability to inhale. A similar episode had gripped her a few nights before when she struggled to piece together her discoveries about Greta and Angela. And now, here again, she felt the impending doom of a panic attack.

Rory ripped the beanie hat off her head and fumbled with the buttons of her jacket. As her pulse raced at an unhealthy clip, she felt cool air on her throat when she unclasped the top of her coat. It provided a moment of clarity and an overwhelming urge to get out of the cabin. Her lungs ached badly enough that she finally sucked for air. With her cell phone flashlight still shining, Rory grabbed the Swiss Army knife from the table, hurried across the front room and through the kitchen. She pushed open the door that led to the porch with a plan to cut across the back of the property, find the stairs to the river, and race to her car. But when she stepped onto the porch, all thoughts of leaving this place evaporated. A woman sat slumped in a chair, a nylon noose around her neck and her hands bound behind her back. The subtle tremor that had vibrated Rory's fingers now rippled through her entire body as she walked closer and realized she was looking at Catherine Blackwell.

The noose around her neck was attached to a rope that snaked upward to a large wooden contraption bolted to the porch ceiling. Rory ran her cell phone light over it. The rope slithered around three pulleys—up, down, up, down—before the other end fell to the floor a few feet away from Catherine. The apparatus took on the shape of an M and Rory instantly remembered it from Angela's drawings. She had discovered a similar tool in her husband's warehouse.

Rory pulled the beam of her light down from the ceiling and hurried to Catherine's side.

"Catherine, can you hear me?"

As soon as she spoke the words, Rory knew they were worthless. The woman's eyes stayed closed, her body was cold. Rory swiped the face of her phone. It took three attempts, her shaking fingers unable to activate the slider. When she finally had the phone open, she hesitated for an instant, contemplating whether to call Ron Davidson or dial 911. During her indecision, she saw the light out in the distance. Through the screen of the porch, out across the back of the property, she spotted a wobbling light. The long beam of the flashlight cut through the darkness and bounced in a rhythmic cadence as the person who carried it made his way toward the cabin.

Remembering her initial view of the cabin from when she had crested the stairs from the riverbank a few minutes earlier, Rory realized the glow of her phone would stand out in the darkness. She quickly doused the light by covering her phone with her hand and pressing it to her chest. Still crouching next to Catherine's body, she turned her flashlight off and dropped the phone in her pocket. Then she turned and ran back through the door and into the kitchen.

As she quietly closed the door to the porch, she saw the bouncing flashlight approaching. The distance had been cut in half, he was perhaps thirty seconds from reaching the cabin. In the darkness, Rory fumbled around the kitchen for somewhere to hide. She realized that she had stopped breathing again and was momentarily distressed at the idea of having to remember to inhale. On the wall adjacent to the porch, she felt the handle of the pantry door.

She opened it and slipped inside just as she heard the outside door to the porch squeak open.

"Have you got one more round in you? I'm sure you do."

Rory trembled in the pantry as she heard Thomas Mitchell's voice.

CHAPTER 42
Starved Rock, Illinois, November 5, 2019

*R*ORY WORKED TO CONTROL HER BREATHING AS SHE STOOD IN THE pantry, the door of which she had pulled to her nose like the lid of a casket. Mold and dust filled her nostrils, and tears blurred her vision. A sliver of visibility was available between the door and the frame. Her sternum ached and her ears thundered with the rush of circulation as she watched Thomas Mitchell prepare a meal in the kitchen. He stood just five or six feet from her as he mixed food in a metal bowl and then ate while he stood, clinically separated from the enjoyment of taste, interested only in the need for sustenance.

He had turned on the lights when he entered the cabin, giving Rory a clear view of the kitchen and porch. As she moved her gaze around, she noticed the red footprints she had tracked across the floor. She looked to the area immediately in front of the pantry and saw the hurried scuff marks she created when she had slid into her hiding spot. Her panic rose, and she concentrated on reviving her lungs and leveling off her breathing. It sounded to her as if she took each breath through a bullhorn, and that any second, Thomas would walk to the pantry, open the door, and discover his prize. She was prepared to scratch and claw, to gouge and punch. She wouldn't hesitate to bite any piece of anatomy that came close to her if she had to. The only thing she wouldn't do was die at this man's hand. Too many other women had. It was why Rory was staring at him now when she could have been racing down the canopied drive and out to her car. It had taken her this long to realize it.

As usual, her conscious mind took a moment to catch up to the small triggers of her subconscious. But she knew now why she hadn't run out the front door when she had the chance. Or why she had turned her phone off rather than dial 911. The same way Camille Byrd's spirit had spoken to her a few hours before, there were others who needed Rory's help. Others who waited for peace and closure. They were buried behind this cabin, where they had lain in turmoil for forty years. Rory could no more turn her back to those women now than she could to Camille Byrd. Rory didn't need Lane or Ron or anyone else to help the women who waited for her. The women needed Rory, and Rory needed to answer their calls for help.

Just as these thoughts materialized in her mind, Thomas placed the metal bowl from which he had been eating onto the kitchen counter and walked toward her. Rory retreated an inch or two, as far as she could in the cramped space, receding farther into the darkness of the pantry. Her lungs became so difficult to fill she was certain her efforts had betrayed her hiding spot. She closed her eyes, waiting for the sliver of light that crept into the pantry to explode as Thomas opened the door. The brightness would be her prompt to attack. To fight like hell. For herself. For Catherine. For the lost souls behind the cabin. Her muscles tensed as she readied to pounce. But instead, music drowned out her heaving breaths.

Her eyes blinked open and she set her gaze back to the crevice between the door and the frame. She scanned the kitchen, but he was gone. She heard Mozart's Requiem fill the cabin, soft at first and then louder. And louder. And louder. Finally he appeared. He walked past the pantry and out to the porch.

CHAPTER 43
Starved Rock, Illinois, November 5, 2019

*T*HE MUSIC WAS DEAFENING IN THE CABIN, BUT HERE ON THE PORCH, it was just right. He hoped it was loud enough to stir her, to bring her back. He longed for the lyrical chorus of Mozart's Requiem to wake her and tell her what was to come. She had barely survived the last round, and he wasn't sure she was still alive. He refused to check now. He didn't want to know if she was gone. He'd missed The Rush more than he imagined, and longed for it once more.

His two leads had run sour. One was too old to offer much, even if he believed she knew the truth. He hadn't the time to elicit it from her. He thought he'd have more luck with the one in front of him, but she proved to be just as useless to his search for Angela. And when he didn't know where to go next, he succumbed to his long-subdued urging for The Rush. Now, as the ode to lost souls spilled from the cabin and filled his ears, Thomas stepped up onto the stool six feet from Catherine Blackwell. He slipped the nylon noose around his neck, instantaneously feeling the surge of endorphins fill his body. Tightening the strap, he slowly eased himself off the stool and watched as she levitated from the chair. It was a glorious sight. Coupled with both the charm of the music and The Rush that surged through his body, Thomas Mitchell slipped off to euphoria.

He closed his eyes for a moment. Despite being out of practice, he reminded himself of the dangers of overindulgence. The Rush was a cryptic practice. It provided the closest thing this world offered to bliss, dangled it on a stick in front of him and begged him to come for it. But Thomas knew The Grim Reaper held that stick, and to abuse The Rush or take too much of it would spell the end. Perhaps that was the lure. Ecstasy and mortality divided by such a fine line.

He was there now, euphoric as his body shook with The Rush. He slivered his eyes open to take in the sight of the woman floating in front of him. He witnessed her magically hanging in the air. It was magnificent and perfect. Until it wasn't. Until a flash of something appeared in his peripheral vision. It startled him. He opened his eyes fully, grasping for the noose around his neck and searching with his foot for the stool.

CHAPTER 44
Starved Rock, Illinois, November 5, 2019

*R*ORY WATCHED FROM THE PANTRY AS THOMAS PULLED A STOOL TO the center of the porch. He fidgeted with the noose overhead. Finally he mounted the stool, hooked the nylon around his neck, and slowly lowered himself off the stool while Catherine simultaneously rose into the air across from him, like a magician levitating his subject. The sight stole what little breath Rory had left.

Through the crack in the pantry door, Rory witnessed the strange scene play out before her. She had reconstructed cases that dealt with the despicable practice of autoerotic asphyxiation, and had read articles about the perverted individuals who reached sexual gratification from its practice. But the scene unfolding in front of her was something entirely different. It was not sexual in nature, but perverted in another, more disturbing way. The high Thomas Mitchell was reaching came not from any perverse use of sex, but rather from the pleasure of watching another die.

Rory saw Catherine's legs dangle limply as she rose, the weight of Thomas's body on the other side of the pulley system dragging her upward. Rory remembered the dual pulley system Angela had drawn in her notes chronicling what she had discovered in Thomas's warehouse. He had re-created that system here in his cabin, and across from him now was his wife's only friend. Someone who he surely believed had helped Angela disappear forty years earlier. How terribly wrong he had it, Rory thought.

As he lowered himself in a slow, guided movement, he kept one foot on the stool as a fail-safe, placing his weight back onto its surface when the tension became too great and he neared unconsciousness. When he put his weight back on the stool, he rose higher and allowed Catherine to sink back to the ground. Rory watched the eerie seesawing while the classical music blared through the cabin.

When she saw Thomas take his weight off the stool again and sink downward, coming to a rest twelve inches from the cabin floor, with the noose tight around his neck and his face boiling to a deep crimson, Rory felt the pull in her chest. It was as powerful as when she was a child at Greta's farmhouse. She quickly pushed open the pantry door, the sounds of her movements camouflaged by Mozart. She reached into the pocket of her coat and retrieved the Dark Lord Swiss Army knife. Unfolding the device, the blade caught the light from the porch. Her movements as she charged through the porch door startled Thomas, who worked frantically to gain leverage on the stool under him. His bloodred face took on another shade, deeper now. Purple.

He worked to gain footing on the stool, his legs flailing until his right foot touched the top surface. If given another few seconds, he would have had the stool underneath him and the pressure relieved from his neck. Rory made sure to take those seconds from him. She walked slowly over to him, their eyes meeting—hers calm and calculating, his bulging and panicked. For once Rory had no inclination to avoid eye contact. She thought of Aunt Greta alone in her room the night Thomas had found her. She thought of the women buried beneath the ground behind the cabin. She thought of Catherine. She thought of Angela.

Rory folded the Swiss Army knife closed. She wouldn't need it after all. Just as Thomas placed his foot on the stool, Rory kicked it out from under him. His body dropped down a few inches, recoiling with the jolt. She watched as he reached for his neck, trying unsuccessfully to pry his fingers between the noose and his skin. As he thrashed about, Rory took a good, long moment to stare at him before whispering in his ear. His bulging eyes appeared to widen; then she turned to tend to Catherine.

She couldn't leave her strung up like cattle. It took a few minutes before Rory had her body lying peacefully on the ground of the porch. Then, with Thomas still meekly thrashing, she walked into the kitchen and lifted the phone from the cradle. The card had been stuck into the crevice between the phone jack and the wall. Rory dialed the number, waited for a voice to answer, and then laid the phone on the kitchen table.

When Rory finally walked from the cabin, she left the front door open. She could still faintly hear Mozart's Requiem when she reached her car.

CHAPTER 45
Chicago, November 5, 2019

*I*T WAS SIX IN THE MORNING WHEN RORY PULLED TO THE CURB OUTSIDE her house. She hurried barefoot up the steps and fumbled with the lock. Inside, she went straight to the front room, gathered newspapers from the bin next to the hearth, and placed them under the logs in the fireplace. She lit a match and touched the flame to the paper, then carefully kindled the fire until it was blazing. More logs went on top, stacked in a precise teepee to allow maximum heat.

Then she undressed and threw her clothes into the fire. First her jeans and T-shirt; next her coat and beanie hat. She waited a moment for the flames to take the fabric. The fire grew strong as it absorbed the clothing. When they were gone, floating up the chimney in small remnants of ash, Rory grabbed her Madden Girl Eloisee combat boots. They were covered in the red clay from her trek through the forest and to the Starved Rock cabin. She placed them in the fire.

Standing in her underwear, she watched the boots begin to melt before she walked upstairs and climbed into bed.

Lane Phillips keyed the front door and walked into Rory's house. It was just before noon and she hadn't answered her phone. He'd called several times. He noticed the glowing logs of a dying fire in the front room.

"Rory?" he called.

No answer.

He checked the study. Empty. The den next. Also empty—besides the dolls that lined the shelves. He walked upstairs and found her asleep. Rory Moore would never be considered a morning person, but sleeping until noon was not common, either. Lane walked over to the bed to check on her. The covers rose and fell with her rhythmic breathing, and Lane couldn't remember the last time he'd seen Rory sleep so soundly.

He noticed the corner of papers poking from under the blanket. He pulled the comforter to the side to find a tattered copy of his thesis. The corners were turned up from frequent readings, the pages crumpled. Lane flipped through the document and saw Rory's notes in the margin of many pages. Toward the end, he found a dog-eared page in the section analyzing why killers kill, and the psychological mechanisms that bring an individual to the precipice of deciding to take another's life. In the middle of the page, a passage was highlighted. He read the yellow glowing sentence: *Some choose darkness, others are chosen by it.*

The page was damp, with circular stains, as if someone had dribbled water onto the paper. *Water,* Lane thought, *or tears?* The doorbell rang and Lane looked up from his thesis. Rory didn't stir. The bell rang again. He placed the document on the nightstand and headed down the stairs. He opened the front door to find Ron Davidson standing on the front porch.

CHAPTER 46
Chicago, November 5, 2019

"*R*ORY?"

Her eyelids fluttered. She heard her name again.

"Rory."

When she opened her eyes, she saw Lane standing over the bed. He touched her cheek.

"Hey, you feeling okay?"

"Yeah," Rory said, sitting up. "I'm fine."

Her mind ignited with quick snippets of her time at the Starved Rock cabin. Of Catherine Blackwell hovering off the ground. Of Thomas Mitchell in his bizarre state of ecstasy. Of her hiding spot in the pantry and the thin slice of light between the door and the frame. Of the classical music. It still rang in her ears.

"What time is it?"

"Noon," Lane said. "Did you hear me about Ron?"

"No, what about him?"

"He's here, downstairs. Said he needs to talk with you. Something urgent."

Rory blinked a few times. She saw her copy of Lane's thesis resting on the nightstand. She had been reading it earlier, before sleep took her to a deep, dreamless rest.

Rory ran a hand through her hair as she nodded. "Tell him I need a minute."

* * *

The three of them sat in the front room fifteen minutes later.

"I got a call early this morning from the LaSalle County Sheriff's Office," Ron said. He was sitting on the couch across from the fireplace, Rory and Lane on adjacent chairs next to him. The fireplace was to Rory's left, Lane's right, and directly in front of the head of Chicago Homicide. If Rory could have chosen, she'd have ushered Ron into the kitchen for this meeting. Instead, when she finally walked down the stairs, he and Lane were sitting in the front room.

"LaSalle County?" Rory asked.

"Starved Rock," Ron said. "We're still piecing together the details, but it looks like Thomas Mitchell killed himself."

Rory kept her face stoic. It was how she would typically react to this news, and she wanted to look typical today.

"How?" she asked.

"Looks like he hanged himself. But details are still coming in. I only talked for a few minutes with the detective in charge. There was another body at the cabin, a woman. It sounded like he tortured her in some way. The county guys are still putting the scene together."

"How'd they find him?"

"He called his parole officer early this morning, about three o'clock. Left the phone on the table while he hanged himself. Least that's what they think. The forensics crew is still putting the scene together. Because he was your client, I thought I'd stop by to let you know. I'm getting ready to head out there now."

Rory nodded. "Thanks." She looked at Lane, then back to the detective. "Sorry I seem off, I'm trying to process everything."

Mostly, Rory was worried that she'd left her fingerprints on the phone or somewhere else in the cabin. Or that she hadn't managed to sweep away the red imprints of her combat boots on the way out.

"Well, there's more to process," Ron said.

"Yeah? What else could there be?"

"The state guys found a plat of survey at the cabin that looks like a map of the burial grounds for several women who went missing in 1979. All the women who were suspected to have been abducted by Thomas Mitchell."

"Sweet Jesus," Lane said.

"Sounds like he abducted them from Chicago, killed them, and then buried them behind his uncle's cabin. When the uncle died, he willed the place to his nephew. Son of a bitch probably knew what Thomas was doing all along."

Rory shook her head. "I don't know what to say."

"My guys will be part of the investigation, since the victims were from Chicago. Cook County Sheriff's Office as well."

"Makes sense," Rory said.

"Say, Gray, when were you last out at Starved Rock?"

Rory looked at Ron. "Uh, you know, the other morning. When Lane and I dropped him off."

"Doc?" Ron asked. "That the last time you were there?"

"Yeah," Lane said. "Why? What's up?"

"Just crossing my *t*'s. The LaSalle County guys are bound to ask. Just giving you two a heads-up. Since you were at the cabin, they'll probably ask to talk with you."

"Sure," Lane said.

Rory nodded. "Of course."

A glowing log popped in the fireplace—a loud crack that caught everyone's attention. Rory looked for the first time at the spot where she had burned her clothing a few hours earlier. A muscle in her neck twitched when she saw the remnants of one of her combat boots sitting on top of the ashes. It was the front half—toe and sole, about four inches of leather and rubber that the fire had failed to swallow. The boot stuck out from a glowing log as obvious as dead fish floating in an aquarium. It was covered in the red dust from the clay terrain of the Starved Rock cabin. She looked at the area in front of the hearth and noticed a faint patch of bloodred dust from where she had placed her boots while she waited for her clothes to burn.

In the split second after the log crackled, and during the time it took Rory to recognize her errors, she saw Lane stand from his chair and grab the poker.

"Whatever you need from us," Lane said, standing in front of the fireplace and blocking Ron's view of the logs. "We'll do whatever helps your guys."

He threw a few slivers of wood on top of the glowing logs, causing a stream of embers to puff from the orange glow. The logs caught immediately and rejuvenated the flames. Rory had a clear view into the fireplace, and watched as Lane put the tip of the poker to the remnant of her cherry-red boot and pushed it into the flames. It caught and melted away to nothing.

Lane threw another log on the fire and hung the poker with the other fireplace tools. Rory watched as Lane slid the throw rug, which lay on the hardwood in front of the hearth, to his left until it covered the smear of crimson.

"Needless to say," Ron continued, "we've got a goddamn mess on our hands. The media are going to have a field day with this. Being that he was your client, the state guys are going to want to talk with you, too, Rory. I'm heading there now, if you want to tag along."

Rory suddenly wanted Ron Davidson out of her house. And the last place on earth she wanted to go was back to that cabin.

"Yeah," she said, nodding her head. "Probably be a good idea."

Lane had sat back down in the chair across from her. He, too, was nodding. They made eye contact, staring at each other with volumes of wordless conversation happening between them.

"Probably a good idea," Lane repeated.

"Give me a minute?" Rory asked.

"Of course," Ron said. He stood from the couch. "I'll call and let my guys know we're on the way."

Ron walked to the front door, his phone already to his ear. Rory continued to look at Lane after Ron was gone. She wanted to talk with him, to tell him everything.

"You better get dressed," Lane said.

Ten minutes later, Rory found Ron on the front porch. He held up a finger as he finished his call. When he slipped his phone into his breast pocket a minute later, he did so with a quizzical look.

"You ready?" he asked.

"Yeah," Rory said, adjusting her glasses. "What's the matter?"

Ron looked down at her feet. "I've never seen you without your boots on."

Rory pulled her beanie cap down on her head. She'd found a

spare in her closet. She had a replacement for her coat, too, which was now buttoned up to her neck. But she had owned only one pair of boots. Ten years old, perfectly formed to her feet, and now melted to a pile of ash.

"Well," she said. "It's a mess out there. I don't want to ruin them."

She walked past her boss and climbed into the front seat of his unmarked cruiser.

CHAPTER 47
Peoria, Illinois, December 5, 2019

*T*WO ITEMS RESTED ON THE PASSENGER SEAT WAITING FOR DELIVERY. Rory pulled to a stop in the parking lot of the Harold Washington Library Center. She picked up one of the items—Camille Byrd's Kestner doll—and carried it into the lobby. She spotted Walter Byrd standing in nearly the exact spot where she had met him weeks before. When she approached, his stare was set firmly on the box in her hands. Rory adjusted her glasses.

"Sorry it took me so long to get this back to you."

"Is it finished?" Mr. Byrd asked.

Rory pointed to the doors of the library. "I'll show you how it turned out. I think you're going to be pleased with it."

They walked into the library and found an empty table in the back corner. Rory placed the box on the surface and opened the top. She carefully removed Camille's doll and handed it to him. Walter Byrd took the doll in his hands, swallowed hard, and ran his hand over the surface of its face. Rory saw the man's eyes glaze over with tears. He looked up at her.

"Thank you," he said. "It's truly remarkable."

Rory averted her eyes and nodded. "I wanted to let you know," she said, "that Camille's case is all I will be working on now. I've got one more thing to take care of, and then all my attention will be on your daughter."

Mr. Byrd looked up from the doll. "Thank you," he said again.

Rory wanted to tell the man that his daughter had helped her in ways that were unimaginable. They were unexplainable as well, and no one would understand how the soul of a dead girl who waited for Rory's help had pushed her to the precipice of her epiphany. So, instead, she said, "I feel a connection to Camille, and a need to help her. I promise I will."

She turned and walked out of the library, leaving Camille Byrd's father holding the now-flawless restoration of his child's doll. Outside, she headed to her car to deliver the second item that waited on her front seat.

She drove the long, straight country road as the barren cornfields blurred past in her peripheral vision. It was late afternoon and the sun was approaching the horizon, sitting out in front of her on the flat landscape. The sky was cloudless, melting from cotton blue to a deep shade of salmon as the day fell away.

The body of every woman who went missing in 1979 had been located behind the cabin in Starved Rock. The identities had been made via dental records, and the victims' families had finally found closure. Sadly, many of the women's family members had passed before the discovery. Most of the parents had died without knowing for certain the fate of their daughters. But their siblings were living and many were present at the press conference when Detective Davidson explained the discovery to the world. The news media covered the story at a frantic pace. Thomas Mitchell, the events of the summer of 1979, and the tragic discovery at the cabin in Starved Rock forty years later would forever be folklore for true-crime junkies. It was sure to be revisited at some point when a filmmaker decided to create a documentary about the case. When that happened, Rory wanted no one knocking on her door and asking questions. She wanted only to be a small footnote in the Thomas Mitchell saga, the attorney who briefly represented him during his parole. She didn't even want that mentioned, but she knew there was no way around it. What she desperately sought was to hide the truth. The truth about Angela Mitchell, her escape to Greta's farmhouse, and the child she bore before she died. A child whose blood ran thick with Thomas Mitchell's DNA.

For Christ's sake, Rory thought, *what a field day the nuts on the Internet would have with all that.*

It was no wonder the people who loved her most took such extraordinary measures to bury the secrets of the past. Rory planned to do all she could to keep them underground. She knew it would take effort. People would continue to dig. There was a buzzing conversation, mostly relegated to chat rooms and Reddit threads, about one victim whose body had not been found buried at Thomas Mitchell's cabin. That of his wife, Angela—the woman who had started her own investigation in 1979 and had become the nucleus of The Thief's downfall.

One phase of the public's conversation fed into the deep sympathy that since Angela's remains had not been unearthed, and now that Thomas Mitchell was gone, the whereabouts of her body would forever stay a mystery. The other dialogue was conspiratorial, with theorists suggesting that there was a simple explanation for why her body was not found at the Starved Rock cabin: Angela Mitchell was still alive. Conspiracy theories always trumped sympathy, and over the past month this discourse became louder and louder until it dominated the conversation. True-crime buffs jumped on the bandwagon to claim that Angela Mitchell was out there somewhere. They promised to keep searching for her.

As Rory drove the lonely country road, though, she knew the truth. She finally understood it all. Not only had she reconstructed Angela's death, but she had pieced together her own childhood. The missing fragments came together in a way that both shocked and settled Rory's soul. It was a reconstruction that had taken a lifetime to assemble. Careful deliberation and months of searching told her she was the only one left who knew the truth, and she had no intention of sharing her knowledge with the world.

She had briefly considered confiding in Ron Davidson, telling him everything. She should have, probably. But the repercussions were too unpredictable. If she confessed to Ron, she feared smart people would start asking questions, and if put onto a scent, investigators would start sniffing. If one of them began to dig the way Rory had dug, she worried they'd find the same lineage she unearthed. It was a secret Rory planned to carry to her grave.

The only people who knew the truth were gone, and she was satisfied that wherever they were now, somewhere off in the by-and-by, they were watching her as she made this final journey. They were proud of her. A deep sense of peace came to her as she drove. It was a reconciliation never before experienced that allowed her to feel free and alive, liberated somehow. She had made her choice, and she was comfortable with it.

The long road came to a T, where Rory turned left. A moment later, the farmhouse appeared before her. She hadn't been here in some time. Aunt Greta had moved to the nursing home several years before, and until today, Rory never had reason to return. As soon as she saw the old farmhouse, though, with its blue painted cedar and wraparound porch, she realized how much she missed it. Her memories transported her to the summers she spent there as a child.

With her mind flooded by flashbacks, Rory turned up the gravel driveway. She parked at the front, where the gravel ended and the never-ending expanse of grass began. A moment passed as she waited for anyone to appear from inside. She wasn't sure how she would proceed if the new owners were home. But what she needed to do could not wait. The pull in her chest was too strong to ignore. After a few minutes, the farmhouse stayed still and quiet in the fading light of dusk, silhouetted by the lavender horizon. Rory looked at herself in the rearview mirror. Even during the long ride out to the country, she kept her thick plastic glasses on her face, and the beanie cap slung low on her forehead. She reached up and pulled them off. Today, of all times, she couldn't hide. Didn't want to hide. Didn't need to.

She dropped her hat and glasses on the passenger seat, and picked up the other item that had made the trip with her. She opened the door and climbed out into the evening. She walked to the side of the farmhouse and into the backyard. The rear porch was to her left, and she remembered in vivid detail the night when she was ten years old, when the buzzing in her chest had pulled her out of bed and into this field during the middle of the night. She remembered the smoky glow of the moon and the far-off thunderstorm that ignited the horizon with intermittent pulses of lightning. Tonight the fading sun burned lilac on the horizon, the sky above a dark cobalt.

Rory found the low, two-tiered stable fence that ran the length of the property. She followed it again now, the same way she had the night the amazing calm had come over her. Nearly thirty years later and Rory finally understood the meaning of that night. The lure in her chest, the magnetism that had pulled her, and the sense of peace that had washed over her when she had lifted that rose and had inhaled the sweetness of its scent.

Rory followed the fence to the back edge of the property, where it turned at a ninety-degree angle and ran off to her left. Once she arrived at the corner of the prairie, Rory looked down at the ground. The only other time in her life when she stood in this spot, she had found the flowers she always watched Aunt Greta pick from the garden. The ones she helped bundle.

The conspiracy theorists could have their chat rooms and threads. They could keep their wild and uneducated ideas about Angela Mitchell and where she was today. None would ever know the truth. None would ever find her. Angela hadn't wanted to be found forty years ago, and she didn't want to be found today. Rory lifted the item she had carried with her from the car—a bouquet of roses tied in a tight bundle. She placed them to her nose, closed her eyes, and took in their sweet scent. Then she crouched down and laid them on the ground.

ACKNOWLEDGMENTS

A big thank you to the following people:

The entire clan at Kensington Publishing, who continue to support my novels in ways that stun me. Especially John Scognamiglio, who has fought for me more times than he lets me know.

Marlene Stringer, agent and friend, who is always two steps ahead of me.

Amy Donlea, who is the glue that holds our family together. Without you my life would be in so many scattered pieces that not even Rory Moore could put it back together.

Abby and Nolan, for being my biggest supporters, for constantly asking to read my books (you're still not old enough), and for all the wild ideas for future novels. Keep 'em coming!

Mary Murphy, for trying so hard to have coherent conversations with me about completely incoherent ideas for a manuscript that was only half written when I started bothering you for help.

Chris Murphy, for suggestions on the final draft, and for setting me straight on Dark Lord stout. We should probably share one soon.

Rich Hills, for the idea. Although I'm sure I distorted and perverted your original suggestion.

Mike Chmelar and Jill Barnum for sharing your lawyering knowledge in order to help me spring a serial killer from jail.

Thomas Hargrove, founder and chairman of the real Murder Accountability Project, for taking my calls and explaining what you do.

And to all the readers who keep buying my books. I'm forever grateful.